MW01245754

Lillie Sue Baby

(Loving Evil People)

By

Pamela Hubbard

In memory of my mother and her inspiration.

Dedicated to my husband, Mark, my three children and my aunt, Sharon Fritz.

With much gratitude to Mark Hubbard for his art work and tech support. Thanks also to Anne Goodrich, Graphic Designer.

Forward

Life is joyous and messy, lovely and horrible. Lillie Sue Walloon's life is an example of human relationships with all the joys and hardships of loving difficult people. It is a story that encompasses the common human experience of family differences, mental illness and the ultimate love between family and friends. It is a warning tale as well as a heartwarming story.

Lillie's story brings tears of laughter and sorrow. From her humorous truck driving baby brother to her loving, good natured father, we find joy and hilarity. On the other end of the spectrum are the difficult to evil men she falls in love with and the consequences of those relationships. Through Lillie's life one can see many aspects of themselves and their own relationships. Perhaps it could serve as a cautionary tale to guide others away from poor choices or to see a situation from another angle. Lillie did everything out of love and fear. She worked hard to succeed and was hit hard with the truth of her choices.

Lillie was raised by a loving, happy, but financially poor family. The Walloon family, except their two oldest children, was content with their position in life. Boyd Walloon was never a wealthy or powerful man by earthly standards, but by the standards of the soul there was none above him. People loved the Walloons and enjoyed being with them. Folks with bigger, fancier homes chose to celebrate at the humble Walloon home; for it was here that one would feel loved and be accepted no matter who you were or what was wrong with you. They were not perfect people, but people perfect to be human with.

A broken heart

breaks other hearts

The pain too great to bear alone

And so

takes hands and pulls along

to share

heartache and pain

P. K. Hubbard

Table of Contents

Lillie Sue Baby

(Loving Evil People)

She woke to the smell of Ajax. Her head was pounding and her sight was blurred. The cold laminate on her cheek felt good and helped to clear her head. Lillie was on the floor after fainting yet again. She had little interest in food and was losing weight. It was decided by her mother that she was overdoing it in her ballet class. Lillie had been taking dance classes in Toledo, OH, a 15 minute drive from her small modest home in Delta. The Toledo Ballet Company had accepted her into their group. It was her dream beginning to come true and she worked and danced with all she had. It was a joy she had never experienced. A true feeling of acceptance, of being part of something. Lillian Sue Walloon, known as Lillie, had always felt like an outsider. Her friends were from middle class and wealthy families. Her own family was content with their lower class position and enjoyed the simple things before it was popular to live simply. Lillie did not fit in to any of these categories, but longed to be wealthy and carefree. How she longed for their cashmere, pearls and circle skirts. They always had fresh, new, white "Bobbie" socks. She rode with a friend, who had what Lillie strived for, to ballet class each week. It was the only way she could get there.

Lillie had taken a job at the local soda shop called, The Palace. She waitressed three evenings a week after school. Her heart would sink when she had to serve her friends, but the money she earned was the only way she could pay for the clothes she wanted, the ballet supplies and oh, the prom dresses. She loved her prom dresses and ballet outfits and paid top dollar for them. She studied, worked, saved, danced and fell in love. Her senior year of high school was exhausting. In addition to her overloaded schedule, she had managed to be chosen as a cheerleader that year. Her schedule was a nightmare and she made it work.

Now, Lillie's parents were good, salt of the Earth, people. Her father, Boyd, was five feet six inches of hard working man, thin of build yet remarkably strong. He had sharp sparkly blue eyes and gorgeous wavy hair. Her mother's name was Thelma. Thelma was five feet four inches and quite heavy set. She was plump to fat her entire life. She had hazel eyes that always glowed with her love and snapped with her mischief. Dad worked 2 to 3 jobs to keep the family of seven fed and housed. Mother went to work once the youngest was in second grade. Most mothers did not work outside of the home in 1950, so it was not spoken of and not something to be admired. A hard job twisting metal into springs to be put into box spring mattresses was her exhausting employment.

Dad toiled lengthy hours in a foundry, steamy hot, then would drive a propane truck to make home deliveries for people to heat their homes with the smelly stuff. A smell so potent that all of his children and eventual grandchildren would end up pairing that smell with their much loved dad/grandpa. To this day, his grandchildren think of him when they smell gas, oil or propane. He eventually worked into a position of gas station attendant in addition to the other jobs. It was this position that ended up giving him a glimpse of a way to a better life. He was able to gradually quit his other jobs after saving enough money to buy into part ownership of the gas station. His hours were long, but it was his station and the money he made put the family in a better position. Lillie's freshman year of high school had been when she watched her father and families' dreams and better life collapse. This may have been the year that she began to fear she was to stay different from her friends and the world she wanted.

Jack

Lillie's oldest sibling was her brother Jack. Jack was beyond handsome. He was adventurous and dangerous. Girls flocked to him and boys tried to emulate him. It was the era of James Dean and Jack was the local James Dean with Elvis Presley looks. The peers fed fuel to Jack's fire. Jack's popularity and devil may care attitude was the male mirror of Lillie's dream and desire to be different and special. They may be poor, but they had a special spark. The two oldest Walloon children, Jack and Lillie, knew they were born to be different than the rest of the family. They could feel the edge of that something special and they would throw everything they could at grasping it. Jack was also admired by his family. He actually was a nice person and usually pretty sweet. He was a quiet boy-man which led others to think he was more deep and dangerous than he truly was. Jack dated several girls and had a great time in school socially. He did okay academically, but was not very interested in most of his classes.

It was a regular Friday night. The Walloon family would have dinner and watch some T.V. together. Jack, as usual, borrowed his dad's car for his night with friends or a date with a girl. This Friday, after Jack dropped his date home, he decided to stop by a friend's house. A couple of other guys were there and talk began about how the youngest, a 15 year old who was soon to be 16, had not been allowed by his family to drive. Joking and teasing led to the kid becoming upset and Jack wanted to make it right. He told the kid, Wendell, that he would take him driving right now. Wow, all were impressed and Jack and the kid left. As they drove, the confidence of this young man grew. He wanted to drive faster. Jack let him take it to some country roads where they could really let it fly. The first hill they flew over was where the inexperience had them careening out of control, then sliding on some gravel. It was all a blur in Jack's mind and he soon realized they had crashed into a tree. What a nightmarish scene. He yelled Wendell's name. He swore and pushed his way out of the crumpled car. "How will I make this up to dad," his brain cried as a million thoughts flooded his mind. Even a pleasant thought of the attention this would bring him with the girls at school crowded its way in. They would flock around and croon over him. As this flashed through his mind, he continued screaming for his friend along with some incomprehensible mumbling and swearing. He saw Wendell lying motionless, but heard a slight moaning. Fear raced its way through his veins like icy water. He felt himself become light headed and, for an honest moment, he felt guilt and fear. He allowed that moment to disseminate, to be pushed down deep into his secret space where all negative thoughts of himself were buried.

Jack felt himself running on wobbly legs. Stumbling and yelling for help, fighting against the urge to scream and cry. He had no idea when he had started to run or for how long he had been seeking help. An older gentleman was grabbing him by the shoulders and shaking him. Jack turned and pointed in the direction he felt he had come from. He could see in this man's eyes that he knew about the accident, that in fact, he knew much more than Jack wanted him to know. He pulled himself together and became "Jack Walloon", high school athlete and all around popular, nice guy. The lie he should tell was battling against other lies and the truth. He was driving, not the kid. He tried to stop the kid, went along to try to get the car back, to stop Wendell. The battle raging in him was all about saving himself. He was young and unprepared for this type of tragedy and at that second decided he would never be unprepared again. He would design himself to be prepared and ready for anything the world would throw at him. He was frightened about what Wendell would say. Jack was just being a good guy to this kid, would others see it that way too?

He ran his fingers through thick wavy hair and walked the road in a circle, being sure to stay back from the accident. Police had arrived and were very focused on the crumpled car with the unconscious Wendell inside. Surely Wendell would back him up with whatever story he chose to tell, he just had to get to the kid and get their story straight. He went toward the car to see if he could connect with Wendell. Cops pulled him back telling him that he did not want to see this. Not want to see this? What? How bad was Wendell? Jack had not seen any blood or injuries, but then he really had not looked Wendell over or tried to move him. He had spooked and run. Run? Had he run like a hero for help or had he run in fear and panic? He pushed the truth of that away, he was going to get help and no one could tell any different. He vowed yet again to himself that he would never run in panic or fear. He was continuing to frame himself, to mold and decide who he would be as an adult. The truth of him left a bitter taste that gagged. He knew that now was the day when he would begin to grow into the image that he had carefully crafted for others to see. Emboldened, he approached the closest police officer. The officer was a seasoned cop and Jack was shocked to see tears in his eyes. Dear God, how bad could this all be? Jack felt outside of his body. He walked zombie like toward the officer. He saw such sadness and frustration on the face of this man. All Jack could get out was a whisper of the word, "What".

Noooooo, God in Heaven, noooo! They were placing a blanket over Wendell's slight body, over his face! Jack knew this kid's parents and was in classes with his older sister. He could not bear the thought of their grief. It was when a policeman came to take him home that he began to shake uncontrollably from the shock. The shock that came from the thought of going home, to see the face of his father. Oh, his father, his ever patient, loving, happy father. He knew he would never forget one bump or turn of that ride home.

There would never be anyone who could understand the depth of his misery and little did he know that it was about to get worse.

Boyd and Thelma

They were content with their lives and happy with each other and their family. Boyd was known around town as "Scrappy" to the point where most folks did not even know his real first name. He had received this nickname during WWII due to being a lightweight boxer for the Army as well as a soldier. Thelma had an identical twin sister that had married Boyd's favorite cousin and they were in touch daily, living only two blocks apart. So when police officers arrived that evening, Thelma began to panic about her family and her oldest son, Jack. The other four children, three girls and the baby boy, were all home and she knew they were safe. Scrappy tried to calm her down, but she was in a state of panic and dread. All evening, she had felt unrest in her soul. She got like that sometimes and often something did go wrong. She felt herself a bit psychic, but she would never speak of it until she was an old woman. Thelma knew Jack was in that police car and that he was in trouble, her dread was deeper than that though. Scrappy kept up his friendly surface, relieved to see his son alive and with no injuries that he could tell, but when he saw Jack's face he knew there were deep emotional injuries. He was more frightened than he had ever been in his life, including his stint in the war. "What in hell had Jack got himself into", Boyd wondered.

The officer approached Scrappy and asked if Jack had been using the family car that night. He then proceeded to explain in detail even Jack had not been aware of, how the accident had taken Wendell's life. Thelma made a keening noise that Jack, Scrappy and even Thelma had never heard before. She felt out of control with her grief and embarrassment. Thelma always found a way to fit in being embarrassed and ashamed, she was raised to do so. The shame she felt now was the most intense of her life. This was so much worse than when her twin sister got pregnant and had to marry. So much worse. Thelma then was pushed to marry Boyd since they were dating. The family had feared that Thelma and her identical twin, Velma, would be confused as to who was pregnant and that it was best if she were to marry as well. That was years ago and it all had turned out just fine. Today was not fine, it was frightful. Thelma had worked with Wendell's dad at the box springs factory. He was a supervisor there and had always been a pleasant man. Now her son was involved in an accident with her family's car that had killed the boy. Living in this small town, she knew that most would know of the accident before they went to bed that very night. She prayed that Jack had not been driving wildly or fast, that it was a pure accident or someone else's fault. As the details emerged, Jack's parents were made to realize that their son had allowed Wendell to drive and Wendell was underage and unlicensed. Jack had no idea of the Pandora's Box of pain he had just unleashed on his family.

Retribution

The lawsuit against the family was quick and harsh. Boyd's insurance would not cover many of the expenses and he would need to sell his part ownership in the gas station that he had acquired only a few years earlier. The town took sides and split friends and family members. Boyd returned to working at the foundry and picked up driving the propane truck, but he never returned to pumping gas. Everyone in the family tried to avoid talk of the station and to not drive by if they could help. It was such a deep sadness for everyone, but their parents did not subject the children to all of the pain they felt. They lost so much, including not having a car for a year. Close family would help out with driving once in a while, but mostly they all walked to where they needed to go. This is when they were thankful for having moved to town a few years earlier as they were close to many stores and their employment. Winter was the harshest time and it angered the kids that Jack did not often help with grocery shopping, especially with lugging them home by foot through the rain, snow and ice. Jack often was not home. They felt he was avoiding the work and grief. In reality, Jack was trying to not bring more trouble to his family. He felt too awful to be around his family, especially his hard working parents. He stayed into the evening with friends and snuck in at night. He asked for nothing and worked a job after school to pay for his own food and clothes. He was filled with joy and relief when he saw his father bring home a used car in pretty good shape. A year to save had paid off well. They did not know that poor Boyd was also saving to buy another station someday, but that was never to be.

Lillie and Richard

Richard came from a family that Thelma referred to as "ten cent millionaires". The family heard her use this phrase often in describing people who acted as though they had more money than they actually had. Lillie liked the calm and dignity that she saw with Richard and his family. They acted like they were better than Lillie and her family and she believed them. They lived in the same neighborhood, had a similar house and car, but were better off financially due to having only one child. Richard's daddy had a little better paying factory position than Boyd. His mother worked in a decent clothing store part-time and made everyone believe that she worked there out of her interest in clothing; because she wanted to. If truth were known, they had made about the same or less money than the Walloon family. What the Walloon children and others did not know was how Boyd was saving for a new ownership of a gas station of his own. He felt, given time, he could make things right. He secretly felt and hoped that in doing this, he could help heal Jack. He knew Jack was suffering greatly and he did not have any idea how to help his oldest son. His wife would listen to him at night and agree and encourage Boyd. She took on a lower paying job as a full time nurses' aide as she could no longer tolerate the conditions under which she worked at the box springs factory. Thelma had worked long hours, had swollen feet and legs, been cut and gouged by that damn wire; she needed out of there.

None of the things her parents did made Lillie feel better. She took her happy, loving family for granted, as most teenagers do. She did not realize the strife and terror that some children lived through. She just knew that she planned on much better for herself and her future family. She did not realize that Harold, Richard's daddy, was a mean son of a bitch to his wife. He spoiled his only child, Richard, whom he felt could do no wrong. Lillie loved that Richard's daddy bailed him out of trouble at school, with sports and at home. She did not see him cheating on his wife and being hateful. No, Sally would have no one know what Harold did to her. She was far too proud and too busy keeping up appearances socially and at her church. Lillie knew none of this and thought she wanted her family to be at least as good as Richard's family. She decided to date and allow herself to fall in love with Richard. He had been after her now since her junior year and really stepped up trying to get her to go out with him since she had made the cheerleading squad that summer for her senior year. She knew that the cheerleading had impressed Richard and his family, yes they were that shallow. Lillie assumed that she would be able to dance, travel and date Richard. She had no desire to marry him until she had obtained her dream. She dreamed that Richard would love and adore her, but she had no idea how he could fit into her plans to dance professionally.

Lillie spent a lot of time with Richard that summer before senior year. Richard had just graduated and landed a job in a hardware store. Lillie had one more year of high school and then planned on staying with the Toledo ballet company until she was good enough to audition for a bigger dance company or the Radio City Rockettes. Her dreams were big and she had the drive and talent to make it. Her body was strong, lean and beautiful and she sort of realized it. Like most teenagers, she felt she was not pretty enough although all who saw her knew she was beautiful. Her little sisters, Sarah and Betty Sue also felt plain. They had grown up hearing their mother tell them, "pretty is as pretty does" and all three girls had interpreted it to mean that they were not naturally pretty, but would be considered pretty if they worked hard enough and were nice enough. Unpretentious Thelma knew her daughters were beautiful in the physical way that she was not. She was proud of how wonderful they were as well as secretly thrilled at their beauty, but she felt it was wrong of her to "let on" about it. She had been taught that letting children know they were good, special or pretty led to sinful vanity and no child of hers was going to be boastful or vain. Thelma also tried to avoid being or acting proud. Pride was unforgivable in Thelma's childhood family.

Thelma

Thelma had been raised poor and to be humble. Raised by the whipping of the razor sharpening belt. Thelma had the scars to prove that she had been raised to behave. How could Thelma understand her daughters' desires to be pretty or to have nice things? They had it great in Thelma's opinion. No one whipped the Walloon children. They were loved, allowed to talk and to laugh. She was proud of the loving home she and Boyd provided for their children. Thelma had had a good life herself, when Daddy and Momma were pleased with her. She played on the farm with her cousins after all the chores were done. She and her sisters sang at church and social gatherings. Identical twins were such a novelty; most people flocked to see them and to be associated with the family. People were always thrilled to see and hear the twins and their sister play the piano and sing with their wobbly soprano voices. It was years before she realized that she and her sisters had terrible voices, yet even after that realization as an adult, she still sang for the pure joy of it. She was a happy woman in her marriage and felt freed from the past constraints of her domineering father. Her main embarrassment was her weight. She had always been over weight and after the birth of 5 children, she knew she was considered "fat". She usually only felt fat in public, so home was safe and joyful. She knew Boyd adored her and was as grateful to her for saving him as she was to him for saving her.

Lillie knew a bit of her mother's past, but it all seemed so story like and hard to believe this happy woman had ever been treated so cruelly. Only the scars on her mother's legs proved the truth of a very strict upbringing.

Dancing

Lillie's dreams were her only goals, she often daydreamed about how she would create her own world with dance. She would leave the small town and relish her visits home, but they would be short visits. Friends and family would see her as the "famous one" that was always classically and elegantly dressed. All would comment on how she rivaled Audrey Hepburn. She would be able to bring her family wonderful gifts. She would stand out among her family and old friends. These were her only reveries. Lillie was different and she could feel it just at the edges of her being. Almost within her grasp, that tangible dream dangled and danced. She had received a good part in the ballet company. She was to dance the part of the Sugar Plum Fairy in The Nutcracker production this December, but practice began this September, 1956. Lillie was young for her class in school, she would be 17 this coming November and graduate this coming May, 1957. She would practice four times a week for ballet and once a week for cheerleading. She would cheer at almost all of the games until December, then she would need to miss two games due to the Nutcracker practices and shows. The adults at school helped her to make it all work out. She was so busy that she sometimes felt ill, yet she was happy and kept pushing through it. Her dancing was praised as her toes bled. She was promised a good career as her feet became disfigured by the shiny pale peach pointe shoes she had worked and saved to purchase. She absolutely loved it all. Blood and pain only served to make her dreams feel possible and just around the next corner.

Excitement was everywhere for Lillie now. She was getting attention from her peers for her cheerleading and most knew of her dancing in the Nutcracker production. She was happy with being in love with Richard. He had been a track star at her school, was a high school graduate and working. This all brought her great satisfaction and popularity. Her one disappointment was that her parents and siblings would not be in attendance at the ballet. They saw her dance around as best she could in their tiny dining room, practicing positions des bras, and getting Richard to lift her and catch her as she practiced pirouettes, jete' petit, pas de deux and all that she could at home. Her siblings, Richard and her father enjoyed it, her mother called it, "showing off" yet Lillie saw pride in her mother's eyes and small smile. Her parents had never gone to any of their children's functions and they would not start now. No one ever begged or asked too much of their parents. They all knew how hard their father worked and their mother had her reason, being obese and embarrassed. They were such loving people though, that none of the children resented their absences in spite of how it made them feel. It was the culture of this family and the times they lived in. Now, Jack, her big brother, would be unable to attend as he had joined the Army right out of high school.

Walloon Laughter, Tears and Family

Jack did well in basic training, not minding any pain or discomfort as he felt it a small price to pay for what had happened to Wendell. After basic, he was sent to South Korea to guard the demilitarized zone (DMZ). He sent home small postcards and very short letters, just enough to keep his mother from going into full panic about his safety. Lillie had heard her mother mention Jack daily on her two to three times a day calls to her twin sister that lived two blocks away. She heard her talk of her fears and saw her cry on the phone and then laugh with her sister as she cried. Yes, the Walloon family often laughed at jokes, each other and themselves. Laughter was frequent in the home and the youngest son had a wicked sense of humor. He was able to have people crying with laughter over a story that others could tell with little to no response. One Christmas, he had purchased extremely huge Christmas underpants for his mother to open. Now, others may find that tacky or mean, but when given by Boyd junior it was hilarious. Thelma laughed, screamed and held them up for pictures that her great grandchildren still look at with glee and mischief. You see, there was a true wonderful part of Thelma that did love herself. She had a fabulous sense of humor.

She was a strong woman, comfortable with herself and her body. It was the looks from outsiders and society that she could not stand. Her family understood this and loved her beyond measure for it. She had no qualms about having a grandchild come hook her bra as she could not reach it. And the grandchildren had no issue with it. They would march up, hook her bra and go back to playing! She would grab that runny nosed grandchild and use her apron or housecoat to wipe up the snot, then send them on their way. Yet, she was always clean and usually wearing some sort of Sear's polyester clothing. The person of Thelma was real, vibrant and you had to love her, you had to, even as you might shake your head or get grossed out. She would nap on the couch after a hard day at work and then make a bologna sandwich for everyone's supper. She made the best ever potato salad that no one has emulated yet. She was not a good cook or housekeeper, but no one cared because she did not care. Children and grandchildren would pick up, dust and sweep without ever being asked, just because that is the vibe in the house, that is what you do when at Boyd and Thelma's house. When Boyd saved up enough money to remodel that small kitchen and enclose the porch with a screen, they felt rich indeed. Everyone was happy for them and piled on that porch to enjoy it. With extended family and friends, that could end up with 15 to 25 people crammed in that small home all at once. People with bigger houses came here to sit on the floor and eat or sleep, because this was a home. Many found it a relief to not have to put up or keep up pretenses. You knew you were loved no matter what was wrong with you!

Propriety Frays

So, Lillie danced in her ballet productions, went to school, went to work, cheered at games and continued to date the sometimes difficult Richard. By December, she was growing tired of him and always having to do things his way. He had become more demanding and not pleased with Lillie's growing confidence. Richard would raise his voice at Lillie when he was upset with her. Lillie always felt that he must be correct, that she just didn't understand. She would end up apologizing and then Richard would be a darling to her. Sometimes, he was so good to her that it took away the awful, niggling feeling that something was not right and good about Richard and his family.

Lillie's mother took her to the doctor to see if they could help with the weight loss and sickness her daughter often felt. After the examination, Lillie was given vitamins and told to slow her schedule down. She took the vitamins twice, then never again as they upset her stomach even more than it already was. She did not slow her schedule and even added prom committee to her list of activities, but that met during school hours so it worked out fine. March brought another big ballet production. This time she was a flower in Swan Lake. Richard was not as excited to help her practice and she was seeing less of him lately. Rumors of him taking another woman to a bar were circulating and she thought they were most likely true. It saddened her, but she knew in a few months she could possibly be busy and travelling with the dance company. She realized that Richard understood this too.

In the middle of a Swan Lake practice, she passed out. This brought her again to the doctor who re-examined her and delivered the scandalous news that she was pregnant. He felt she was about two months along and should have a late September or early October baby. She was shocked, scared to death to tell her parents and Richard, but relieved that she could graduate in May without anyone knowing her situation. Then the realization hit her hard, the dance company! It was this truth that brought on her crying in the doctor's office. Her mother came in and collected her. The doctor told Thelma about the baby and she too cried, but reassured Lillie that the timing was good. Thelma was relieved that Lillie could get married quickly and maybe people would not focus too much on the timing. She could not understand Lillie's true devastation. Lillie would not consider releasing the baby for adoption, so her dancing dream crashed. Then Lillie did what she did best, she put it out of her mind. She continued with her life as though nothing had changed. Her parents did speak with Richard's parents and with Richard. They agreed a quick marriage at the end of May, just after graduation, would work perfectly. Richard was angry, but went along as he felt it was the socially correct thing to do. He knew he could not ruin his family's carefully kept appearance of propriety. Sally would never recover from it and he did love his mother. His father had taken him aside and explained that marriage did not mean that Richard couldn't have fun with other women, he just had to be careful. So a May 26th wedding was planned with very little input from Lillie or Richard.

Richard dutifully took Lillie to the senior prom. Lillie was gorgeous in her frosty peach prom gown. The gown was strapless and tight in the bodice, but full and swishy over the stomach that was just beginning to get a little round. Her tummy and waist were still much smaller than most girls her age. Lillie continued to wear her regular clothes to school since circle skirts were popular and she had not really added much weight to her frame yet, just a roundness to her normally flat stomach and breasts. Her dancing had kept her tiny and firm. Her muscles were strong. She loved her dress and shoes, many pictures were taken that night. Lillie felt proud and happy. As Richard drove her home afterward, she made sure to keep the talk light and steered him away from baby and wedding talk. She wanted to be a normal high school girl for a bit longer. Graduation was coming up so soon, just two weeks to go until the May 23rd celebration. Lillie had put in a few extra hours at the Palace to get the right dress and shoes for her graduation day.

On May 22nd, Lillie felt very different. She told her mother that something was not right with the baby. She was feeling movement, but her back hurt so much. Thelma said it was from too much dancing and working at the Palace. Lillie did not go to school and that was rare. Graduation was tomorrow and she was hoping to be better by then. That night she did begin to feel better and was able to go to school the next day, her last day of high school. Spirits were high and all of her friends were so happy. Lillie realized that she had been the only one of her friends to have plans to leave their small town and to have a different life. Now she was just part of them, no different, not special. In fact, she had not felt the edge of that special glow in the last few months. She was close to four months pregnant and only family knew. This was not something she had even discussed with her best friend. She still spoke of traveling with the dance troop and trying out for the Rockettes when she was with her friends, even sometimes with Richard she would forget and talk about dancing. Then she would see the deep sorrow in his eyes. A sorrow for himself, not for her. It was then that reality would crash around her with such force she could feel the wind being sucked from her lungs. She would struggle for air, for equilibrium. They did not know then that it was a panic attack, only that she was "upset". What a tiny word for such a decimating feeling. She didn't want this world and Richard did not truly want her.

It was Lillie's world that had been rocked and ruined, not the others involved in this mess. Richard could still be Richard, keep his job, his goals and his dignity. Her family would move on normally with their lives with their married daughter living near. Her friends' plans would all stay nicely in place. Only she would experience the dramatic changes. Changes to absolutely everything she was and had planned to be. It was this thought that brought her to her knees in the senior hallway. What was happening? No, it wasn't the thought, it was the pain. The worst pain ever. She could not compose herself, could not regain her dignity. This was not ok. This was a scene and Walloon women did not cause scenes! Her parents were called. She had been taken to the office with the suspicion of appendicitis on her teachers' minds. She and her parents thought it could be that or maybe a miscarriage. They took her home, but the pain was unbearable and she screamed out loud. Thelma called for an ambulance. She knew her daughter was losing that baby. If they could keep it hushed, everyone would think it had been appendicitis. Her heart soared with hope, yet there was sorrow at the thought of losing that little grandchild. She had been warming up to that thought, her first grandbaby.

The ambulance arrived and they whispered their fears to each other and to one attendant and begged him to keep it a secret. He vowed he would and they could see the shock and fear in his eyes. He had gone to school with their son, Jack. He had known the boy that had died. They could see this ambulance attendant felt sorry for them. Thelma and Boyd did not want his sorrow for them, his pity, but what could they do? They smiled and Thelma rode with Lillie. She told Boyd to stay home. They didn't want to be a spectacle at the hospital and there was nothing he could do anyway. Lillie was shocked to see her mother in public. Thelma avoided it so well. Sometimes she even sent others to the store for the family needs, but Thelma worked at this hospital as an aide, so she felt somewhat comfortable there. And she loved, loved, loved this daughter of hers. She was worried and scared. Lillie could see the fear and hear it in Thelma's high pitched nasal voice, a voice she only had when there was fear or tragedy. Now, Lillie began to panic.

She was ripping apart, so this is how it felt to die. She knew that the baby would die, it was only 4 months in gestation and now she would die too. She began to think it might be an ok way out of this situation. She could go to heaven with her baby and maybe not disgrace her family. She could go to heaven and get away from this pain! She heard the attendant say that he saw the baby's head. Oh God, not here in the ambulance. She did not want her baby to die here, but she did not know why she felt so passionate about it. Soon, she felt herself not resigning to death any longer. She was fully focused on needing to push. They were in the emergency room now and nurses and a doctor were yelling things at her, but she had no idea what. She was in her own little bubble of intense pain and pushing to get that baby out. She heard crying, was she crying? What was that, who was that? There was a baby being held in front of her. She asked the baby if she was going to die now. A nurse told her that no one was going to die. Lillie was confused, the nurse was smiling and holding a real live baby. The doctor looked shocked and shook his head. He mumbled something about going to tell her folks. Lillie was very confused. She was a child trying to be pulled together and mature. She felt unfocused and saw her body shaking. The nurse reassured her that the convulsions were normal after giving birth. Another nurse brought over smelling salts fearing that her patient was about to pass out. Lillie wanted to pass out and wake when she may be better able to sort all of the facts.

The baby cried, this child was real and alive, demanding attention. Lillie reached for the infant, just as the nurse turned and whisked the infant out of the room. The doctor came back to speak with Lillie, assuring her the baby was alive, healthy and, to everyone's surprise, full term. He went on about never seeing such a case, asking her if she did not notice missing periods. Lillie came alive with a protective vengeance she never knew existed. She told the doctor that her periods were often irregular and spotty, many dance friends had told her they experienced the same from the rigors of dancing. She then demanded that her child be brought back to her. The old physician was not used to demands and not happy to have delivered this child out of wedlock, calling the infant a "bastard" in his mind. He told her that she would see the child when he decided it was best, he then turned and left. Lillie felt empty, sick and nauseous. She also felt controlled by others. These were in conflict with the inexplicable joy and power she felt as well.

An hour later, a nurse's aide returned with the infant. She had a smug look as she passed the baby to Lillie. She said, "It's hungry" and left. Alone with this little stranger in her arms, she was amazed at the love she felt, but that sharp, "It's hungry" comment made her realize that she did not know if this baby was her daughter or her son. She unwrapped the crying infant to see. Her heart leapt, this baby was a girl. She had no names picked out, she had not had long to know this was happening and most of that time she forced herself into such denial that naming a baby was impossible. She tried out different girl names and nothing seemed right. This baby was now screaming and Lillie had only a surface knowledge on how to feed it, no, not "it", her. How to feed her? She held the baby to her breast and the infant tried to suckle, but things did not seem right. How could her mother have done this with 6 babies, one having died only weeks after being born? That baby would have been Lillie's older sister, but Lillie may not have been born if Lucy had lived. Lillie was conceived two months after Lucy's death and that may not have happened if she had survived. She unhappily remembered the story of her father hearing the news of little Lucy's death and how he then fell down the stairs of the house. His grief was as intense as his love was strong. The baby had died during a nap, just stopped breathing, just stopped living. It made Lillie shiver and draw her new baby closer.

Thelma walked in on a sobbing girl with a crying baby trying to nurse. She was competent in this area and instructed her daughter on what to do and how to do it. Both finally stopped crying as the feeding began. Thelma was also filled with love, she reassured her daughter that it would be ok, that people would forget in time. Lillie knew exactly what her mother meant and that she meant to be comforting. Thelma was in love with this bundle of baby, happy and deeply humiliated at the same time; her daughter knew it. Boyd came in after work, her dad was pure joy. When she told her dad the baby was a girl, he cried and called the baby Kimmy Lou. So that was the perfect name for Lillie to give her child, Kimberly Louise. Boyd was always giving his loved ones nicknames and no one knew how they came about, they seemed to just slip out of him naturally and then stuck. He called his kids, Squirrel, Baby Boydbert, Rabbit, Old Long Legs, Jack was always Jackie, Old Blue Eyes and Lillie Sue Baby is what he called Lillie. Many of his friends were "Ol' Whatchamacallit". He had a cousin he called Poke and so many others. He was adored by the entire town.

While she held her new daughter, her classmates were having their graduation ceremony. Lillie had given birth just hours before the graduation had begun. The graduating class of 1957 was small enough that her absence would be obvious to all, especially her friends. Talk of her collapse in the senior hall and then her absence at graduation had some thinking that she had to have surgery for appendicitis, but that belief was quickly dispelled as gossip in a small town moves faster than anything else, especially when it is true. Before the graduation was over, half of the adults in the small town knew of baby Kimmy's birth. By that evening, everyone would know that the "appendicitis attack" was an illegitimate child. Now, many people in town were married due to unexpected pregnancies, but they had all had the decency to get married before the child was born. For an actual baby to be born to an unmarried woman was unheard of in most situations in 1957. For a woman to not realize how far along she was in her pregnancy was rare and this unfortunate circumstance was the reason for the biggest shock gossip around town.

So where was Richard? The gossip must have gotten to his family by now. Oh, how shocked and upset Sally and Harold must be. Lillie was terrified of the situation with her "in laws to be" as much as it gave her a certain satisfaction to think of their discomfort. This would definitely cause a ripple in their perfect reputation. A reputation, she had come to realize, they did not deserve. Well, visiting hours were over, so she knew that she would not see Richard until tomorrow and that was fine with her. She was grateful for the time to collect her thoughts. There was no wiggle room on hospital visiting hours, doors to the public were closed and locked promptly at seven p.m. and would not open until seven a.m. Lillie was alone with her baby to feed and care for the girl until the nurses showed up to take Kimmy to the nursery, where they would maintain her until the morning. It was important for the new mother to get her rest. Lillie knew that her daughter would get a lot of attention. She knew any staff that could would get up to the nursery to see her "bastard" child. Such a novelty. Everyone would want to know the full details. Amazed that the mother's maiden name appeared on the baby's chart and crib. How uncouth it seemed to them all.

As it happened, the Sullivans did not show at the hospital. Flowers were sent with congratulations and good wishes, but no Richard or his parents in person.

Nurse Cranky Pants

Thelma was relieved that the Sullivans did not show and cause a "commotion". Richard kept himself busy at home after work so he could dodge uncomfortable questions. Everyone knew he was the father, no paternity test would be needed. When Lillie received flowers from Harold and Sally, their note had read that they had a room ready for the baby and expected her and the baby to live with them as soon as she and Richard were married. It was all decided and quite frankly, Lillie never thought to question the plans made. She felt ashamed and was quite aware of the social expectations of 1957 in the U.S.A. She embraced the norms of the day and was aware of her aberrant behavior, a situation she surely did not choose out of any type of rebellion. It was because of her lack of backbone, her lack of being able to stand up for herself, which was the reason she was in this very situation. Richard was charming and pushy and she had given in to him all summer. This is when she had become pregnant. During the school year, she had kept herself busy enough to avoid any more sexual advances, for the most part. So she would follow the plan made, but was surprised at how well her heart took all of this. Somehow, having this small being, she was adjusting to the changes in her own plans. She knew it was this new love she had inside of her that was responsible for her satisfaction with her entire future being changed. Her dancing could wait and perhaps there could still be a way for her to become a professional dancer in time. As soon as this daydreaming brought her hope, in came the cranky, self- righteous day nurse. Her humiliation returned anew with the looks and comments from this woman. She wanted to be able to stand up to people like this and to let them know that she was better than this situation she was in, that her daughter was better than this treatment being dished out. She sat silently and took whatever meanness came her way.

Thelma had arrived during Nurse Cranky Pants' tirade about mothers that are too young and she too kept her peace. Lillie knew she would, it's probably where she got it from herself. Walloon women and most of the men kept their peace when others were mean to them and Lillie saw this as a weakness. She decided it was because they were poor and had no way to truly stand up against those in better positions within society. She made a new declaration to herself and her child to get out of this position, to rise to a position of power and use it to be kind to those less fortunate. She would be sure to have her children raised with more money and better social standing. She might even become a "ten cent millionaire" she didn't care, she was desperate to never feel this way again. "That's enough of that now!" came a stern voice across the room. It was Thelma speaking directly to the nurse. This nurse would be Thelma's superior at work, but now she was crossing the line with her daughter. To Lillie's surprise and joy, the nurse actually apologized and left the room. Thelma acted as though nothing had happened. When Lillie voiced her surprise at her mother's action, Thelma said simply. "Well, we'll have none of that around this baby." Lillie saw her mother with new eyes and with amazing pride. She saw how this whirlwind of a baby, an utter amazement of life, brought out a side of Thelma that Lillie had never seen. This was a protectiveness paired with a dignity that Lillie began to see as priceless. When her mother then turned to the baby and cooed, "Aren't you a pretty little thing?" Lillie was shocked. Had her mother talked to her like this when she was a baby? She could not imagine it. Thelma was kind and loving, but not complimentary to gushing. No, never gushing! Yet, here she was, cooing and gushing over this surprise child. This infant that had rocked their lives, brought unwanted attention and even caused quite a scene was being adored by a woman who avoided attention at high costs.

On the third day at 5:07p.m., Lillie's parents took her and the baby home. She ate supper at the family table while the newest member of the Walloons slept in a bassinet that had been used by all six of Thelma's babies. At 7:00 that same evening, Richard arrived. He held the baby and seemed quite taken with his new daughter. Lillie felt so relieved to see that Richard was happy. He told her and her family that he loved this new little family of his. He asked if she was ready to be married soon and of course she was. Richard left after about an hour's visit.

A Family of Her Own

Baby Kimmy was 15 days old when her parents were married at the court house. Her birth certificate could now be changed to reflect her father's last name. This was not at all the way things had been planned, but Lillie was over the moon with joy. Lillie had taken to calling the infant Kimberly as others still called her Kimmy. Lillie wanted to begin to embrace a sophisticated lifestyle and felt that "Kimberly" was more acceptable to that life. Soon, all but a few people called the baby, Kimberly. Of course she was still Kimmylou to her grandfather and on occasion he would even call her "Kimmzywimmzy", no one knows why. Whatever struck Boyd as a good name to call you, that's what you got called. Lillie moved into Richard's parents' home for the next several months as they saved up to rent an apartment. They had found a nice upstairs apartment in an old farmhouse that was not far from town. The family that owned it was very welcoming and sweet to the young couple even though they knew the truth. So it was planned to be there home in a few months. Lillie could not wait. While she truly appreciated how accepting and loving Sally and Harold were with their new granddaughter, she was weary of the constant advice and not so slight reprimands. Sally did bring home beautiful clothing for the baby from the clothing store she worked part-time at. She appeared to enjoy spending some of her money on the darling little girl items. Sally had also created a sweet little nursery in the corner of the large hallway upstairs. She made it very clear that when Richard and Lillie moved out, they were not to take the nursery items. She wanted them left there for visits. Lillie asked Richard later why Sally would want to keep that when they were only moving ten minutes away. He shrugged and said they would just have to save up for a crib they could not afford.

Lillie was grateful to an older girlfriend when she offered to loan some nursery items to them for the new apartment. When she shared this news with Richard in front of his parents, she was surprised to see Sally bristle and scoot to the kitchen to sulk. Why would she not be happy, unless she did not want them to move? Looking back it did seem that Sally had tried to discourage them from leaving with all of her good reasons for them to stay and save money, get help and to give them time to learn how to properly care for an infant. Yet it was her very actions of "helping" that was driving them both out. Harold was also getting grumpier toward Lillie and had begun making her wait on him and run errands. As always, he was fine with Richard and frequently praised him for any little thing he did and Richard did do very little at home.

One evening, as Lillie was rocking her baby upstairs, she overheard Harold and Sally arguing. Harold was telling Sally to back off of Richard and let him leave. Sally was sobbing that she could not let him go, that she felt they were still too young. Lillie heard Harold gruffly tell Sally to shut-up and then there was a slap. She was sure that would be the end of it, but there were more slapping sounds and muffled crying. Lillie didn't know what to do. She put the baby down and crept to the stairs. Harold saw her peering down and began to run upstairs, shouting for

Lillie to keep to herself and mind her own business. Harold raised his arm to slap Lillie. She was petrified and stunned. Her action surprised Harold and herself. She stood tall, stuck out her face and said, "Make it a good one then." Harold stopped, put his arm down and proceeded to call her many horrible names. He told her that she was obviously a whore who had trapped his son. She was a gold digger in his opinion. What? A gold digger? Lillie turned toward her baby and silently prayed that Richard would not be like his father. They were so alike that this thought, almost a prayer, made her shiver. She heard Harold come up behind her and was surprised that this was not over yet. Harold grabbed her hair and pulled hard. Lillie clasped her hand over her own mouth hoping not to wake her child by screaming out. She could feel and hear his ragged, angry breathing. "You mind yourself and keep your place or you will be sorry, you understand?" he said in a quiet voice. Almost a laughing superior sounding voice, Lillie later decided. He then shoved her hard and she fell to the floor, shocked. Lillie had never been treated like this, she had never been verbally or physically assaulted and was in a dream like state when she saw Harold walk to the crib. He leaned over and stared. "Pretty baby", he said. "Next time, have a boy, a good, handsome, strong boy. Then you may be worth something." he strode away and down the stairs as though he were a king. As though he was right and had to keep them in line. Bitterness and bile crawled its way up her throat and into her mouth. She was sick to her stomach with him. This was awful, he was awful. She had renewed love and concern for Sally. Is this what she put up with? Is this why she didn't want them to leave? Perhaps, Sally felt things would be worse if they left, although Lillie had never witnessed Richard defending his mother, Harold was always in a better mood when

Richard was home, so there could be something to this fear of Sally's.

Lillie discussed the episode quietly with Richard when he got home. They had taken Kimberly for a stroller ride around the block. She spoke softly so that nosey neighbors would not hear. Richard appreciated his new wife's discretion. He appeared visibly shaken as Lillie described the physical and verbal abuse she witnessed and then experienced. He tried to dismiss it as perhaps too many beers, but admitted to having seen his father this way before, though not often and never more than one slap ever. He thought his father had only hit his mother that once, but Lillie's suspicion was that Sally was great at hiding it from everyone. That afternoon, Lillie had come down to Sally's red cheeks and swollen eyes. She asked if Sally was ok. Sally had said that she had cried too hard over a simple argument, that she had rubbed her cheeks too hard while crying and had bruised them. She was pretty convincing. Sally was known to be anemic and to bruise extremely easily. Lillie could see how well the cover ups must have worked for her and for Harold. For his part, Harold was very charming and well liked in the small town. There were rumors about his infidelity, but he was liked. He was able to hide the devil inside with Sally's help and now he fully expected Lillie to continue that tradition.

Richard told Lillie that the Musburgers had their apartment ready early and that they could start moving in that week-end. This made them both happy, but Lillie's heart was heavy for strained and sad Sally. This went far in explaining and excusing her mother-in-law's penchant for being critical and controlling. Lillie would try to be more supportive of Sally in the future. She also made a strict decision to guard Kimberly from her paternal grandfather. She would keep a close eye on the two when they were around Harold. It was obvious that Harold had little to no respect for women.

As the couple packed and prepared to leave with their new baby, Sally fussed over every detail. Richard and Lillie had found a used couch, chair, kitchen table and chairs for free from family and friends. The nursery was outfitted with the furniture from Lillie's friend. The Musburgers had said that they could use the washer and dryer on their enclosed porch out back. Lillie felt they had all they needed and both of them were very pleased to be moving in by the end of June. Their baby would be one month old when they moved. Climbing the outside stairs to the second story was so much work with all of the furniture and boxes, but once it was done and they were alone they were very pleased with themselves. They would sleep on the couch until they were able to save for a bed of their own. That was another item that Sally would not part with and Lillie's parents could not part with. The bed Lillie had slept in growing up was a double bed, but she had always shared it with Sarah and sometimes Betty Sue as well. Sarah now had that bed to herself as well as the room. Lillie realized that she had never slept alone or had her own room her entire life. She would have to be sure to ask Sarah how it felt to be in her own room and alone in a bed. Richard had always been alone. This is why she felt he needed time away from her sometimes. He was good to her, loved his daughter and worked to provide, but seemed aloof at times. He would stay out all night, ending up at his parents' house to sleep in his old bed alone at least once a week. Those were difficult nights for Lillie as she was afraid and jumpy all night. She felt so vulnerable and like she was in total charge of protecting her baby, there was no way she could sleep much at all.

A Curious Picture

Jack was coming home for Christmas this year. They were all excited and anxious to see him. Lillie had sent pictures of her new family and hoped that Jack felt differently about Richard by now. Jack and Richard never got along in high school. Jack was one year ahead of Richard, but had no respect for him at all. They had been involved in two fights during their high school years, both occurring off of school grounds. One time Harold had called the police citing Jack for assault. That went nowhere fast when witness after witness blamed Richard for the altercation. She wondered why Jack and Richard had to be like that. Anyway, plans were being made so that she and Richard could be with Jack during the visit. She was so proud to show off her baby and was excited for Jack's arrival. He had spent the better part of this year in Korea. He had moved up the ranks quickly and had just become a sergeant. Reports sent home were vague, but did refer to winning some battles that were hard fought. Jack also had sent a curious picture of himself outside of a Korean home with his arm around a young Korean woman. This had prompted giggling from Sarah, Betty Sue and Boyd Jr., but Boyd Sr. told them that Jack was only friends with the South Koreans and this was probably a friendly family to the G.I.'s. That was how it had been for his buddies and himself during World War II. He had fought all over Europe and had some terrible experiences, but he always reported the European people as being helpful, taking them in to feed and protect the G.I.s. His children listened to him and knew he spoke the truth, but something about the way Jack had his arm around this young woman and with no one else in the picture seemed odd, it seemed intimate. To top it off, Jack had a beautiful smile on his face, a smile no one had seen since the horrible accident. Thelma kept the picture close and looked at it often throughout the days leading to his visit. Lillie looked at the photo and had her suspicions about Jack's relationship with the woman in the photo. She observed how the woman leaned toward Jack, the way Jack had her nestled under his arm with his other hand on her waist. This was more than a friendly family dinner. Jack looked happy, looked comfortable and at home with this foreign looking young woman.

Jack arrived home 4 days before Christmas to a happy and excited family and group of friends. Jack's girlfriend from high school was there as well. They had never officially broken up, but had decided to see others while Jack was in the Army. She flung herself into his arms and Jack looked surprised and uncomfortable. The entire 6 day visit, Jack was extremely quiet and uncomfortable. One could see the love in his eyes and that he really was happy to see his family, yet at the same time the distance Jack had created between himself and others after the accident had only grown deeper. Boyd Jr. tried to talk with Jack about what the Army was like as he was interested in the Army or Marines for himself, but Jack was quiet and changed the subject every time. Boyd Sr. told Boyd Jr. to not talk about the Army and having to leave again, Jack was probably trying to put having to leave again out of his mind. Boyd Jr. was just 10 years old, but he completely understood and that understanding made him sad for his big brother. Boyd Jr. was not happy about his sister's new baby either. Now Kimmy got the attention that he used to get. He decided that he would call her "Kimmy" forever, since it seemed to irritate Lillie.

Pranks

Boyd Jr., called Babe by his family, had always been a prankster and the quick witted comeback king, but now he began to "up his game" so to speak. He did this subconsciously to get the attention back on him. He had been the "baby" and the center of everything at least that was how he saw it. Now, with this infant around, everyone went straight for the baby and talked about the baby and bought stuff for the baby. Ahhhh, "for the baby", he was tired of it! His family soon became afraid to walk into a dark room or sit near him due to his many pranks with fake spiders, dog doo and puke. Next, he set his sights on terrorizing the one and only family bathroom. There was an opening, like a window, high up in the side wall of the restroom that faced into a side hallway, very strange and no one knew why it was that way. Thelma said quite a few homes in the area were built this way and thought it was because it gave the person inside another exit if the door was stuck or due to a fire. That window became little Boyd's perfect "window of opportunity" for pranks. This window was large enough for one to crawl through, but up high enough that people walking by could not see in. To get out one would need to stand on the edge of the tub and climb through, so it had never been a real problem for the family until now. Things would come flying through at them as they sat on the commode. During a bath, with the window directly above the tub, fake spiders would dangle down, cold water would be dumped onto the person soaking below. What really creeped out visitors, would be the fake faces on sticks that Boyd Jr. had designed. He was a master at edging the "head" up just a bit, so just the top would show and then sneak it down and wait for a long time before sneaking it up yet again. People sitting on the commode would get a glimpse of the head creeping up and wonder if they were imagining things, until they could deny it no longer and just knew that someone was spying on them while they pooped. It was unnerving and one was in such a delicate position, you couldn't always just get up. Boyd Jr. knew when to stop and sneak away, leaving the flustered and sometimes frightened person wondering. Family soon knew who was up to this and would yell at him to stop and chase him. It was wonderful fun and attention that served only to keep him at it. Friends on the other hand were frequently confused and that brought Boyd joy as well.

Jack and Gyeong

Jack heard about the increasing pranks and witnessed them, but was never the butt of these jokes. Somehow, everyone knew better than to prank Jack. Although he was so happy to be state side, Jack did have a secret longing to get back to South Korea. He was stationed in Soule and was battling to keep the people of the Northern part of Korea from sneaking across the divided country. Some tried to cross to see family or to get out of the north due to lack of food and communist government. Some groups of North Korean soldiers were ordered to try to cross to attack or to be spies. What Jack did not know was that this demilitarized zone would last for a very long time. For now, Korea was just two separate countries that both sides wanted reunited as one.

He did have a secret from his family and felt that perhaps only Lillie had guessed at it by the look in her eyes. Jack felt like all would work out well when he was in Tague, Korea, but here at home in Ohio everything looked different to him. He began to realize for the first time that in order for his relationship with Gyeong to work, he would need to stay in Korea. Although Gyeong was a main reason for Jack's desire to return, he secretly admitted how wonderful it was to be admired by his Captain. Jack would never say this to anyone, but he was a great soldier. He did not know why for sure, but it may have been his lack of fear to die. His fellow soldiers trusted him and looked to him for guidance and answers. This is part of why he began to rise through the ranks quickly. He loved the training, the discipline, the adrenaline, he loved it all, except for the thought of killing someone in battle. He felt he could do that without batting an eye when faced with the moment, but something like that weighs very heavily on a soul. He hated the thought of potential death of his fellow soldiers even more. It was a wonderful feeling to be so important, needed and good at something. Yet this also brought about the possibility that he may actually have to kill at some point in his Army career. He felt that he deserved to suffer as he still fought a lot of demons from Wendell's death. It was a Hell to be relived over and over and Jack felt he deserved this. But everyone craves love and peace. Gyeong brought Jack that.

Gyeong had been helping her parents with their barley fields. They also had wheat fields, but the young sons took care of those. Gyeong had two younger brothers, Hoon and Hwan. They estimated their ages at 14 and 16 years of age, but birth records were not kept and birthdays were never celebrated in Korea. Gyeong was between 18 and 19 years old and Jack was 20. She had seen American soldiers protecting her country and her people and grew to admire them. Gradually, she became used to their peculiar looks and actions. Her family, as were most Korean's, was Buddhist. She did know of several families that were Christian converts, particularly Protestants. Sixty nine percent of Koreans were Buddhist and only 22% were of a Christian faith. The fact that the American soldiers were most likely of some Christian faith did not bother the Yoon family. It did not change their beliefs or ways. Jack was not accepted as a possible suitor at all. The Yoons were not happy with how close Jack and their daughter were becoming. Family forbid it to go any further and Gyeong complied, at first. She was a good girl. She was honest, but she was in love for the first time. Jack was handsome even by her Korean standards. She had seen a few American movies and knew that he was handsome by American standards as well. He was happy when he was with her. He had begun seeking her out whenever he could get away. Teague was a full day's trip from Soule, so as the Americans had begun to assist building new barriers, their visits had become fewer. Jack used any leave he had to come visit, once being able to stay only an hour before having to begin the trip back to Soule.

Her English was becoming so much better and Jack's Korean was basic, enough to get by. Gyeong spent a week with Jack in Soule, just before he left to visit the states for Christmas. When she returned to Tague, her family would not let her back. She was tossed out to survive on her own. She had disgraced her family by being with a man overnight, by leaving for Seoul on her own. Jack did not discover this until he arrived back to base. Gyeong had had little money as it was. She took a train headed back to Soule until her money ran out. Then she walked and ate out of trash cans or fields. Arriving in Soule, she begged the American soldiers to have pity on her. She promised them that Jack would repay them any money. They hid her in a shed and kept her fed and safe. Jack was going to have his hands full when he returned. To his fellow soldier's surprise, Jack was happy to have Gyeong there. He paid them back, got a small apartment for her and happily took care of the girl.

The U.S.A. sent fresh soldiers to help the South Korean army guard the Demilitarized Zone. A few miles with barbed wire fencing was all that separated the countries physically, but the political and belief system grew to be hugely separated. Jack knew his time in Korea was coming to a close. He had been with Gyeong for a few months now and was able to visit frequently since her move to Seoul. She had a job in a small factory making clothing and seemed happy to Jack. Gyeong felt that Jack would stay with her. Jack wanted to stay with her, but he was owned by the United States Army and he had no say or choice. He held her so tightly and cried for the first time in more years than he knew. She knew this was a bad sign. Her heart ached so, like never before. She had a secret and was not sure if she should share it. In sobs and gasps, she told Jack that he was going to be a father. She needed him to stay and help her. He vowed that he would find a way. If the Army did not let him stay in Korea, he would leave when his time was up and come back for her. He would live in Korea or take her to the U.S., but she would need to give him time. She smiled and promised she would, she had to, Korean woman having biracial children from American soldiers were nothing new and were not respected. Their lives were difficult and their children's lives were miserable. The biracial children were seen as servants at best. Jack knew it would not be much better in the U.S.A., but it would be better than staying in Korea at that time. Jack and Gyeong said their good byes. Jack snuck to Taegue to see the Yoon's, Gyeong's family. They were not happy to see Jack, but served him tea and some kimchee with rice. They were polite. Then Jack told them about Gyeung and begged them to take her back to the farm where they could protect her until he got back for her and the child. He cried and hated himself for it. Tears were not respected anywhere and certainly not here with Chul, Gyeong's father.

Iseul, Gyeong's mother, began to scream. She shouted loudly in Korean and fell to her knees. Jack was destroyed to see her this way. He told Iseul that he loved Gyeong and would be back for her as soon as he could, but it may take one to two years to work it out. She grabbed him by the shirt and made him promise her over and over that he would come back for her daughter until they were both exhausted. Iseul sat at her small table, with her knees curled to her chest and her head on her arms and sobbed. Chul looked lost and then angry. Wisely, the boys stayed outside and eavesdropped. Jack caught glimpses of their angry eyes and a small part of him quickly wished that they would kill him as he came out of the small house. Chul dismissed Jack with a quick nod and a grunt that sounded like he would take his daughter back. In what little Korean he knew, it sounded like they were going to pass off Gyeong's baby as a Korean soldier's baby. A soldier killed in battle. He pieced together Iseul saying that with Jack's dark looks, the baby would probably look Korean. It was all they could hope for. Jack was leaving when he felt a rock bang into his back, then another into his head. He stopped and waited for the attack. As he turned, he saw a Korean insult from the boys' arms and hands. He saw tears in their eyes mixed with the anger and humiliation he had brought to their small family. He felt like the bastard he knew he was. Jack continued on his way back to base. He flew for the states tomorrow.

A Difficult Goodbye

Jack held Gyeong all night. They spoke of their plans and she shared that the baby should be born around early June. Jack felt more love for this woman than he had ever known was possible. He felt that he could make this work for his child. It would all take time and patience and money, lots of money to get things arranged to bring them all to the United States. He pulled himself together the next morning. They both put on happy faces. Gyeong wanted Jack to remember her as the happy, pretty woman she was. Jack wanted Gyeong to see his happy face as a promise that he would be back. Gyeong was relieved that Jack had made going home a possibility for her. She promised not to embarrass her parents by ruining the lie they were telling the people of her village near Taegue.

They kissed goodbye. Gyeong spent the next few days holding her stomach as she packed her few things and listened to plane after plane flying out. She would not leave until they had all gone. That way she would know that she had heard Jack's plane leave. She ached so bad for him that she thought she might die or kill the baby within her from all of the grief she felt. She wondered how people could live through such sorrow, her face was swollen from all of the crying. She forced herself to eat for the baby, but only ended up throwing up due to so much crying and distress. She packed the beautiful silk hanbok (traditional Korean dress) Jack had bought her as well as the few other pieces of clothing she had. She packed the few photos she had of them together along with the

Christian necklace that Jack used to always wear. He had left it behind on the table for her and the baby. Her bag was light and Jack had given her enough money for a train ride and gifts for her parents. The money he left was all that he had and it would last her almost a year. She walked to the train station, excited to see her family and with hope in her heart. She smiled at everyone she passed. They probably thought she was a crazy woman.

Gyeong's father was angry when she returned. She knew he would be, but had hoped for better. Her mother was glad to see her, hugged her and then backed off and kept her distance. Hoon and Hwan were excited and hugged her a lot. They knew the truth, but were happy to discuss the lie as though it were real too. A brother-in-law dying in guarding the DMZ had brought them some measure of admiration from their school friends, especially since many of them had lost loved ones to the war as well. The baby was seen as a promise of hope and regrowth for the Korean people. Woman carrying babies from dead soldiers were given a certain amount of respect since they brought this promise forth from their own bodies. The villagers were kind to Gyeong, her friends and brothers were good to her. She felt special until she looked into her parents' eyes. The truth of a half American grandbaby was very upsetting to them. Even if no one found the truth out, they knew and that was devastating to them all.

Back in base in the United States, Jack spoke with his commanding officer. He was informed that bringing Gyeong to the U.S. was a bad idea, but possible. The higher rank he held the more likely it would be that he could bring her home. It would be faster as well. Jack was not too far away from becoming a captain, so that gave him hope. He trained in the states and was sent to Europe for a time. Before he knew it a year was up, he was a captain now and his child had been born in Korea. He heard nothing in response to the few letters and money he had sent to the Yoon address. He thought surely Gyeong would contact him. That she would find a way. His grief and desperation turned him into a mad man by the time he was sent to Vietnam.

Lillie and a New Baby

As baby Kimberly grew, Lillie saw Richard become more comfortable as a husband and a father. They had turned a corner in their relationship and both were very happy with their life together. The small apartment was comfortable and Richard was saving for a house. He had spent their first house savings on a nice new car for himself, but had reassured Lillie that he was determined to get back on track for the house. She accepted what he decided on the surface, but it bothered her more than she let anyone know. She was a bit too much like Sally in wanting others to think she was doing well and was happy. Thelma had also been guilty of raising children that did not complain or share their problems with anyone. So Lillie, true to her nature, continued on against the small discriminating voice in her head when Richard proposed having another child. He was hoping for a boy this time and he let everyone know it. Surprisingly, Harold, Lillie's father-in-law, was completely smitten with his granddaughter. It had been Harold that had told her she should have a boy next time several months ago, but now he adored the little granddaughter so much that he told Richard to never mind about having a boy, that this little girl thing was pretty wonderful. Lillie had been amazed at Harold's transformation around Kimberly. He doted on her and any bad mood he was in would melt away instantly. Sally loved having the little girl around as she had never had a daughter of her own and she loved the man that Harold became around the little one. Kimberly had the best clothes and carriage. She was played with and sung to by both of her grandfathers.

Boyd, Lillie's father, would sit on the floor and sing to the first grandbaby. Even Boyd Jr. had begun to lose the jealousy around Kimmy and began to enjoy his toddler niece. He was proud that Kimmy screamed and laughed at the sight of Boyd and Boyd Jr. All could see that these two were favorites of the little girl. She would snuggle and rock with her aunts and grandmas, beam at her Grandpa Harold and jump and scream at the sight of either Boyd, Grandpa or Uncle. There is a purity of soul and love that children and babies seem fabulous at detecting and Kimberly knew her Grandpa Boyd and Uncle Boyd were pure, unselfish, loving people. And they were absolute fun as well.

So Lillie was lulled into a peaceful joy at the thought of Richard wanting another baby and, by proxy, wanting her. He began coming home earlier and staying with Lillie and Kimberly more. He seemed to enjoy family outings. He did not play with his daughter, but appeared to enjoy her. He did not take care of his daughter, buy her things or talk to her much, but he watched with love in his eyes as she played alone or with other family members. If the toddler was cranky or crying, he usually found a way to leave or get outside. No, Richard would not be inconvenienced or irritated. He would escape every time and he always had been this way. He never had to put up with any trouble or issue. His parents had bailed him out of any trouble or situation that he had not wanted to deal with. Having Kimmy had even been smoothed over and made easier for him by his parents and Lillie. For Richard, having another baby was interesting and a chance at having a son. He thought he wanted the relationship with a son that he and his father had. Harold knew that Richard would struggle with forming that type of relationship as he had recently begun to realize how ruined and spoiled Richard truly was. Harold had approached Richard about having just the one child and not going for a second. He tried to explain the positives about having only one to care for and provide for. Richard had his mind made up. He wanted a son, but what if this second child was another daughter? Richard did not want that at all. He did worry about that a bit, but continued with the determination to have his way. Lillie convinced herself that Richard would love another little girl once it was born, she was sure of it, so she convinced herself to go ahead and try to get pregnant as Richard wanted.

This pregnancy was completely different. Lillie was tired and getting bigger in her 6th month than she had ever been during her first pregnancy. Her breasts were larger than ever and Richard loved that, but then her belly began to catch up and he lost complete interest in Lillie and the baby to be. He was rumored to have been with several different women in several nearby towns. Lillie was heart sick and knew it was most likely true. Here she was, bigger than she ever thought possible, exhausted and alone with a toddler that could be very demanding for attention. Kimberly was a sweet, but busy little girl that had been the center of all adult attention. Lillie's sisters, Sarah and Betty Sue would come over and help out as much as they could and Lillie was grateful for that. The problem with them being over so often was that they soon realized how much Richard was absent. This news was shared with the rest of her family resulting in their anger and resentment toward Richard. Lillie tried to downplay it. She made excuses that he was working overtime for the new house they finally had bought. Her family knew better. The house was one of the least expensive in the town and Richard spent a lot of money on entertaining himself. Lillie and Richard had to borrow half the down payment money from Boyd Sr. In addition, Richard had recently bought another new car for himself. Lillie had no car for herself, but that was common during the 1950's and 1960's. She also had no money for herself, only just enough for groceries.

Lillie was hot, sweaty and 9 months pregnant that August when she found herself in labor. She called Richard at work and explained that she needed him to take her to the hospital. She felt a small part of her wonder if Richard would come and get her. To her relief, he sounded excited and happy. She heard him yell out to his boss, she heard his boss yell out a congratulations to Richard. The line went dead and Richard was there by her side so quickly she knew he had sped through town. It pleased her greatly. He held her gently around her back and led her to the car. Even in her pain, she took time to relish his touch and care during this moment. She realized how much she had missed his touch recently or even the chance to look at him. Richard put Lillie in the car and ran back for her bag. At the hospital, as she was wheeled away, it dawned on him that he did not know where Kimmy was. He called out to Lillie and she reassured him that the neighbor, June, had Kimmy and would take her to Thelma for the night. That Thelma and Lillie's sisters would be able to care for the toddler for the next few days was a huge relief to Lillie. She could never do all of this without them.

A Different Birth than the First

The Sullivans were at the hospital this time. Harold and Sally came as soon as Richard called. They were in the waiting room with Thelma, Sarah and Betty Sue. Boyd Sr. was at work and Boyd Jr was in school. No one spoke in the waiting room for the first hour. When Boyd Sr. came in after work, the mood lightened considerably. He had such an infectious smile and good natured personality that all relaxed and began to speak to each other politely. The Sullivans and the Walloons did not dislike each other. They lived in the same neighborhood and had some of the same friends, but travelled in different social circles. Thelma and Boyd did not like the way Richard treated their daughter and they both were often cool and abrupt with him. They had little idea of how poorly Richard did treat Lillie and how little time he spent with his wife and daughter. Boyd and Thelma would be supportive though, if this is what Lillie wanted. No one in that waiting room had any idea how tortured Lillie had been to give up dance except for her sister Sarah. Sarah and Lillie didn't talk about it much, but they had a special connection. Sarah knew how miserable her sister was, in spite of the joy Kimberly brought to her. She knew that Lillie would go back and do things very differently if she could. Sarah desperately hoped this baby would be a boy. She had heard Richard's comments and had heard him speak about wanting only a son this time. He was determined that having a son would bring him joy and a relationship he greatly desired. Both Richard and Sarah errantly thought that a boy would make the little family happy, as Richard could have his son and go off on adventures and Lillie could have her daughter to spend time with and perhaps teach her to dance. Sarah and Lillie thought Kimberly could have the life that Lillie never got the chance to live.

That evening a nurse came into the waiting room with a little bundle of blue for the Sullivans and Walloons. They could look as the nurse held the baby before taking him to the nursery. They were all quiet with awe. They were polite and appropriate. They caused no scenes. When the nurse left, they spoke excitedly and congratulated Richard. There was much joy and love in that little hospital waiting room in small town Ohio. They shook hands. Thelma was allowed to see her daughter briefly. Lillie looked exhausted but exuberant. Thelma was so very happy for her and felt that things were definitely headed in the right direction for the entire Walloon clan. She was unaware that her Jack, now safely stationed in Germany, had just received orders to deploy to Vietnam. He had a week to visit family before he left. He knew he would use that week to go to Korea.

Lillie relished her time in the hospital with her little son. Richard came every day after work and twice brought Kimberly to the window outside of the hospital so they could wave and blow kisses. Lillie thought they had turned a corner. She was thrilled that Richard had taken it upon himself to bring the little girl, how thoughtful of him. Then just as quickly, she realized it was probably at Sally's suggestion. Even so, he had done it and looked happy. She prayed these changes in Richard would stay. Perhaps he had just needed time to mature and adjust to family responsibilities. They had many friends their ages that were married and having children, it was normal now. They were not the main gossip anymore. Lillie did not realize how much talk occurred behind her back when she went in public with Kimberly. Most of the family was unaware of the ongoing gossip about the birth of the little girl that then led to the gossip of Richard's womanizing. Sarah, Betty Sue and Boyd Jr. knew all about the gossip though. They had not been spared and heard it from their friends in school. The friends had obviously heard it from older siblings or parents. It was tough on the Walloon children and they avoided talking about or mentioning Lillie at all costs.

It was day three and time to pack and go home with her new son. Richard would be in after work to pick them up and take them home. She was so very happy. Her little guy had been so contended and peaceful. He already seemed like a much easier baby than her daughter had been. Even nurses commented on how sweet and kind of sober he was. He was very awake and aware, just more contented. Lillie had everything ready to go a bit early so that she could hold her son and rock without interruption. She knew that with her little girl at home, she would be interrupted a lot. They had decided to name the new baby Matthew Richard Sullivan. This baby had a name that would not need to be changed, his father's middle and last names were his from the beginning. This child was, dare she think it even, not a bastard. She rocked and waited. Supper was brought around and the nurses ordered her a tray as she was still waiting for Richard. He had to be there soon. He had been off work at three and now it was five o'clock. She nibbled at the food, too concerned to eat. The nurses reported that they had called his employer for Lillie to see if Richard had to work late. She was wild with anger and sorrow. If there had been an accident, she would have known, so where was Richard? She would not cause a fuss. She would not be the subject of new gossip. Lillie expertly put on a calm and happy face and asked the nurses to call Boyd and Thelma. Surely Richard was busy getting the house ready and had lost track of time. The nurse smiled with a hint of pity, she had called the home number repeatedly with no answer. She blessedly made no comment or mention of their attempts to find Lillie's husband and left to call the Walloon home. Boyd and Thelma arrived within ten minutes. Boyd was excited to see the baby again and Thelma had her socially appropriate face on. She smiled and acted like this had been the plan all along. God bless her mother for naturally pulling this off. Lillie knew her mother would not make a display of herself. This would not turn into the horrid exhibition that Lillie had dreaded. They packed up and received well wishes from all of the nursing staff. Lillie climbed into the front seat with baby Matthew on her lap. Thelma got in the backseat, no easy feat, and they drove Lillie home. Grandma Sally was there with Kimberly so there was an excited homecoming from her daughter. She quietly screamed with her little hand over her mouth. Sally had trained the little girl well. She hugged Lillie's legs and kissed them repeatedly. When Lillie sat down, Kimberly slowly crept in to look at her new baby brother. She was all smiles and wiggles. She brought him toys and helped with bringing blankets and diapers. This was how Lillie imagined it to be minus Richard. She looked at Sally, but did not ask about Richard, she would not show any weakness, she thought it best. Thelma and Boyd had helped get things put away, kissed everyone and then gave Sally a ride home. Lillie was now alone in her new house with her new baby and a two year old ball of energy. Where could he be and what was he doing. She lied expertly to herself that Richard was planning a surprise, had forgotten or had gotten to the hospital just after they left.

Lillie laid Matthew in his bassinette and tucked Kimberly into her bed. She was able to read two stories that helped the little girl go to sleep. She sadly thought how odd it was that Kimberly never asked where her daddy was. With the house quiet, Lillie laid in her bed and cried hard for the first time in a very long time. She had not cried this hard since realizing her dancing was not to be. She cried herself to sleep with the baby boy Richard had so desperately wanted sleeping in the room beside her. She awoke around midnight to the sound of Richard coming in, it was obvious he was drunk. She heard a car pull away and knew that someone had brought him home. She took the baby into Kimberly's room and sat in the rocking chair and nursed. She kept very quiet and hoped that Richard would not come up and look for them or wake the little girl. She was afraid of the truth and did not want to face it. She stayed in that damn hard wooden rocker all night and held her baby and stared at her daughter.

In the morning, Lillie heard Richard getting ready for work. She waited until he was gone and went and got a stash of diapers to keep in Kimberly's room in case this happened again, she would have supplies there too. She found some pillows and borrowed some more pillows from her mother. These she placed in Kimberly's room to soften the rocker for future nights. No one asked about Richard except Thelma. In the privacy of her home, Thelma could be a force to be reckoned with. She told Lillie that she was having none of Richard's cheating and drinking. She was done with him and he had better keep his distance. She told Lillie that she should come home and get those babies away from that situation. She was livid and wanted to protect her family so much. It was maddening how much she wanted to intervene but did not have the power to make things right for her children. And now she had grandchildren to worry over. It was almost too much to bear. She had not foreseen how desperately she would love and want to protect these grandchildren. With the great love came such great pain. Lillie wept a little bit, but told her mother that Richard was still immature and just need time to adapt. She reminded her mother how much Richard had wanted this little boy, so she was sure he would come around. It quieted her mother who was not convinced at all, who felt tigers don't change their stripes. This story Lillie tried to sell her mother actually ended up convincing Lillie that things would be ok and it calmed her to repeat it to herself often.

Korea

Jack took his family week before deployment to go to Korea. He knew he needed to see Gyeong and connect with her and his child. He sent a letter to his parents explaining that he was being sent to Vietnam, but he did not mention having a week leave. He did not want to upset his mother and make her feel rejected or unloved, but mostly, he did not want to try to explain Gyeong or even mention a baby. He had heard a lot of news from home regarding Lillie and Richard and knew that his mother had her hands full of worry and upset. He wished he could hide Vietnam from her, but that was not possible, he could not directly lie to his parents to that degree. He needed them to know where he was. He was scared to go to Vietnam. He was a captain now and would be in charge of many lives. That responsibility scared the shit out of him and that is what would end up making him a hero. He had received a letter from his mother months ago where she had shared a worry, a nightmare that she kept having. She was so glad to know he was on desk and training duty in Germany because she kept having images of Jack being chased and shot at by "Koreans" as she called them. She saw him running through a jungle and she knew he was afraid. He was yelling at men to follow him. It scared her so much, but then she would realize where he was and would relax. Thelma did not know that Vietnam was where the jungles were, not Korea. Thelma also did not pay much attention to current news, she had her hands full with work and family and Lillie. She never allowed herself to think that Jack might go to actual battle. When Jack had received news of his deployment to Vietnam, his mother's letter from months ago came to his mind, front and center. Somehow that woman always knew things ahead of time. He had seen it on many occasions. He would over hear her speaking to her sister about a "dream" and then something very similar would happen in the next few days or months. She had dreamed about Lillie not being able to dance, that her legs were missing, months before they had found out Lillie was pregnant. And now, his mother saw him running scared. He vowed to conquer his fear.

Jack boarded the plane to Korea. This was an army plane, so luxury was not part of the flight experience, but affordability was. This trip had caused him to save a bit more money, but resulted in him having to send a little less to the Yoons. He felt bad about that and hoped it had not caused a hardship for his child and Gyeong. He wrote short notes and hoped Gyeong found an American to read them to her. Although she had learned to speak English quite well, learning to read and write it were very difficult. The Korean alphabet was much more direct and was in symbols. As he flew closer to her, he felt his joy return. He was afraid, but hopeful that she would still want him, still understand him. He prayed this visit would bring her reassurance of his love and comfort. He wanted to plan their future together. He wanted her to encourage their child to learn to speak English well and maybe begin to read and write English from the Americans stationed in Seoul. He allowed his mind to wander as he flew to her.

As Jack collected his small bag, he noticed the people of Korea's kindness and politeness. He felt oddly at home due to the familiarity of it all and the love he had for Gyeong. Grabbing his bag, he ran to find transportation to Taegue. From there he would most likely walk to the small farming village. The train was long and slow. A trip that could take two hours always took at least five or more. As they neared Taegue, Jack grabbed his bag and prepared to disembark. He jogged from the train station down the road leading to Gyeong. Now, it felt like every minute leading to see her was a minute too long. He had written of his arrival, had even had a little help from a buddy to put some words in Korean to help her understand that he was coming to see her. As he jogged he imagined her waiting impatiently near the house. He saw in his mind's eye a slight look of approval and admiration on Iseul's face. Father Yoon, Chul, was another matter. Chul meant "Iron" in Korean and Jack saw Chul as set in his ways as though forged in iron. He did not imagine acceptance on any level from Chul. Mostly, he thought of Gyeong.

As he approached the house, he saw no one waiting. He felt as though he was running toward a ghost town. He walked around the house and checked the sheds, no one. He began walking the fields and saw no one. He was so disappointed he wanted to cry. He went and waited at the house. Evening came and he saw the family walking toward the house. He stood and instantly knew that Gyeong was not among them. They all walked toward him like frozen statues, obviously displeased at seeing him there. He asked about Gyeong and only the youngest brother spoke. "She not here", Hwan said. "Where is she, where is the child", Jack demanded. Hwan explained, in broken English that was much more advanced then Jack had even hoped for, that Gyeong had married and left the village. Jack gasped audibly, how could his Gyeong marry someone else? He kept quiet and listened carefully to all that Hwan was sharing. After Gyeong was married, she left for another village that was far away. They had not seen her for over a year. They had not heard from her for 11 months. Iseul was very worried and sad. Chul had demanded that she marry an older gentleman of some wealth. He said it was to be done to bring the family honor. Iseul disagreed, but could say nothing against her husband's wishes. Jack had Hwan repeat several sentences to be sure he was really understanding this horrible truth.

He could not seem to get any of the Yoons to respond to his questions about the baby. They would just speak of Gyeong as though they did not hear parts of his questions. He knew they were avoiding talk of the child. He pursued the questioning more directly resulting in silence from the family. His frustration and anger only brought about Chul ordering Jack from the house, ordering him to leave them alone. Jack left the small home and walked about 100 feet from the house to the creek that ran slowly and sadly through the country side. He sat by a tree and imagined Gyeong sitting there as a child, then, with tears streaming down his face, he imagined her as sitting there with his child in her arms. Sadness permeated this place. Perhaps it was just his mood, but he felt a great sadness surrounding the entire area. He was sure it was emotion left behind by a broken and grieving Gyeong. He found himself curled on the ground, grasping the ragged weeds growing there and gasping for air. He was in complete shock and grief that mimicked how he would have felt if he had been told Gyeong had died. As he lay there, he realized that this grief may actually be worse than that of grieving her death. He had deep worry that made him ill at the thought of his love being miserable and at the wonder of what had happened to his baby. Yes, this was a horror that Jack had never anticipated. He could not move. His discomfort or physical needs did not even register. He was alone in a way he had not known existed. Constantly, Jack was running plans on how he could find her in the few days he had left through his mind. His body may be motionless, but his mind was busy and frantic. As a foreigner, he would have significant difficulty foraging through this part of the country.

Jack gradually became aware of a presence. Slowly turning his head, he saw Hoon. Ja Hoon was Gyeong's youngest brother. Hoon was still in high school and other than throwing rocks at Jack, he had never interacted with him. All seemed to refer to Ja Hoon as simply Hoon. It was an unusual name by Korean standards. As it turned out, Hoon was an unusual boy. Quiet and wise, Hoon was very observant. He was a very loving person and no one knew how heartbroken he was over his sister's despair and disappearance. His parents thought he knew nothing about Gyeong's pregnancy and forced marriage. His parents also did not know the extent to which Hoon had learned English. English was taught in his high school by an excellent teacher. Hoon then had gone on to practice with soldiers from America whenever he could. This had resulted in Hoon being quite fluent. He had a goal to attend college in the United States and perhaps to live and work there after college.

Hoon knelt down close to Jack, he spoke quietly, almost a whisper. He spoke English clearly and quickly, surprising and bringing hope to Jack. He told Jack to stay hidden somewhere for the night and tomorrow they would venture to a place he had heard of in conversations about Gyeong. He said he could not promise anything, but together they would look for answers. Jack thanked him and took the food Hoon held out to him. It was Hoon's dinner, Jack did not know it was all Hoon would have had for the day. Jack ate and was led to a beaten down old shack among some shrub. He was told to please not move from the shed until Hoon came for him. It was essential that the Yoons not know that Jack was still in the area if Hoon were to be able to get away for the day tomorrow.

Hope rose and fell all night in the little shack. He truly believed and trusted Hoon to be on his side although he was not sure why the teenager was. Along with hope mingled wretchedness and tears, Jack was miserable, hopeful and in a hurry. He came to the conclusion that sending Gyeong to her family was most likely the worst thing he could have done. Instead of serving as protection, her parents had profited from her return. They had probably kept the money he had sent and also gained money from the older, wealthy man they had married her off to. And then there was the child, what in Heaven's name had they done with the child? Perhaps they had sold the baby. Korean families would often take in an orphan to serve as playmates for their own children and then as servants as they grew. Orphaned children were not adopted in the fashion of the United States of America and were considered second class citizens. This thought all but destroyed him. Perhaps the baby was in an orphanage, but that would not be much better at all. There was still the possibility that Gyeong had the child with her, how would a new husband handle that. Also, not a popular or acceptable custom for a new husband to accept children from another man. What if the baby had simply died in birth or shortly after? That was a bit more tolerable to think on as then he knew the child was not somewhere suffering or miserable. All of the options seemed too sad to have happened to someone he loved so deeply.

Just as dawn seeped through the cracks in the shed, Jack saw a shadow at the shed door. Hoon motioning for Jack to move quickly and quietly. The two of them walked in silence until they were past the small farming village. Hoon spoke first, telling Jack that this trip they took would most likely bring bad news and that there was almost nothing to be done about a marriage unless Gyeong's new husband had died or would kick her out. Hoon made it clear that he and his family had been given very little information. They all had travelled to this next village to visit Gyeong and her new husband when she had stopped writing. Upon their arrival, Gyeong and her husband were nowhere to be found. Only a few villagers recognized the name of the wealthy man. They told the family that he was powerful, a merchant and someone to fear. Most villagers appeared too frightened to speak out about him or his family. No one admitted to knowing where he had gone after leaving their village. Hoon was hoping to speak with some of the younger kids, kids his age. He hoped they might not be so careful with their words. He shared that he was glad Jack had come back in time to go with him, but more than anything, Hoon was happy that Jack had truly loved his sister so much. He could see now that the love his sister had spoken of was a true love and it had made her incredibly joyful and content.

This walk had given them both insights into each other's worlds and had served as a time to bond. Jack promised Hoon that regardless of the outcome with Gyeong, he would help Hoon out when he came to the United States. Hoon and Jack shook hands on the promise and each felt a bit closer to Gyeong's love with the promise in hand. Jack could see just the slightest resemblance to Gyeong when Hoon finally smiled for the first time. It broke his heart with the familiarity. If the baby had been a boy, would he have looked like Hoon? Jack thought so. It brought a small measure of comfort to have this young man connect him to Gyeong and the baby.

The village was not just farming. Upon arrival, Jack notice nice looking buildings and what appeared to be stores. People here seemed to have a little better lifestyle than at Gyeong's little farming village. There were many cars and bikes. People were on the streets talking, smiling and conducting the day's business. He followed Hoon down a side street to a small building that resembled a school. Hoon indicated that he wanted to stay there to catch some kids he kind of knew. He was hopeful that they could give him some true insight and not just gossip. He was hopeful for so many things, he wanted the truth and he knew these peers may know things that their parents would not share. Chul had forbid him to speak to any of the teenagers. He had demanded dignity and composure and would not have his family running around causing a scene and more gossip. When Jack heard this, he could not help but think of his own mother. She was always concerned about what the neighbors would think and about keeping a low profile.

A few teens began to wander out of the building toward them. They smiled at Hoon right away and came up to speak. As it turned out, Hoon was quite well known here and well liked. He spoke quickly in Korean and Jack could not make out the conversation. Also, several of the teens engaged Jack into a conversation to practice their English on him. This further distracted Jack from picking up on anything being said in Korean. He would have to trust that Hoon was giving him all of the information. They were there for about 30 minutes when the kids began to leave. They had to get home for chores and jobs.

Jack could see the sadness in Hoon. This was not what he had hoped for. The teens had spoken openly with Hoon. They were relieved to finally be able to share the truth with him. From what they knew, Gyeong had been taken to France with her new husband. They said she never appeared happy and often looked afraid of him. They also shared that the baby had been taken from Gyeong and put in either an orphanage or a hospital. They were not sure where, but knew it was far away from what they heard from their mothers. It was even possible that the baby died. That not knowing was still the hardest part. They did have more knowledge, but that did not bring them closer to finding Gyeong or the baby. One teen felt pretty sure that the child had been sent to an orphanage in Seoul. Jack said he was going to leave that night to get to

Seoul and begin checking orphanages and hospitals. More people spoke English in Seoul due to the American soldiers stationed there to guard the DMZ, so he hoped he would get along ok without Hoon there. Hoon gave Jack an address to mail information to him that was not his home address. He told Jack that he would then be able to see what Jack wrote. He confirmed that his parents had most likely kept any money Jack had sent and they never shared information or mail with their children. Gyeong had been taken away, probably to France. Their child was most likely alive and out there somewhere. He was in a nightmare and had no idea how to get out.

Seoul, Korea

The train from Teague to Seoul pulled into the station on a rainy and windy afternoon. The weather matched Jack's mood and emotions. He grabbed his bag and went to a hotel. Here he looked into the mirror and saw a disheveled, humbled and depressed version of himself. He cleaned up and lay on the bed for a bit just to stretch out, but sleep came upon him in desperation. Jack's body had been on the go and without sleep for far too long. He awoke in the middle of the South Korean night. It was still raining and the wind howled. Jack grabbed his jacket and went out. He walked and smoked. A few bars were open and Korean and American soldiers mingled. He went in. It was like old times. A few drinks in and he had the fleeting feeling of needing to get back to the apartment to be with Gyeong. The slap of reality sent him reeling back onto the street. He walked to the old apartment that he had shared with Gyeong. It was dark and quiet and new people lived there now. He kicked himself for not just leaving Gyeong there. He had sent enough money to support her staying there with the baby. He should have kept her there. He was certainly misguided in thinking she would be in danger staying in Seoul alone. She would have had his money, his letters, and friends. She would not have had to doubt his love and she would be there waiting for him now with their child.

Jack somehow managed to get back to the hotel room in spite of his despair and regret. He made a vow to himself, Gyeong and God that he would not stop searching. He waited in his room and watched the sun come up. He spent the morning and early afternoon searching the hospitals and the only orphanage he could find. If his child was in any of them, he would not be able to find out as the records kept were very few with no identifying information allowed regarding parents. Walking to the Army base airport, he felt a small tug on his heart. A tug as if to say to him that he would never be back here again. He brushed that off and vowed he would do whatever it took. He would return. Captain Jack Walloon straightened his back and his uniform. He was very handsome, strong and determined. He was all business now. He was in control of his emotions and switching gears into becoming the leader he needed to be. He pushed down the sorrow and the fear.

Lillie 1959

Lillie was a busy mom of two little "buggers" as Boyd called them lovingly. It was nearing Thanksgiving and Jack would not be able to get home for the holidays. Lillie had heard some news about Vietnam and it made her worry for Jack. She had learned that the first American soldiers had been killed in the conflict. A Major and a Master Sergeant had been killed during a guerilla strike at Bienhoa. This brought the danger of war to the forefront of all the minds of the Walloons. Thelma was especially sick with worry. She could often be heard on the phone with her sister saying things like, "Lord have mercy" and "Keep him safe Lord, keep him safe" in her high pitch nasal whine. All would silently agree with her pleas as they passed by. Any neighbors that were silently listening in on the party line would also bow their heads with a silent prayer as well. The telephone was located in the dining room by a large window. One needed to pass through the dining room to get to the only other rooms on that level, the kitchen and the living room, known as the front room. The stairs to the upper level were also accessed through the dining room, thus privacy on the phone was not possible or even considered needed. Large heat and air vents connected the dining room to the upstairs hallway making listening in inevitable even when upstairs.

This air vent between the upstairs and lower level had been the source of some of Boyd Jr.'s pranks. He would drop things and water onto unsuspecting individuals standing below. Once he had convinced his sister, Betty

Sue, to slide down the vent to the lower level. He made it sound like such fun, that she and her friends had actually removed the covering grates and slid down. Landing caused each one a great deal of pain and they were upset with Betty Sue's baby brother, but could not tell on him for fear of being punished themselves. It later became a story to be shared and laughed about at family gatherings.

Lillie and Richard 1961-1963

Lillie had convinced her husband and her father to help her build a dance studio in the old garage in the back of the house. Richard always parked in the road in front of the house until winter. Then he could park in the drive. This would help them bring in extra money as Lillie could teach dance. She would be able to do something with all of that training and skill and they could really use the money. Richard did help at first. He cleaned out the garage and helped Boyd bring in the needed materials that Boyd had paid for. Boyd began much of the basic work and some specialized work was brought in. Within a few months the garage was transformed into a dance studio. Signs were made and advertisements run in the paper and on the local news. Lillie was surprised with a beautiful sign for the front of the studio by a dear friend who was quite an artist. Lillie's Dance Studio was written in large fancy letters with tap and ballet shoes on the sign as well. It was very professional looking and made Lillie very proud to hang it, which she ended up on a ladder next to her brother to assist in the hanging of the sign. Thank God for her family.

Lillie began getting requests for lessons and she set her schedule up. She had a variety of ages of children and one class she set up for adults. The money became pretty good and people loved her classes. Kimberly was now old enough to attend and to watch the classes. She was four years old and very social. She knew when to talk and laugh and when to be very quiet. The first dance recital was held at a local elementary school. Costumes had been purchased or made, background had been designed. Richard even made some large trees that turned out quite nice. Kimberly and her mother were going to dance a hula at the end of the recital to a Hawaiian song. Lillie and a few friends made the grass skirts and bikini tops for the hula. Lillie also would dance in a short ballet with a few of the more advanced students. Richard showed up for the recital and stayed for the entire show. He was getting a lot of attention and slaps on the back, so he was pleased with Lillie's adventure. He seemed to continue to enjoy the dance studio attention, he felt a bit like a celebrity in the small town. So, when the local parade was being planned, Richard signed up Lillie's dance studio for the parade. He built the float with the dads of the students. All of the students road on the float and waved. It was a joyous time in Lillie's life. When pictures were printed in the local paper, Lillie's float was front page as many of the towns' children were on it. The laughter spread when people saw that the sign on the float had blown in the breeze and the "io" of studio was not seen, thus rendering the float, "Lillie's Dance Stud". It was the local inside joke for a bit and Richard loved it.

Richard soon began to disappear again and come home a little drunk at night on a more regular basis. Lillie was very unhappy in her marriage and Richard had begun to make her skin crawl when he touched her. She knew he was with other women and on the prowl again. She did confide in her mother and sisters on a particularly distressing night. It was cold and beginning to snow. She had asked Richard to shovel coal into the furnace before he left for work and he had not. Now, he had not come home after work and the furnace was out of coal. The children had been whiney all day with colds and teething for the baby, Matthew. Lillie was tired and so sad that her marriage was like this. She had called Richard at work to remind him to come home after work to shovel the coal and he had said awful things to her. His boss had heard and had come over after work to shovel the coal, but Lillie had been too proud and said that Richard had shoveled the coal in already. It was obvious to them both that she was lying. She then went to the basement and figured it out for herself. She was crying from exhaustion and sorrow. This upset the children even more, but she just could not hide it today. Kimberly went to the basement with her while Matthew played and whined in his playpen. Kimberly was crying just a little bit too. Lillie opened the furnace and shoveled coal, somehow managing to get the coal dust on her hands, arms and pants. This angered her and she slammed the furnace door hard. The door smashed her finger and took off the nail. She screamed, the kids screamed. Wrapping her bloody, throbbing finger in a towel, she finally convinced Kimberly that it didn't hurt, that it had just surprised her. It hurt like hell. Her entire arm began to throb and she was becoming nauseous from the pain. She called her dad to come and get her. He took the kids to Thelma and Lillie to the hospital. This should be her husband with her, she thought, not her dad. Shoot, if she had a real husband, she would not be in this pain.

She cried as Boyd drove her to his house. He knew she needed to get it out. He asked her nothing. He told her what a great mother she was and how proud he was to have her for his daughter. Which, of course, resulted in

Lillie crying even more. She loved her parents and she just wanted to be like them, not like Sally and Harold Sullivan! She had prayed to be like the Sullivan family and it had now come completely true. She had had no idea what she had been asking and praying for. She did not want this for her children. She did not want this for herself or her poor parents and siblings. So it was on this desperate night that she confided in her sisters and parents. Boyd Jr. came home and heard about it later. The result was even more anger and resentment toward Richard than before. Boyd Jr. begged her to come back home and offered to help with the kids. Such a sweet boy. Boyd Jr. was now 14 years old and loved by everyone just like his father. He did struggle in school having a form of dyslexia that was not recognized in the late 1950's and early 1960's. Sweet Boyd Jr.'s face broke her heart even more. He had a friend across the street that was another wonderful kid. His name was Tom, but everyone called him Baby Tom and would forever call him that in this small town, no matter how old he got. Now, Baby Tom had followed Boyd Jr. in, so he too knew the story of the day. Lillie pulled him aside and asked him to not tell anyone, even his folks. Baby Tom agreed and then offered to be of any help she needed, especially if it meant helping her move stuff home. Lillie cried again. Why could she not have kept an eye out for a young man like these two to marry? What had she caught herself up in?

Lillie and the children spent the evening with Boyd and Thelma and then she had Boyd drive her back home. The kids needed their own beds, she said. She needed to think, she said. This was just a really bad day, that's all, she said. Bathing her babies and singing them to sleep relaxed her. She laid on the couch with her bandaged finger propped up and hoped that Richard would not come home, but he did. She pretended to be asleep. Richard woke her up. He had heard about her accident and had been sent home from the bar. It sure was a small town. Richard acted like he cared. He acted like it was all her silly mistake. A bad accident that had nothing to do with him. Lillie said she was fine and rolled over and "fell asleep" on the couch. Richard went upstairs to bed. She knew he would not peek in to check on his beautiful, innocent, sleeping children. And he did not.

Days and months went on with Richard being Richard. He had an intense selfishness that was played out daily in little and big ways. One day, Richard had come home with a burger and fries from the local diner. He took his food and sat at the kitchen table. The children saw and smelled the food and Kimberly asked for some. Richard told her, "No, this is my food. Have your mother make you some food if you are hungry." The kids really wanted some French fries. Lillie told them she did not have any, but they could have some potato chips. Kimberly and Matthew began to whine. They wanted French fries, not chips. Lillie, exasperated, asked Richard to just give them each a few fries. He refused. Now the whining turned into tears. The parents thought it was because of the fries, but deep inside the children were beginning to recognize the rejection from their father. He had always run hot and cold with his attentions toward everyone, his wife and children included. Lillie had been desperately sad about it for some time now, but no one had recognized the grief and sorrow in the children. Matthew was somber and quiet. Kimberly whined and was clingy to her mother. At two and four, they knew life was stressful and unhappy when their father was around and they were not all that thrilled to visit their grandma and grandpa Sullivan. The children only experienced true carefree childhood and pure love when they were with their mother and her side of the family. Lillie did her best to calm the children, but their whining angered Richard and he began to gather his food to leave. Lillie tried to stop him, but he grabbed the broom she had in her hands and used it to shove her to the wall with the handle in her stomach. It knocked the wind out of her and she sucked air hard to try and get a breath. When the air finally returned, Lillie screamed, the children screamed and Richard left with his food.

Lillie picked up the phone to call her parents yet again, but then she stopped and put the phone down. She could not keep running to her parents like that. She knew it was solving nothing. It certainly was not helping her relationship with Richard. So she decided to call the pastor from the church they had sporadically attended. He agreed to meet with her to council her. He asked that Richard come too, but Richard had refused. Lillie got a friend to watch the children so that she could go to do some "shopping". She had decided that she needed to keep her problems very quiet and to work on them by herself. She never stopped to see herself becoming like Richard's mother, Sally.

Lillie met with the pastor who listened as she shared her problems and cried. He prayed with her, but then encouraged her to go out with Richard more. He explained that if she could not get Richard to stay home with her, then she needed to go to where he was. If that meant to bars that she was not comfortable with, then that may need to be what she had to do to save her marriage. So Lillie vowed to try something new and was amazed at how much better she felt to have changed her way of attacking the problem. Richard was surprised but happy when Lillie offered to get a sitter and go out with him. Things did begin to get better between them, but Lillie was often miserable driving a drunk, loud and obnoxious Richard home from the bar.

Richard and Lillie got along better and even took a trip to Florida with friends. And while all were pleased with the peace in their relationship, it was wearing on Lillie to always give in to Richard's way of doing things. She felt her strong, confident self fade away. She began to doubt her decisions and was unable to make plans without first going through Richard. Children can sense that deep unhappiness and Lillie's children were no exception. They became even clingier and had horrible fits of crying when their mother left with their father.

Kimberly had started kindergarten and appeared to enjoy going. Her teacher told Lillie that the little girl was very polite, but very quiet. They had a difficult time getting her to speak loud enough to be heard. They decided that she was a very shy child. Morning kindergarten was fun for Kimberly and she was home before her father got back and before her brother awoke from his nap, which gave her time with her mother. Lillie's sister, Sarah was now married to a local boy and they bought a little house not far from Lillie. Sarah was pregnant and Lillie was happy to be able to help her out for once. Kimberly and Matthew loved going to their Aunt Sarah and Uncle Jerry's house. They felt loved and cared for there. They pealed with laughter at their Aunt Sarah banging on her ceiling with the broom handle to get the birds out of the attic. They stayed here when their dear mother, Lillie, had to have all of her teeth removed. Richard had brought Lillie to Sarah's house and placed her in the guest room after her teeth were pulled. Sarah was to take care of Lillie and the children while Lillie's mouth healed. Lillie had to have dentures at the age of 22. The story was that she had a gum disease, which was partly true. The rest is that her teeth were just more easily knocked loose during one of Richard's famous belligerent, drunken rages. It was easier at that time to have the teeth all removed for dentures. Lillie would most likely have been able to keep her teeth until she was in her late forties or early fifties had it not been for Richard repeatedly hitting her in the face that night.

Lillie and the children stayed with Sarah and Jerry every evening and all night. They would go home for clothes and supplies during the daytime when Richard was at work. It was during this time that Lillie became aware of even how much more she was controlled by Richard than she realized. Sarah did not work and Jerry's job did not pay as well as Richard's, yet Sarah had her own car and such freedom. Sarah had more cash to spend then Lillie ever did. Now, Lillie wondered where all of the money for her own little family was going. She knew, deep inside, she knew. Richard not only drank it and gambled it away, but he used it to date and entertain women. She did not even have charge of the money she made teaching dance.

Richard had successfully convinced her that it was needed for expenses. She shook with anger, but kept it to herself. Sara knew more than Lillie thought she did. The entire town knew more than Lillie thought. Politeness and respect for Lillie kept them from ever bringing it up to her.

Lillie eventually moved back with Richard. He had cried and made promises. He had taken her and the kids to the zoo. That was all it took for her to give "the rat" yet another chance. All went well for a few months at home, but not at school for Kimberly. Her first grade teacher now reported that the little girl would not speak in class. If she was forced to speak or join in, she would cry. Kimberly did have frequent ear aches and sore throats. She missed a lot of school. She stood alone at recess and watched the other children play. Once, a boy had approached her to play chase with the group and Kimberly had cried. She was sent home for the day. Lillie knew her daughter was being damaged by the stress at home. Richard had now allowed Lillie to keep most of her dance money and she was hiding it away for an emergency or for that unbidden horrible future when Richard left for good. Kimberly had to have her tonsils out and that missed time added in with her absences and her immaturity resulted in the school informing Lillie that the little girl would have to repeat first grade. This knocked the wind from her. How would Kimberly do better next year? What if this behavior continued? Lillie was frightened for her daughter. Her son had been diagnosed as delayed in development by her doctor. Could all of this be the result of the chaos at home or were her children truly defective? This was a thought she would never say aloud.

When the Sullivan's got wind of the information regarding their grandchildren, they were outraged. They blamed Lillie for not being strict enough. Harold began paddling Matthew for small errors or infractions. He paddled Matthew for bed wetting as well. Harold was determined to correct this problem with some serious discipline. Seeing her brother spanked by her grandfather upset Kimberly to the point of tears and shaking, but she knew better than to say anything. She tried to play with her brother and to keep him away from her grandfather. Lillie sensed the children's discomfort and fear of being left with their paternal grandparents and so she successfully kept them away from the Sullivan's unless she was with them. Richard was more and more argumentative with Lillie and more antisocial with the children.

One day the Walloon's were visiting at Lillie's house with the family to celebrate Kimberly's birthday. The Sullivan's were over and Aunts and Uncles were stopping by as well. The house was decorated with balloons and streamers. The cake was beautiful. Kimberly had opened her presents and thanked everyone. It was a beautiful day outside and Richard asked Kimberly if she would like to take a ride in his new car. The little girl felt like a princess and although she was a bit uncomfortable being alone with her own father, she jumped at the chance to sit up front. Richard turned on the music and sang to her. They rolled down the windows and drove through town. Richard shared his candy bar with his daughter and she knew then that he really loved her now. Finally, her daddy really loved her. She was so proud pulling up to the house and getting out of the car. All of her relatives were smiling and waving at her as though she really was a princess. Her birthday had changed everything. She knew that she was now like the other kids at school. That she was loved and cherished too. That she had real value. This was her daddy that took her in his new car, in the front seat. Her daddy, who never shared anything, had shared his candy with her. Everything was alright now. She wanted her mommy and brother to know that everything was going to be alright now.

The Leaving

She awoke to a banging sound. Sleepily, Kimberly got out of bed and padded down the hall and then down the stairs. She heard muffled arguing. Following the voices, Kimberly saw her parents in the driveway. Her daddy had two large bags and was putting them into the car. Her mommy was crying. What the girl did not know was that her father had not come home yet again last night. She also did not see the woman in the passenger seat of the car. The same seat that Kimberly had sat in yesterday feeling like a princess. She heard her mother say something about the kids. She could not hear her father's words. They sounded like a low rolling thunder in the distance. A thunder that warned of an incoming storm of giant magnitude, it sounded like a gale full of blusters, threats and tornados. Kimberly could tell things were changing fast and she could feel the winds of trouble like never before. She would not go to school again today.

Lillie walked back toward the house and the little girl ran upstairs to her brother's room and crawled into bed with the sleeping Matthew. He looked so peaceful and innocent. He had no clue that the horrible, bad tornado was on its way. Kimberly could hear her mother crying in the kitchen for what seemed a long time. She was sure the time to get ready for school had long passed. She felt her brother begin to wake and she shushed him. He was only 5 now, but he knew to be quiet. Matthew was not in kindergarten yet as Lillie had decided to wait until he was 6. That way she hoped he would be more prepared and less delayed as well as maintain the 2 year gap in grades as in the chronological years between the kids. When Lillie came upstairs to check on the kids, she found them playing quietly in Matthew's room. She went silently to her room to get ready for the day. She had a dance lesson with the adults this morning to give and then several after school lessons today. Lillie then cleaned and dressed her children and gave them breakfast. It kind of felt like a regular day to the kids.

Lillie had the kids play in the yard during her first lesson and then they packed up to go visit Aunt Sarah and Uncle Jerry for the day. Lillie and Sarah sat in the kitchen discussing life and kids. Sarah had a little boy that was 3 years old now and Lillie's children loved playing with him. Sarah was very pregnant with her second child. Betty Sue would be graduating from high school this year, Boyd Jr. was 17 and would graduate next year. Jack was still in Vietnam most of the time. They had recently received a letter from Jack indicating that he was dating a woman from a tiny village north of Angola, Ohio. He had not shared her name.

Jack, the Vietnam Years

Jack had gone to fight in Vietnam after searching South Korea for his true love and their child. He had racked his brain on how to handle this further. With no names to go on, he felt a trip to France would be futile, still he longed to go and dreamed that he could find Gyeong somehow. Then what? Could he even begin to get her back? He spent long hours trying to devise plans to steal her away. Then the war began to escalate. Jack was given charge of a ground infantry that was on the front line. Their orders were to get behind enemy lines and to send back information. They often found themselves in miserable and inhumane conditions. The heat and mosquitoes were unbearable at times.

Jack took his leadership seriously and his men were confident in his ability. He saw the trust in their eyes along with their fear and homesickness. He was young, but man, these guys were just babies. Many were only 18 years old and away from home for the first time. When they had dangerous missions or marches, Jack made sure that he went first. He put himself in harm's way before he would ever send one of his men. It was not a lack of fear of death as much as a "what do I have to lose" attitude that pushed Jack to do daring things. He had made some daring rescues, had led his men behind enemy lines and to overtake hills and towns in a way that fostered absolute trust among his men. The result was that more of his men made it out of those battles alive and intact. The absolute pain of watching his men die or become injured was so jarring and awful that Jack did everything he could to lead them out of danger as quickly and smartly as he could. Jack had a talent for having a clear head under pressure and was credited with great bravery. He knew that his reasons were selfish and yet also that he had very little to lose by being brave and going the extra mile. Jack did not accept his talent and intelligence for war. He was brilliant in battle, but saw that brilliance as a result of his sorrow and anger.

Jack had begun to see a woman from a small northern Ohio town, but she was merely a distraction to his intense ongoing pain of losing what he considered to be his family. He did not fear losing her or for her to lose him. She had been married before and had a young daughter that was very obnoxious. If any woman came his way that he felt may be able to compete at all with Gyeong, he quickly walked away. It felt like it was cheating on Gyeong to find someone that was able to replace her. The very thought made him ill.

Jack ended up receiving many medals and commendations during his Vietnam years. He was angry that his thoughts and pain of losing Gyeong and the baby were beginning to weaken. He felt that his heart or mind or something evil in him was betraying him. He did not deserve nor want happiness and peace. A small true part of him knew that both of them were suffering in their own ways and that he should continue to suffer as well. Vietnam turned into one hell of a long battle that continued to bring distraction and honor to Jack.

Boyd and Thelma to the Rescue

Lillie knew she could not continue in her marriage or in her giving dance lessons. She had been quietly packing and selling items. She gave her students notice of her closing down with no reasoning as to why. She simply stated that she would be moving. She sold all of her dance studio supplies, keeping only the beautiful sign her friend had made for her, "Lillie's Dance Studio". Once she felt things were in place and that she and the children were calm, much to her surprise the children had been calm and happy since their father's more permanent departure, she contacted her parents. She asked to move back home so that her father could sell the house he had bought for them. At least he could get his money back. She had already found a job at a pharmacy in town within walking distance from the Walloon home. No one in the entire Walloon family, or the town for that matter, was surprised to see this divorce begin. All who knew Richard and Lillie felt this separation was long overdue. More people were aware of Richard's behavior than Lillie ever realized.

Lillie and the children were unreasonably happy as they moved back to Lillie's childhood home. The three of them shared a small bedroom and the entire family at home now consisted of them, Boyd, Thelma and Boyd Jr. Betty Sue had moved to Toledo to live with a cousin and work as a secretary upon her recent graduation from high school. Betty Sue was a sweet, loving young woman who had inherited her mother's weight issues along with the sunny disposition of her father. So, one really had to love her. Except, no boys or men did love her in the way Boyd loved Thelma. Betty Sue passed away the spring before she turned 20. She had an undiagnosed heart issue that resulted in her collapsing at work one morning and dying at the hospital. The family was grief stricken and pulled together to mourn the loss of this darling human being. All the family and close friends worried over Thelma and feared that this loss would be so great that she too might pass away. Thelma grieved hard, but found joy and comfort in her family. Her love for "her people", as she called them, kept her going. Boyd was stricken with deep grief as well; and clung to his wife and children to find the strength to heal.

Lillie was embarrassed to be in her position, two children, living back home, working a low level pharmacy job, impending divorce and loss of her dance studio. She realized that she should be very sad, but as she walked to work, even in the rain, she was amazed at the freedom she felt. She was awed that she still felt happy and filled with hope. It was then that she learned the lesson all good mothers know, if your children are happy, you can be content even in not so perfect circumstances. Matthew and Kimberly were happy and relaxed as she had never seen them before. They were filled with joy and anticipating the summer trip to Missouri with their grandparents in a few weeks. Lillie, the children, Boyd Jr. along with Boyd and Thelma were all going to drive to Missouri to see the sights and to visit family. At least two adults would be smoking most of the way. Boyd smoked and drank coffee incessantly and Thelma smoked occasionally (so did Boyd Jr., but not in front of his parents, he was still 17 and in school.) So the car would be filled with happy people, unbuckled (seatbelts did not come in cars yet), breathing in hot air and cigarette smoke. The children would scream for their grandpa to drive faster and faster and he would. With the windows rolled down, the breeze brought a freedom and healing that was needed.

As they packed the huge trunk with suitcases and food, the kids ran around the small backyard singing made up songs. Lillie had encouraged them to eat, go potty and run. She knew the car ride would be the longest they had ever had. Boyd Jr. even got the children involved in a game of tag and running around the block. Soon, they were all scrambling into the car, laughing and talking all at once. The children sat in back with their grandma and mother. Once in a while, one would get to ride up front between their grandpa and uncle, giving Thelma and Lillie a bit of time to stretch out. Mostly, the children slept, but when they were awake they were happy and content to just be with the people that loved them most of all. Once in Missouri, they saw many sights, a zoo and had picnics. The family they visited had a pony, so nightly pony rides were the normal event for the children. One day, they decided to go visit the Mississippi River. Boyd had told the kids many stories about the "Ol' Mississip" so they were excited to see it. They were warned that it would look like flowing mud, but that sounded cool to them.

They had left early in the morning on a weekday to see the river. They followed the other family to an area where there was a park by the river. This time Boyd Jr. drove and

Boyd senior was the co-pilot. As they entered the parking lot, they could see it was on quite a steep hill. Once they began to park, Boyd Jr. yelled to his dad to be careful when getting out due to the steepness and to be careful not to fall. Well, Boyd had lost most of the hearing in his left ear during World War II due to a bomb explosion near him on that side. That was the reason Boyd Jr. yelled and also the reason that Boyd Senior did not hear the warning, although one would think Boyd would see the steepness for himself, he did have a tendency to be distracted at times. Upon Boyd's opening of the door, the family watched as their patriarch was yanked from the car by gravity. The family heard Boyd yell, "Whaaaaa..." Cigarette still in his mouth, he began to roll like a log down the parking lot. He rolled for quite a distance, picking up some speed as he did so. His family got out of the car and yelled a variety of non-helpful things. He rolled, the Winston in his mouth, until he hit the back tire of a parked car. Now, to know the Walloons is to know that they are laughing so hard that they cannot breathe. They are very worried about their loved one, but laughing insanely. Boyd Jr. and Lillie are running toward their father as he is dusting himself off and cussing up a storm. He knows they are all laughing, so refuses to look at them as he continues to smoke the now smashed cigarette and cuss. Boyd Senior's cussing is mild. He says stuff like, "Dag nab it all" and "What in the hell..." and "My God..." Boyd was never a vulgar man, even during his combat times. He walks with his children up toward the rest of the family, puffin' and a cussin' along the way, and sees that his grandchildren have inherited the sick sense of humor the rest of the Walloons seem to have. They were gasping for air and Thelma was pink to red with tears of laughter streaming down her face. Her right plump hand covering her mouth and nose.

Boyd Senior was a bit embarrassed and trying to "tough man" it out. They walked over to look at the park and opened the thermos for some coffee for Boyd. The kids went off to play on the swings and all began to calm down. They enjoyed the visit and knew that a memory had been created, little did they realize that even Boyd's great grandchildren will laugh at this story and grow to love and adore this great grandpa they never met. Thankfully, Boyd was a fit and spry man for any age and he was uninjured except for bruises on his right elbow and both knobby knees. Boyd was also thankful that the other family missed the incident but, of course, heard about it in great detail a few times before they all left the park.

The ride to and back from this trip was filled with the many stories from both Boyds and the many old songs sung by Boyd senior with others joining in occasionally and all enjoying the "show". The radio was difficult to get stations on long trips, but with the two Boyds in the car, no one would have wanted it turned on anyway. The children felt such joy seeing their mother laugh and relax that they did not want the trip to end. They both had learned to try to watch out for her and to make her happy, especially Kimberly. Little Kimberly also felt a great pressure to protect her baby brother and try to keep everyone happy. She began to become a story teller like her father figures, her grandpa and Uncle Boyd. When she succeeded in making people smile or laugh, she felt fabulous and smart. She didn't realize what a chatterbox she was at times and how the adults often humored her. She did not realize how hard they all worked to keep her and Matthew happy and at peace.

Boyd often sang songs from the military as well as other older songs. One of the children's favorites was "Sweet Violets". Boyd would start out singing and they would join in on the chorus, "Sweet violets, sweeter than all the roses, covered all over from head to foot, covered all over in.....(big pause suggesting a swear word) shwwweeeeet violets, sweeter than all the roses...". Another much loved song was, "Dance with the Dolly with the Hole in her Stocking". The children fell into an easy pattern that summer and the following school year. They would awake to the "tink, tink" sound of their grandfather stirring his coffee repeatedly as he added cream and sugar. They would come down to the smell of bacon, eggs, coffee and cigarettes. Sitting at the counter and eating with their grandpa before he left for work and watching their grandma move leisurely about the kitchen and then joining them at the "eating peninsula" that jutted from the wall. They loved the swiveling stools and conversation. Boyd would get up to leave and kiss everyone goodbye. Next, their mother would come down dressed for work and grab some food. That summer, they stayed home with grandma on her days off and went to Aunt Sarah's on the work days. They loved being both places and found plenty to keep them entertained and happy.

One summer evening when everyone was home and talking on the back porch, their father, Richard, showed up. It was obvious that he was unexpected. He said he wanted to see his children. Kimberly was excited and felt loved. He wanted to see them. The adults were saying no and negative things and she could not understand why they would keep him away from her. Her darling grandfather yelled at Richard, "Over my dead body are you a gonna' take these kids, way you are, should be ashamed a yerself!" As she cried and watched from the little yellow chair, it became obvious to even her little eyes that her father was drunk. Kimberly pulled her long dark blond braids over her eyes. The father she dreamed of loving her wanted her now, but he was drunk. Now huddled against the back corner of the screened in porch, Kimberly and Matthew cried as they watched their father scream and become an angry, belligerent man they knew all too well. Their grandma was shaking and whining in her high pitched voice of worry, "What is wrong with you Richard, you was raised better'n 'is." Thelma had called Harold to come and get Richard. Harold arrived, but now the children had to watch their paternal grandfather yell at their mother and much loved maternal grandparents. Richard was furious and now everyone was frightened of what he might do. Grandpa Walloon was fit and spry and ready to defend his family, Thelma was gently holding him back and crying. Lillie was crying and trying to reason with the Sullivan men. It was Uncle Boyd, at just 17 years old, that called the police to the house. He was afraid of the impending violence and what might happen if the Sullivan men did get their hands on the children.

In a circus of crying, screaming and flashing lights, the children watched their father being arrested for drunk and disorderly conduct. Harold was now in a rage, but left to get money to bail Richard out as soon as possible. Thelma took the children in to watch television and prepared them both bologna sandwiches with ketchup, her specialty. As the children watched their precious family calm down and get back to normal, they too calmed down and went back to being kids. Unknown to the children was their mother's deep fear of what was to possibly come next. She knew Richard was not to be trusted even sober. She should have reported the domestic abuse according to her attorney. She needed to have a record showing Richard's unfit behavior toward her and the children. Her attorney explained that Richard's behavior was neglectful toward his children. Richard was emotionally and physically abusive toward her. The truth of it all was that Richard was emotionally abusive to everyone that loved him or had to be around him for any length of time.

At this point in time however, the children were safe in the Walloon home, watching The Lawrence Welk Show and eating Circus Peanuts candy provided by their grandpa. Boyd Walloon had certain loves. Circus Peanuts candy, black licorice, cigarettes, his thumb being rubbed or "flicked" and saving money to buy small middle class treasures such as vacations and soon a summer cottage. He had given up the saving for his own business. His family needed him too much and often. He adored being able to help out as best he could. Thelma went along with any of Boyd's wishes as she cherished his love of his family and she totally trusted him.

The court granted the divorce of Lillie's marriage to Richard and ordered child support payments from Richard. Richard paid twice and not without being argued into paying. He came to get the children on several visits that first summer. He always picked them up and drove them the three blocks to his parent's house, where he may or may not eat dinner with them, before leaving the children with their paternal grandparents for the week-end. He would pick them up Sunday morning and drive them back the three blocks to the Walloon house. During the visits with their paternal Grandma and Grandpa Sullivan, the children spent much of their time playing board games and coloring with their grandmother. Grandma Sullivan did seem to love them and want their visits. She was always a bit upset with the "messes"" children make, but was good to her grandchildren. Harold doted on his granddaughter and kind of ignored the much wanted grandson. He was proud of how handsome the boy was and did mention that he was a strong little guy, but then that was about all he had for the boy. He enjoyed singing and dancing with little Kimberly and telling her stories as Matthew sat on the floor nearby. Harold was upset and concerned about Matthew's ongoing bed wetting. One particular morning at the Sullivan house, Matthew wet the bed and Grandpa Sullivan found out. He took his four year old grandson downstairs after his bath and spanked the boy hard. Kimberly came running in and screamed for him to stop and cried. Harold stopped when he heard her screams. Matthew was crying pretty hard, Grandma Sullivan assured both children that spankings were needed for children that wet beds and that Matthew needed to stop doing that. Now, Matthew had been spanked before by his mother and his Grandpa Walloon, but those were more like warning swats. They got his attention, but did not make him scream or cry and Kimberly was never alarmed by those spankings. This felt very different to her and seemed mean. Even as a little girl, she wondered how one was to know they were wetting the bed if they were asleep. How could it be right to hurt someone who did something while sleeping? She became more frightened of her paternal grandfather and did not feel safe anymore with her grandmother. She made sure to tell her whole family what had happened that week-end and they listened to her. It was during this telling of the week-end that it came to Lillie's attention that Richard was not spending time with the children, much as she had suspected. She thought at least they got to see their grandparents, but this was not turning out ok. A long talk with Harold and Sally Sullivan seemed to work and they promised to not spank, but to allow her to spank when they reported the "wrong doings" of Matthew. So future visits were a bit better for the children.

"Tiny" and the Tornados

Lillie had agreed to date a man known around town as "Tiny". Tiny was a divorced father of three young sons. He was not a tiny man, but rather a medium height, muscular man with a bit of fat on him. He had brown wavy hair much like Jack's hair. He was handsome in a rugged way and dressed very nicely, often in a suit. He and his family owned a local insurance company and were very well off financially. It was on a date with Tiny that Lillie insisted on him taking her home when the weather turned bad. Now, Lillie loved thunderstorms, but something about this weather seemed wrong. She was desperate to get back to her children. Tiny was good natured about it and drove her back to her parent's home. The weather had become more violent and news casters were advising people to stay indoors.

When Lillie entered the house, she saw her parents, brother and children sitting around the dining room table. The adults were playing games with the kids to keep them calm and distracted. The dining room was in the center of the house and the table was away from most of the windows, so it was a fairly safe place. The basement of the home was what was called an "old Michigan basement" and not a great place to be unless a tornado was coming. Well, old Tiny made himself at home at the table and joined in the game. At first, one might think what a great guy he was, but Tiny was a man who knew how to manipulate people and get what he wanted and he wanted Lillie. He laughed and talked and appeared to enjoy Lillie's children. He finally convinced the crying and frightened little Kimmy to sit on his lap. The little girl was terrified of storms and this storm was loud. The thunder and wind were equally deafening and shook the house. She was frightened by the storm and the stranger who insisted on holding her. He felt creepy to the child. Kimberly dutifully sat on his lap and quietly cried, feeling a bit of relief though, now that her mommy was with her too. Lillie and her family were a bit annoyed by Tiny's bossy behavior. They were also concerned about the way he doted on Kimberly and completely ignored Matthew. Tiny was completely taken by the little girl in a way that did not feel right to anyone at the table. When he left and the children were in bed, Grandpa Walloon forbade Lillie to see the large wealthy man again. Lillie let him know that she totally agreed with him and was very concerned regarding Tiny's behavior.

As they watched the evening news, they were made aware of the devastation caused by that storm. They heard about the many tornados that the storm had spurred. They realized how blessed they were to have been spared major damage in their area. Throughout the Midwest, 271 people had been killed by over 47 tornados. The storm became known as the Palm Sunday tornados.

Tiny called twice and the second rejection from Lillie made him quite angry. He slammed the phone down and never called back, much to Lillie's relief. Tiny was not used to rejection. His mind was reeling from the idea that a poor church mouse, like Lillie, would not be chomping at the bit to be with him. She was beyond beautiful, but she had 2 kids and no money. "Who did she think she was," Tiny wondered. He was done with her.

The Ohio Flamingos

Matthew and Kimberly had worried for days after the storm about the flamingos. "Flamingo's, live Flamingos in Ohio?" one might ask. "Silly children'" one might say. Yes, flamingos did live in this small town in Ohio. A wealthy couple that had remained childless had taken to housing two live flamingos year round. The birds lived at the couple's private home. They had a special side yard designed for them with a large indoor area that was connected to the home. This met the flamingos' every need. These people had the special brine shrimp that the flamingos needed to eat to keep their pink color delivered frequently. They also had a special blue-green algae delivered for them as well.

This couple lived on a main street leading into town and the birds could often be seen, on suitable days, outside in their special yard wading in their special pond. People driving or walking by could see these beautiful creatures preening and strolling about. They became known as, "our flamingos" to the locals. Fortunately, the flamingos had been taken to their indoor shelter and saved from the storm. Their outdoor area was cleaned up from the storm quickly and the flamingos made their grand appearance reassuring all that they were well. People could easily spot the birds through the tall chain linked fencing. They were outside often in warm weather. No one ever bothered or harmed them. These flamingos were a point of pride and well protected. The couple even provided for their care and housing to continue at the home after the couple's deaths. All of the inheritance went to caring for the birds for years until the last flamingo died. Any remaining money went to the library.

Tom

Lillie had been dating another local man that was a couple of years younger than she was. He had known her in school, but with the age difference they never were friendly. She knew of Thomas Rollins from school and from the community gossip. His family was well off financially, especially his grandfather. Thomas was known to be a very clean cut, clean shaven and somewhat handsome boy. He was tall, thin and well mannered. Lillie had been dating him for quite some time before she introduced him to her children. Tom was recently divorced with a son and daughter several years younger than Kimberly and Matthew. Although he was younger than Lillie, he exuded a maturity and confidence that she found attractive. He seemed like he would be a stable and suitable step-father and husband. Soon, they were all taking small trips to the zoo or to his parent's lake house. The children were very quiet around Tom. They were shy children, but Lillie did not notice their reticence to be with this new boyfriend. They sensed a strictness about him that neither child could put into words and they never wanted to upset their mother, so when she had Tom pick them up in a truck to move some things, they said nothing and just went along. Tom played some music in the truck and bought them both their own candy bar. Kimberly sat in the middle next to Tom and began to think her fear of him was silly. He was so nice to both of them. He was really nice to Matthew. He let them take drinks from his pop bottle. No one had ever let the kids have a whole candy bar! They began to reason that Tom must be nice and rich, if he could afford to get them each their own candy bar, yep, he had to be rich. Oh, they were so innocent.

When Thelma met Tom, she was impressed due to how well dressed he was and his great manners. After he had gone she said, "He looks like he just stepped out of a band box". This was a complement that Thelma used rarely for only those extremely well dressed and groomed. Boyd, Boyd Jr. and his new girlfriend liked Tom as well. He had an easy smile and appeared to be comfortable around them. Lillie would continue to date him now that she had everyone's input and apparent approval. Things moved quickly from there on and Lillie was soon explaining to the children that she and Tom would be married and they would all be moving to Elkhart, Ohio before the 1965 school year began.

Poke

They would finish most of the summer with their grandparents, taking road trips and singing along with grandpa. Stopping for smelt or ice cream was frequent on these road trips. The children usually opted for a burger or chicken over smelt, but their grandparents loved smelt. As they would drive through the countryside of northern Ohio, their grandfather would shout out points of interest that usually were graveyards or old factories. He would say things like, "Over there is where old whatchamacallit is buried. What's his name mama?" Thelma would often remember and tell him. Or he would say, "Now that's where your great granddad worked 'afore he left for the fire station." The children were more fascinated with all of their grandfather's attention than with any of this information. On occasion, they would visit relatives that were flung all around within a short drive. One of their favorite stops was to visit their great grandma and great grandpa Walloon. This visit took them to a lake that was fun to play around, but mostly the children were fascinated by a man who was their great uncle. He lived in a small shed just outside of their great grandparent's small two bedroom cottage. This great uncle was called Poke and they never knew his real name. For many years, they believed his true name was Poke. It was their grandfather who had given him that nickname many years prior and it was all many people knew the man by. Poke was always smiling and loved talking to the kids. He would play marbles or jacks with them and always had gum and candy to share. Poke also had a nasty habit of chewing tobacco and spitting cans were all around the yard. Those spitting cans turned many stomachs with contents of thick brown spit from Poke's tobacco or "chew" as he called it. Aside from that one awful habit, Poke was pretty much the perfect adult in a child's mind. It would be many years later before the kids would realize that good Ol' Poke really had the mind of a child. This is why he lived in a small shed right by his sister. He needed her to provide for him, feed him and in general take care of him. She did this with only a little complaining about his chewing. The chewing tobacco was provided to him by all the male relatives. This chewing and spitting is why he lived in the little shed and not the house. Poke lived a quiet life of reading comics and fishing. He enjoyed visits from children more than anyone knew. They brought joy to a very lonely heart.

A Stepfather

Lillie and Thomas Rollins were married on a Friday afternoon by the justice of peace at the courthouse in town. Only her sister, Sarah and her brother-in-law, Jerry were present as witnesses. Tom was an only child, as had been Richard, so he had no siblings to bring as witnesses. Tom was obviously very proud to have such a beautiful wife. He was enchanted by her every move and Lillie knew it. It made her feel safe compared to the way Richard had made her feel. She was, however, attracted to many of the similar qualities that Tom and Richard shared. Their upper class status, confidence and what appeared to her to be a higher class way of carrying themselves with a bit of arrogance that Lillie found very attractive. She knew that Tom was different from Richard in ways that would make him more suitable in her opinion. She was excited for this new life with her children.

Following the ceremony, Lillie and Thomas took a trip to Florida while her children spent the days with their grandparents, aunts and uncles as usual. They really missed their mommy. They were so lonely at night that their grandparents had them sleep with them. Kimberly slept with Thelma in the room that had been Lillie's and the kids. Matthew slept with his grandpa in the master bedroom. This brought great comfort to the kids. They would compare the snoring sounds made by their grandparents the night before and argue over who was snoring the loudest. They would also discuss which grandparent's farts smelled the worst. Matthew would later make up a song about "Little bubbles" that was all about horrid smelling fart bubbles. The kids would sing it all day right in front of the grown-ups and no one knew what they were really singing about, which brought them great joy. One day, Thelma decided to paint the room that had been Lillie's. This meant that Thelma and Kimberly would need to sleep in the room that had been Boyd Jr.'s.

Boyd Jr. had joined the Marines after graduation and his room had been empty all summer except for his bed. What none of the adults knew, was that in his teasing Boyd Jr. had ended up terrorizing the children with some pretty scary stories about a small door in his bedroom. This small child sized door had fascinated the kids and Boyd Jr. found it a perfect solution to keep them out of his room. He told them that all the grown-ups will say that this is a door to the attic. He said that they would tell the kids that so they would not know the real truth and be afraid. He told them that he had to keep the door locked or horrible mean dwarves would come out and kill the family and quite possibly eat them all. He said these dwarves would bang and scream at him all night trying to get out. He was used to it and would growl back at them, but that often made them meaner and so he had stopped growling and banging at them. He said that if they smelled the kids they would get stronger and might beat the door down to get to them. He promised Kimberly and Matthew that if they stayed away from the little hall that led to his bedroom and never came in that the dwarves would not know they were there. Whenever the children heard the slightest noise from upstairs, they knew it was those mean dwarves trying to get out.

So when Kimberly was informed that she was to sleep in there with grandma all hell broke loose in her. She screamed and cried and told her grandparents the entire story that her Uncle Boyd had told her. Grandpa promised that there was nothing up there, but she knew he was trying to trick her into not being afraid. So, her grandpa took both kids up to that room. He was going to unlock that "dag nabbed door" and show them the truth. They were so scared that they could barely walk. He brought them in and the only reason they could even tolerate going in was because they trusted their wonderful grandpa. They feared that perhaps he just did not know the dwarves were real. Grandpa walked over and showed them the door was not locked. He turned the white glass knob and opened that little door. It squeaked and both kids screamed and jumped back. They could see a beam of light and lots of dust. As the door opened wider, they saw some old furniture and boxes and no mean dwarves. Still, they wondered if the darned things were just hiding and waiting for grandpa to leave. He went into the attic and attempted to coax the children to come in a bit. Still no creatures, but they could be hiding. Grandpa walked out and shut the door. He could see the kids were still frightened.

That night, grandpa went into the room with the little door and had Matthew sleep with him there because both children had told him that grandpas could fight the creatures, but not grandmas. They all slept soundly and awoke alive. Matthew claimed to no longer be afraid, but he would not go in the room alone. The little door would cause ripples of fear for years to come, but they had learned to be a bit braver and were proud of themselves for facing the dwarves down.

Irish Hills

Boyd decided a family trip was in order. They were headed to Irish Hills and the Mystery Spot in Michigan. The children bounced up and down at the announcement of the trip. They stood in the very tiny strip of backyard and talked and sang about the car trip. The O'Brien's lived next door. Martha O'Brien was a small, very pale almost albino girl of six years old. She yelled over the fence for the kids to go out front as the wooden fence was too high for the children to see each other over. Martha met them on the side walk, pushing up her big thick glasses as they slid down her small nose. She was a very over protected little girl that did not take family trips, so she was always eager to hear about the Walloon trips. Martha's mother had been attacked by polio as a child and was left with crippled legs. She and her husband had three children with Martha being much younger than the first two. This all resulted in Martha being an odd child and difficult for children to relate to, but all three children were kind to each other. Matthew and Kimberly shared their excitement with her and then blew bubbles and played out front until Martha was called in by a shrill metal whistle that her mother used to summon the child.

Early one morning, the kids were awakened for the trip to Irish Hills. This trip included their Aunt Sarah, Uncle Jerry, cousins; Brian, three years old and Renee, one year old. They travelled in two cars and stopped on the way at a scenic spot to have lunch and stretch. Cousin Brian was a very active boy and required a great deal of supervision.

His mother had purchased something that looked like a halter and leash to keep him safe on trips, but with quiet sober Matthew around, Brian stayed in the area to play with his favorite cousin and the leash was not needed yet. Grandpa Walloon joked with the little boys to run over to a construction area and get the crane to help get "mama" out of the back of the car. Everyone cracked up knowing full well how difficult it was to get Thelma out of the backseat where she had been riding. Often one or two others would help her out.

Upon arrival to the Irish Hills, the children were in awe of the many sights and people. They paid and were assigned to a group to take the tour. Aunt Sarah snapped on Brian's leash and placed baby Renee in the stroller. Grandpa Walloon and Uncle Jerry talked and smoked nonstop through the tour of Irish Hills. When Grandpa Walloon was asked to sit in a chair nailed to a wall, he smoked and laughed. When Uncle Jerry poured water that ran uphill, he kept his cigarette hanging from the side of his mouth. Everyone in the group cheered and talked with the Walloons. Everyone that came into contact with the Walloon group seemed to have a better time and to be a bit happier. The children began to notice that more people were joining their group along the tour. The guide commented on having "the most fun ever" with this group. Oh, they were a loud, laughing and wise-cracking group that brought out the freedom and fun loving parts of all people.

The Big Moves

Tom and Lillie were back from their trip, aka the honeymoon. They packed up the children and moved them to table top flat Elmore, Ohio. This was only an hour away from their hometown, but felt very far to the children. They liked the duplex that Tom had rented for the family. There were children to play with and school was starting soon. Tom had a new job and was pretty happy with the changes in his life at that point. The kids were still shy around him, but were beginning to come around. They were not allowed to call him Tom so they didn't call him anything. The neighborhood kids called him their dad and they just let it go as they did not know how to explain their situation and did not want to cause trouble for their mom. That was another change, they were no longer allowed to call their own mom, "mom" or "mommy". It was "mother" now. Tom preferred the term "mother" and Lillie told the children that she did too. If they slipped, they were corrected and made to say, "Mother". This felt like another loss to the children and no one adult even thought about it. They wanted to say mom and mommy. They did not argue the point or even mention it fearing that it would bring tension or sadness to their mother.

The children rode a school bus for the first time. They were quiet, well behaved children. Most adults admired the children's wonderful behavior and patience, not realizing it was borne of confusion and being frightened of their circumstances as well as the step-father that now mascaraed as their real father. In school they were called by their step-father's last name even though they were still legally Sullivan. They were soon encouraged to refer to Tom as "dad". The children first tried out the "Dad" name for Tom at school. It was more natural there as that is how all others referred to him. Calling Tom "Dad" also was probably made a bit easier by the fact that they had no real deep emotion or bond with the word. Their own biological father had been so involved with himself that he had never forged a true paternal relationship with the children. When the emotion most children feel for a daddy was felt by either child, it was connected to their relationship with Grandpa Walloon. He was and would remain their father figure for their entire lives. It was most likely this connection with their grandfather that kept the children sane through all that was to come.

They had attended Westmore Elementary School for all of two and a half months when they were told that they were moving to Michigan. Kimberly was in second grade and sat on the slide at the school's playground during recess. It was here that the child froze in thought, at the top of the slide. She felt overwhelmed at moving again, yet was happy to get away from all of these kids that she did not know. She had not made one friend. Teachers ignored her due to her looking fine on the outside and behaving so very well. Kids ignored her for the same reasons in addition to her quietness. She sat there frozen, wondering if her new school would be as desolate feeling, emptiness and loneliness filled her during the school days here. She felt a hard shove from behind and scooted quickly down the slide with tears flowing down her cheeks. She was embarrassed by crying in front of the other children and was afraid to look at them. When no taunts or teasing started, she looked around and realized that no one even noticed her at all. She wiped her eyes and sat on a bench and waited for the long recess to stop. She saw her teacher appear. Teachers never came outside, but this one did and she asked the little girl to come help her in the classroom. Now, she was content to be in the classroom. It was good to be quiet and helpful. Kimberly did a few chores for the teacher and began to feel a little bit better about herself until she heard her teacher whisper about the recess incident to another teacher, she was again mortified and felt completely stupid. She told absolutely no one and her mother then believed that all was well. Matthew seemed to have made friends and was not too excited about the move, but he was a get along kind of kid and not about to cause trouble for anyone.

Tom had left a week prior to the move. Lillie packed while the children finished their last week at school. She was excited and happy about the move. She knew this job would bring in much more money than the job Tom had at the local Firestone. This new job was the executive position he had been hoping for. She did not realize that the position required a four year college education and that Tom had only completed one semester of college. She only knew that she was headed in the direction she desired for her family. The kids were happy because their mother was happy. Friday after school, the children said good bye to neighbor kids while their mother said goodbye to the other mothers. Kimberly, who often listened in to adult conversations and learned more than she should at times, sat quietly by her mother. She heard the other women say how lucky she was to get her own house. She heard that Michigan was a beautiful place and she heard that Tom was such a handsome and charming man. Little Kimberly thought, “Yuck, he is not handsome!” at the same time she became enamored with the thought of going to Michigan. She had been repeatedly reassured that they would visit the grandparents every week-end. Now, she was excited about that except for the fact that “grandparents” now included the very fat, very arrogant Tritches. All Kimberly knew at that time was that she was extremely uncomfortable around them and that their “niceness” seemed fake to her. Even though the new Grandma Tritch was not as fat as her Grandma Walloon, she seemed far flabbier and not as pretty. She was bossy to the kids and to her mom and that bothered her a great deal. This new grandma was even bossier than her Grandma Sullivan had been. Grandpa Tritch was actually Tom’s step-father and he really did not like Tom, even the kids could tell, but he was very nice to Lillie and the kids. Grandpa Tritch was fun to listen to. His voice was a growl that rumbled from his large overweight frame. He was a hunter and fisherman. He ate huge portions of food and prepared dead animals for Grandma Norma Tritch to cook. They lived on the outskirts of Delta, on a lake in a small two bed one bath house that was well built and fancy by lake- house standards of the day. They had a huge three car garage that was bigger than their house. Their yard was not large and left the kids to play on the front yard by the lake.

Saturday morning brought Tom and a large moving truck. The household items were packed into the truck and Tom was driving ahead to show the truck to the new house. Tom said this is how one lived and moved when you were an executive. The children were going to leave a bit later with their mother in her car. Tom left after hugging the kids for the first time ever. He was happy and they were all hopeful for good things to come.

Lillie and the children travelled to a small town in southern Michigan carefully following Tom's written directions. As they turned onto the street where the new house was, they were met with new rambling ranches and old nicely kept farm houses. There was a golf course on their left and the directions said the house would be on the right side across from the golf course and a white farm house. Lillie slowed and found the house. She pointed it out to the kids who immediately began bouncing and singing, "We're rich, we're rich, we're rich!" over and over as she turned the car into the long driveway. The moving truck had been unloaded and furniture had been somewhat set up. One could see by Tom's face that he was very proud of himself. One could see by Lillie and the children's faces that they could not believe their fortune. It was breathtaking both inside and out and Tom was pleased with the impression he had made on his new family. The children ran from room to room and squealed with delight. They had never been in such a beautiful home. They ran outside to explore their new seemingly huge yard and met their one and only neighbor kid. At least the only one close enough to play with. Little Miss Kelley Moore was in first grade and was the same age as Matthew although Matthew was in kindergarten. Kimberly was in second grade, due to repeating first grade. Kelley was wearing a rain coat and boots on a very sunny and nice end of October day. The children would soon learn of her great imagination and have wonderful adventures.

Kelley's parents, Mr. Edward Moore and Mrs. Eleanor Moore, were as too old to be parents as Matthew and Kimberly's parents were too young. Lillie was 25 and Tom was only 23. They appeared to the citizens of this small community as simply very youthful looking parents and pawned themselves off as age appropriate college graduates with school aged children. Matthew and Kimberly were entered into Gier Elementary school as Matthew and Kimberly Rollins. A story about the birth certificates being lost during the move placated the officials for the time being. They were instructed to write their names as such and practiced writing those new names at home before going to school the following Tuesday. New school clothes had been shopped for and purchased that Monday so that both children went to school looking very proper and well off. Kimberly's new teacher was an older, tall, terribly thin woman named Mrs. Tindal. She looked imposing and very serious. She rarely smiled, but took Kimberly under her wing and was very considerate of the new student's feelings. She placed her with buddies that had to stay with her always and then miracle of all, she placed the little girl in the top reading group. Kimberly had always struggled in school. It could have been due to lack of ability, but most likely was due to turbulence at home and possibly combined with the predisposed expectations of the local school's knowledge of her birth and family situation. But here in this new place, she was a new creature and she felt wonderful. She quickly discovered that she could read and write very well. She loved Mrs. Tindal dearly for creating this new academic world. She adored that teacher in a way that Mrs. Tindal would never know. Such gratitude to an otherwise serious no-nonsense teacher would never be surpassed by any following teacher. Even though she was only eight years old, Kimberly knew that Mrs. Tindal had just changed her world in a very important academic and social way. She now began to thrive and learned to love being at school, even though she felt that perhaps she had tricked her teacher and school in some way. Deep inside, the little girl knew she was inferior to the others, but she was so relieved to be viewed as "normal" and "above average". Kimberly began to make many friends. Children wanted to be around her and she did not know why. Her new clothes and confidence were attracting these friends and she knew she would never be lonely or alone in school ever again.

Visiting Ohio/Family

True to their word, Kimberly's parents took the children to visit their relatives in Ohio every week-end. Most of the time was spent with Grandma and Pa Walloon, cousins, aunts and uncles, but some time each week-end was spent at the Tritch house. Grandpa and Grandma Tritch were fun characters to observe, but not very lovable people. They often spoke as though they were arguing yet somehow got along with each other well. They never appeared to really love one another, but more like a formation of a union or some type of agreement. Though they shared a bedroom, they did not share a bed. Each had their own bed. The Tritches were proper at the same time they were a bit slovenly. Stains always covered their shirt fronts after eating and Grandma Tritch was usually eating and cooking. She wore pin curls when she got home and her hair was going so thin that you could see her scalp. Norma Tritch was a nurse, an RN, at the hospital and always had interesting stories about people. Peter Tritch worked at a factory as a floor manager and complained constantly about everything. Peter was the type of man that would make Thelma Walloon say, "Give that man a dirty look". His loudness and complaining were the characteristics of men that had Thelma disgusted and often saying this phrase. Since both were extremely overweight, they could be heard breathing loudly and often made a snore sound as they exhaled. Pugs were the only dogs allowed in their home and they each had one. Once they had three pugs snoring along with their breathing and one could feel the floor vibrate. The dogs had gotten used to the frequent yelling in the house and slept right through it. These little beasts were spoiled rotten and not always nice to visitors. Matthew and Kimberly loved animals, but learned to leave the little pugs alone.

In contrast to the yelling and complaining at the Tritch house was the Walloon home. Everyone in the Walloon family enjoyed each other with true love and care. The family enjoyed making other members laugh, often at stories and at times at each other or themselves. They never felt laughed at. Often the telling of family jokes had outsiders saying, "...you laugh at your grandma, grandpa, mother? That's not nice." It was not that way at all. The Walloon family members felt and acted as one unit, an inseparable unit. What is funny about the "me" is funny about the "all" and therein lies why no one ever felt laughed *at.* This unity happened naturally and without forethought or planning. It was born from the relationship of Boyd and Thelma. Born of their oneness with each other and then each of their children and grandchildren. It was a "way" of loving that carried into the generations of their grandchildren's lives. Now, that oneness did not protect them from becoming angry or frustrated with each other at times, but they never felt hurt by each other and the anger never lasted long. In turn, they were a unit bearing each other's sorrows if those sorrows were shared or known about. They were not perfect people, but people perfect to be human with.

Grandpa Walloon had again worked hard and saved enough money to buy a small, but darling, old cottage at a lake. It was only a 20 minute drive to the cottage from his home. He was as tickled as a man could be to announce this new purchase to his family. His children would bring their children to the cottage almost weekly. The siblings would visit and laugh as the cousins played and found trouble to get into. Well, the boy cousins anyway. The girl cousins were all rule followers. The boys would sneak into the dark, damp and moldy wooded area at the lake's edge and start fires, catch things and get hurt. The girls would play at the beach or in the yard and help with carrying things for Grandma Walloon. Grandma often needed her purse or "pocket book" as she called it, brought to her. She needed towels and tissue and food collected and brought in or out. Grandma was not about to bother getting up with so many young legs around to run and fetch. The children thought their grandparents were very old, but in truth they were just 46 and 47 years old when they purchased the cottage.

One could hear the delighted screams of joy across the lake when Grandpa Walloon needed a "favor". He claimed to need some candy very badly. He had a pocket full of change as he walked out of the little yellow cottage and called for his grandkids. "Kimmsy wimmsy," he would say, "I need you and the kids to go get some penny candy." The shouts of joy would begin at that announcement. He might say, "Now take Ol' Blue Eyes with you (Sarah's oldest daughter of 6years old) and Ol' Trouble Maker there (Sarah's oldest boy of 8) and get all o' you a bag and one for me too." This would be followed with children running for the old row boat, the older grandkids buckling the younger ones into life jackets and then themselves. Somehow, Ol' Trouble Maker would grab a too small or too large jacket and cause delay. The kids would start to get grumpy as he messed up the order of things and usually tripped on the way to the boat. He might even think he was cute and pull a prank or fall in the water, thus causing more frustration. Once all were loaded, Kimberly and Matthew usually took on most of the rowing as they were older and stronger. Ol' Trouble Maker, also known as Brian, had lost an oar once when he rowed, yet he often still got a turn to row with close eyes on him. Oh, the joy of penny candy was hard to beat. The little gas station/store was across the end of the lake and almost a straight shot from the cottage. No one worried about the 4 and sometimes up to 6 kids in the row boat. They counted heavily on those life jackets and Kimberly to make them all safe. Upon arrival, the rowdy bunch of kids that had just been singing and laughing and yelling in the boat, became reverent and quiet as they entered the small store and stood in front of the candy counter. The people working there knew that these were "Scrappy's kids", as they called them. One by one each child's order was filled and paid for with hushed voices and respect. Matthew and Kimberly would then order their grandfather's bag of candy. Now, each candy piece was one or two cents and had to be ordered one at a time and each little brown paper sack was always more than half full. Grandpa Walloon's bag was filled with a lot of black licorice candies and something called Horehound lozenges, which he had directed the kids to get, along with various other candies that he let them choose for him.

The children would then pile back into the boat, still having their life jackets on as they rarely took the time to remove them and go into the store. The trip back was quieter with various candies being sucked and chewed on.

All had learned to try to make their candy last the day except for Matthew and Brian. They would then end up begging the others for candy and would be given one or two from each girl's bag with no animosity. As they would row closer to shore, they could see their beloved grandpa walk toward the lake. He would grab the boat and yank them up on shore and help each kid out. He would get his bag of candy and be in as much glory as the kids. Grandma Walloon would get her fair share, usually the candy the kids had selected was what she wanted and Grandpa would keep his licorice and Horehound lozenges.

It was on one of these lazy summer day trips to get candy when the children saw a bit of excitement on shore in front of their cottage. As they got closer, their grandpa did not come out to get them. They pulled the boat up and put the anchor out before running up to the cottage to check out the commotion. Upon arrival to the center of the adults, they saw their Uncle Jack, a fancy woman and a small confused dog. Uncle Jack greeted the kids with a rare smile and introduced them to "Nicki" a tiny, well-groomed Pomeranian. The children sat on the grass and ate their candy while playing gently with Nicki. The kids were all laughing and talking, except for Kimberly who had gone into listening mode. She overheard the adults talk about Jack not being able to take the dog to Germany. That he and Vera would be moving there for at least a year with the Army. She heard that Vera was not even taking her own daughter and that the girl would be staying with her grandmother, known as Mama Bell to everyone. Kimberly was intrigued with idea that a child could be away from the mother. She was amazed at how happy and relaxed Vera appeared, the woman was absolutely giddy over the thought of going to Germany even if it meant leaving her own child! Kimberly knew that her mother and any of her aunts would be devastated with such a plan to leave their child for an entire year.

Jack and Vera donned bathing suits and at this point Tom had his speed boat at the lake along with Grandpa Walloon's pontoon and rowboat. Much of the day was spent on the water and the family had a wonderful time. At one point, Jack had taken Nicki out at the beach to let the pup swim. Nicki was placed in the water that was about shoulder deep on Jack. When Jack let go so the dog could swim a bit, it sank like a rock! Much screaming and panic ensued from the women and children. Jack dove under and came right up with the little dog. Nicki was still paddling his little legs in doggy fashion and looked like he was swimming in air. It was decided that all of the dog's hair had weighted him down when it got wet. Nicki was not allowed to enter the water, but he really never tried much after that episode. After that bit of terror, Thelma (not an animal lover at all) became more agreeable to keeping the poor dog when Jack went overseas. As evening set, the Walloon siblings decided to take a last farewell cruise together on the pontoon. Grandma and pa would watch the kids. Vera's daughter had arrived that afternoon and now sat among the children seeming quite comfortable and at ease with all of these strangers. Grandpa had warned his four kids and their spouses that the pontoon was small and only built for 6. The eight adults got on and included the neighbor, Baby Tom, on the boat as well. Now 9 full grown, supposedly intelligent adults, were on an old pontoon built for 6. The women sat on the men's laps or on the floor. Jack said as long as they kept the weight even and most toward the back, so the pontoon tips stayed above water, all would be fine. They pushed off and began to motor away. The pontoon waited until they were toward the middle of the lake yet still in front of the cottage before it gave up and began to sink. It had not helped that the women had all moved toward the front of the pontoon to see something being pointed out to them. Men began diving off in hopes of saving the boat. Women screamed and laughed. On shore, Thelma panicked and wailed in her high pitch nasal whine, "Lord have mercy"! The boat did appear to lift up a bit, but then the pontoons quickly became submerged. Now the women were jumping off and swimming toward shore. It was a disaster waiting to get worse and no one was laughing now. Children became frightened when they saw their mothers jump in the lake without life jackets, the life jackets that had been preached to them even though they too could swim. The men swam to the pontoon in an effort to raise it and swim it back to shore. It appeared a lost cause until Captain Jack Walloon, USA Army, began organizing the men and shouting orders. Soon life pillows were thrown to the women and the men grabbed some life jackets and flotation devices. Jack swam around ensuring everyone's safety. He then grabbed the motor of the pontoon and the men grabbed the sides they were ordered to and began to swim the pontoon toward shore. And as they did, Grandpa Walloon was heard repeating, "Well, I'll be damned!" over and over until they got that pontoon to shore! Another impossible battle for Captain Jack Walloon accomplished. And boy oh boy were those some proud men when they brought that thing in. Such back slapping and chest puffing had never been seen around this family before. Thelma laughed and cried. The woman were thrilled and talked all at once. The children went from fear and tears to excitement and pride in their family. Neighbor's that had been jumping in boats to try to get there in time to help, came over and laughed and talked into the wee hours of the night. The adults also made arrangements for the children to be taken to Mama Bell's place for the night. The adults decided to stay up all night and give Jack a farewell party. Grandma and Pa Walloon went to bed in the cottage as the adults built a bon fire, let the kids burn some marshmallows and then took them to Mama Bell.

Who Peed the Bed?

They had never been to Mama Bell's before. She was more enormous than their grandmother, but seemed super sweet. Papa Bell was frail and thin. He had gone to bed early as he was often ill. The boys were put to bed on the couch and the girls went upstairs to Sabrina's room. Now they saw where Sabrina lived. She was usually at her Grandparent's house and visited her mother. Her mother leaving to live in Germany did not seem to bother her. It was very odd for Kimberly and Renee, Sarah's daughter, to stay with strangers. They had just met Sabrina that evening.

The Bell home was as modest as the Walloon home. It was only three houses away from the railroad tracks. All three little girls were to sleep in Sabrina's bed with Sabrina. Sabrina seemed delighted to have company and they all put on their pajamas, brushed teeth and washed up together in the small bathroom. Grandma Bell yelled up her goodnights and turned off the downstairs lights. The boys were already asleep which was very fortunate for Mama Bell! Sabrina directed, yes directed in a voice that sounded like an order, them to bed. She put Kimmy by the wall and Renee in the middle and she sat up against the headboard on the end. Renee was excited about a new baby her mommy was going to have and wanted to talk about it, but Sabrina made it clear that the girls needed to stop talking and be quiet. The light was on and she made them sit up for the "reading of God's word". Sabrina then began to read from the Bible. She read for a long time and when Renee began to doze off, she woke her and told her it was disrespectful to fall asleep during God's word and that they would go to Hell if they were disrespectful. Next, Renee had to use the toilet, but Sabrina would not stop reading her Bible and told her she had to wait. Renee was 6 years old and knew that she could not wait much longer, so Kimberly told Sabrina that it was mean to make Renee wait and that she should go potty and then come back to listen to the Bible. Sabrina actually said, "No, you will both go to Hell if she leaves." Now the girls did not believe they would go to Hell for such an offense, but they were both afraid of Sabrina. She was bigger, bossy and very mean looking. Soon the inevitable happened, Renee wet the bed. Oh my word, the horrors for them all. They all got wet with warm pee. Sabrina was outraged, Kimberly was angry at Sabrina, yet still afraid, and Renee was in tears and very embarrassed. Mama Bell heard the commotion and was none too happy to have to climb those stairs to check on the situation. She was sweet when she realized that the bed had been wet on. She thought Renee was cute and told her not to worry, that those things happened sometimes. The girls were too shy and scared to tell Mama Bell about Sabrina. Sabrina was acting all innocent and helpful. Mama Bell had her do most of the work in cleaning up and enlisted all of the girls to remake the bed. Kimberly and Renee would later laugh at how much work Sabrina's meanness had made for her. Mama Bell had everyone march to the toilet and pee before going back to bed. The girls were thrilled to go home the next morning and told their mothers the entire story. The children were reassured that they would never have to spend time alone with Sabrina again.

The story circulated around the Walloon family and somehow Renee was made to feel like a hero. All were concerned about Sabrina and her unconventional upbringing and did not want any more issue with the Bells. Sabrina, for her part, was a lonely and confused child who put forth much bravado in order to survive her feelings of abandonment. She had visited her father on two occasions and did not know if she would ever see him again. He was not a mean man, just ambivalent about being a grown up, let alone having a kid. Her mother, the flamboyant Vera Bell, had grown up poor, much poorer than the Walloons. She had overcompensated by becoming focused on portraying herself as well-off and adventurous. If living an interesting life required her to leave her child, she would do so. She did love her daughter very much and it broke her heart to leave her, but she reasoned that it was best for Sabrina to stay with Mama Bell than to traipse around with Army brats. Vera did feel happy living on an Army Captain's salary as it was more money than she had ever had. Still, she always felt the need to impress and in that way she was similar to Lillie although no one would ever make that connection. Vera was showy whereas Lillie was classy. Vera took pictures of herself when visiting European mansions and passed several off as being part of her new home in Germany. She bought flashy clothes and jewelry on the cheap, but acted as though they were designer. She was friendly and usually smiling and laughing. Jack enjoyed the larger than life distraction of her and loved Vera for that as well as for her enthusiastic love making. He never confronted or exposed her in her lies and exaggerations and she loved him for that. She also adored his handsome face and great physique as well as his Captain status. She was Thelma's living definition of a "ten cent millionaire", but Thelma would never call her that to her face. Vera was a bit artistic, painting landscapes, and family had seen her art work, but while in Europe she "painted" much improved landscapes and even did a portrait of a German woman. She sent photos of her art work to family and friends back in the states. Unfortunately, only one painting was brought home from Europe and the others were given away or sold, as her story went. Most people suspected the paintings were from other homes or museums where she had photographed them as she never painted like that once back in the states. She claimed to be too busy and just not as inspired. She grieved about having to leave her baby grand piano behind, although she did not play. She did convince Jack to ship her Mercedes Benz to the states from Germany when they returned a year later. Vera had sent several pictures of this beautiful car to her in-laws. On the back of one photo, she had described the car and its color and then added, "Isn't it just pure sex"? Sarah and Lillie had wondered, "Now who writes that to their mother and father in-law"? The entire Walloon clan had decided that the car was a fake another one of Vera's tricks. Vera claimed that she and Jack planned to drive it to the Walloon home where family had gathered to greet them upon their arrival back to the states.

The Walloon family was gathered in the dining room eating and talking. Much talk was speculation on what Vera would be wearing and claiming as truth. This was a moment of mean humor at Vera's expense. They soon heard the crackle of gravel under tires and knew that Jack was home. They all got up and scurried through the kitchen and out to the screened in porch. It was here that they laid eyes on the beautiful dark metallic green Mercedes Benz parked behind the humble home. No one could believe how gorgeous that car was. No one had seen a car that expensive in real life. Vera floated on the honest awe of the entire family. One could see on her face that she had lived for this very moment. Her silky scarf billowed in the breeze, her “designer” sunglasses covered her eyes and she looked and felt like the million dollars she always wanted. Jack, as usual, was very quiet as Vera went on and on about the troubles getting the car shipped here, the expense and hassle were worth it as she had no intention of leaving her “baby” behind. She was very proud of “Honey” as she always called Jack. “Honey made sure that my baby was on the ship headed for the U.S.A.,” she gushed. And as their usual selves, the Walloons acted in honest joy and shared their admiration of the car. Though they may have spoken poorly of Vera, they wished her only good things and were happy for their brother, son, uncle; Jack. Jack took turns giving rides and allowing the adults to drive if they wished. It was a happy time and for her part, Thelma was secretly proud imagining the neighbors seeing this car, with her son, at her house. She wanted them to know that Jack had pulled himself together, that he was surviving well after all they had gone through with him.

Sadly, little miss Sabrina was not with them although Vera and “Honey” had spent the night at the Bells’ house with her. She did not fit into the image Vera had of making her grand arrival to the small town. She also knew that Jack did not want the little girl around much and she was willing to sacrifice time with Sabrina if it meant keeping Jack. He had made it clear to her before they had gotten involved that he was troubled with her having a daughter and that he did not want to raise kids. Vera never knew of Jack's true love in Korea. She never knew of the depths of hell he went through searching for his lost love and his child. She never would know. As false as Vera was in her flashy lies and mannerisms, so Jack was in his quiet refusal to share any real past or present feelings.

New Cars/Keeping Up with the Joneses

Tom Rollins had loved that new Mercedes Benz and it made him very dissatisfied with his 6 year old Ford. He had a handsome new family and home. He decided a new car was in order. Tom purchased a one year old Buick and felt very satisfied, even though it was nowhere near a Benz. He gave his wife the old Ford he had been driving and traded her car in as part of the deal on his new car. It was an upgrade for Lillie, but she was secretly seething. She could see how happy all of this car business made Tom and she did not want to rock the boat, it took so little to bring him to anger and make him restless. She smiled and thanked him. Lillie thought this was a purchase that should have been discussed. Certainly he should have consulted her about her car. She had purchased that car and it was in her name. She realized that he had to have forged her name on the pink slip. How dare he? Slowly, it dawned on her how much freedom she had given up without even thinking about it at the time. Tom was providing well, but he called all the shots and made all of the decisions. He had interviewed out of town in Elkhart before they were married and gotten the job with Firestone without checking with her about a move. He had found the job in Michigan without informing her and then had selected and purchased a home without her. What had once seemed romantic and exciting was in truth Tom not valuing her opinion. She had learned that if she voiced an opinion, it caused an argument. She simply had to agree with him and keep the children quiet and happy, then all would be well. She made the decision to go along with Tom without question in order to live the better financial life that he brought. She quietly grieved losing her right to make decisions, have an opinion that she could share and her old car that she had purchased on her own after her divorce. She thought this was a better life for her and the children so the loss was worth it. She also enjoyed knowing that she had material things that her former classmates had, she even had it better than most of them. Lillie had kept in contact with an old friend from high school and knew what had happened to many of the people she had so envied in school. She looked forward to attending her high school reunion this time. At least, she would arrive in a pretty great car wearing pretty great clothes.

Under Tom's Thumb

Lillie had gone back to work the first summer in their new home. She had hoped to take more time to be with the children before returning to work, but Tom had begun to talk to her about getting back to work now that they had "settled in" as he put it. She had to hire a sitter for the kids for the days she worked her new job. She worked in the pharmacy at the hospital as an assistant. She enjoyed this position and her co-workers, but didn't like leaving the kids with a sitter all summer. Tom seemed relieved to have the money coming in and that made Lillie a bit nervous about all of his recent spending. She was happy that her money gave the family budget some help, but she was kept in the dark about the financial situation.

The new sitter's name was Gerri and she was great with the kids. She was a teenager with access to a car thus she provided her own transportation and could transport the kids if needed. Gerri had long red hair and was very skinny and tall. She played with the children and fed them good lunches and snacks. At first, she did not need to worry about any discipline. Matthew and the neighbor girl, Kelley Moore, were a bit adventurous, but always listened to her. Kimberly was Gerri's little helper and would never want to upset her. As the summer wore on, Matthew began to test the boundaries and limits. He also was feeling the strain of living under the constant criticism and correction of Tom. He hated to be bossed in such a loud voice. He did his best as a little 7 year old to sweep the pebbles off of the driveway. Those never ending pebbles that blew from the "modern" flat roof of their new home assured his chore would never be done. He would sweep the driveway only to be corrected by Tom and often scolded for not getting them all. Tom found fault in Matthew's dirty socks, grubby hands and adventurous spirit. He was in reality a well behaved boy, but he was a boy that loved to play and explore. Kelley was a great partner for Matthew as far as girl playmates went, as she was adventurous and spoiled. She played "Barbies" with Kim and guns and war with Matthew. Kelley helped Matthew and Kimberly build forts under the decks of both homes. She then had a great idea to build bathrooms with toilets of rock circles in those forts. Both Kelley and Matthew would use those fort bathrooms and pee and on occasion poop in the rock toilets under the deck. Kimberly found it very gross, but did not tell on them right away. Part of their fort was also a bug hospital and they all loved to catch bugs, build little homes for the bugs and try to pretend they were saving the bug as a "bug doctor". They all loved this game and played it often. The problem was that Kelley and Matthew hated to take time out to go into the house to use the toilet and the play toilets were filling up fast. They just built more. One day, Lillie was on the deck and complained of the horrible odor from around the house. At first, she and Tom had thought it was from a farm down the road that had horses, but as the stench intensified, she knew it was from around her home. She mentioned something to Tom that evening and he said he would check it out tomorrow after work. That scared Kim as she knew the horrible screaming that would come from Tom if he found out what Matthew had been doing. She quickly told her mother that night and promised to have the kids clean it up, but it was a big job for little kids. Kimberly asked Gerri to help, but when she saw how much poop there was, she refused. The kids moved what they could with spoons from the houses and threw the poop into the field out back. When Lillie came home, she crawled under with a shovel to try to finish up shoveling out the poop before Tom got home. They got the Rollins' deck cleaned out, but did not finish the Moore's deck. When Tom got home, he was told that the smell had gone. He walked around the house and peered under the deck. There were the small rocks left over from the "toilets", but all was cleaned out as far as poop. Tom flew into a rage. He wanted those rocks out from under that deck now! Why did they make this mess and what was wrong with them? He yelled and fussed all through supper and the rest of the evening. Lillie tried to reassure him that the kids were just playing "fort", just being kids. Tom was not having it, he wanted things kept up and clean. Only God knows what would have happened if he had known about the pee and poop. This was often Tom's reaction over small infractions, real or imagined by him.

Half Adopted

The children's father, Richard, rarely saw them once they made the move to Michigan as it was an hour and a half drive one way. The visits with their father had always been strained and usually they spent most of the visit with their paternal grandparents, especially Grandma Sullivan. Richard was arriving on the next Friday to take the kids for a visit to his place in Toledo. The children were both nervous and excited. Kim was excited to get away from Tom, but she also was proud to show off her beautiful new house to her father. She did not understand why she felt that way, but she hoped it would hurt him and at the same time make him want them back for good. Although she really did not want to live with her biological father, life did seem better with him than with Tom for the kids. Basically, Kimberly just wanted her father to really want his kids back and to miss them so much that it hurt. She wanted a father's love.

When Richard pulled up, Kimberly could feel her mother's nervousness at letting the children go, but fake smiles were put on all around, except for somber Matthew. Matthew kept a very straight face, but if the truth was to be known, he was a bit afraid to go with his father. It had been over 9 months since the kids had seen him and that is a very long time in a child's mind. Richard pulled into the drive in a new car and hopped out looking quite handsome. After some brief hellos, the children were ushered to the car with their little bags of clothing. Kim sat in back and Matthew rode up front. Richard played some music and told them how "cool" his new place was, but that he was going to have them visit with his new girlfriend and her three little boys so they would have someone to play with. Oh, he had not changed and he did not miss them to the point of any type of pain. This is what registered loud and clear to Kimberly. Matthew and Kimberly were thinking the same thing, they did not want to meet three little boys and play with them, which was pretty stressful along with a new "girlfriend"! Kimberly knew her mother would never had agreed to this and she was worried about the situation.

Richard drove them to visit with their paternal grandparents first. They had dinner and it all felt so strange. It had been a long time since they had seen each other. Grandpa Sullivan took a lot of pictures of the kids. Then early that evening, they were loaded back up to drive the half of an hour to Richard's girlfriend's place. They were told they would love her because she was a teacher and she loved kids. Kimberly thought, "Why would a real teacher date someone like Richard"? In her mind, teachers were too classy and noble to hang out with Richard. She decided that this teacher did not know how mean her daddy could be nor how drunk he could get.

They pulled into the driveway of a nice home. Richard got out and carried the overnight bags into the house. The children were all introduced and the teacher seemed nice and kind of pretty, but not nearly as pretty as Lillie. How could their dad want this lady over their mom? The children were led to a basement playroom where they were to play with the little boys or watch T.V. A sitter was hired to take care of the kids for the night while Richard and his teacher girlfriend went out for a date. It all seemed wrong and wild to Matthew and Kimberly. It was way too late to go out for dinner, so they knew the adults went out to drink and party. Kimberly was very concerned for their safety, but did not know what to say or do. She wanted to call home and she knew Tom and Lillie would come and get them, but she did not want to cause suffering or trouble. The sitter was nice enough and Matthew had started to play with one of the boys so Kimberly tried to relax. Soon, the boys were led to their rooms to sleep and Matthew was put in a bunk with one of the boys. Kimberly was given one of the boy's rooms to sleep in by herself. Thank goodness she did not have to sleep with the little boys. She could not fall asleep and was awake when Richard and his girlfriend arrived home. They were a bit loud, but seemed ok. Kimberly had tried to sleep again, but was so very sick to her stomach. She ended up running to the restroom twice to vomit. She had never vomited alone before and it was strange to take care of herself, but she was proud that she could. She definitely did not want Richard or the strange new girlfriend to come in and take care of her. She got a cold wet wash cloth, like she had seen her mother do, and placed it on her head and went to bed. She must have fallen asleep quickly after that because she awoke to Richard standing over her telling her breakfast was ready. He asked why she had a wash cloth on her head and she had simply told him that she had not felt well last night. She did not tell him she had vomited, she did not want to be a bother or upset him. They had cereal at the table with the other kids and then were loaded back into Richard's car for the trip home. They only really saw and visited with Richard in the car and most of that time was spent listening to music and not talking.

As they pulled onto the long street where they now lived, Matthew began to cry. Kim was shocked to see the tough, somber little boy cry. She knew he did not want to go home to Tom. Richard did seem slightly taken aback to see the tears and sorrow. He asked Matthew why he was crying, but the boy would not answer. He just sobbed. It broke Kimberly's heart. It broke Richard's heart and made him feel things he did not want to feel. Richard asked Kim why Matthew was crying and she said the only thing she could think to say. She told Richard that Matthew was going to miss Richard and that he did not want to go home. She wanted to say so much more. She wanted to explain what life was like with Tom and how miserable he made the kids feel. She wanted Richard to step in and be a great father, but even at her young age, she knew Richard was not that kind of dad. She knew Richard truly did not want to know and that he would only cause trouble and not save them at all. She knew it would cause fighting and arguing. She knew it would break Lillie's heart and hurt her pride. So Kimberly said nothing more. Little Matthew wiped his face and scrambled from the car as soon as it pulled into the drive. Kimberly said her good byes and wished for a hug and kiss from her dad, but that was not to be. If she had approached Richard for a hug, she knew he would comply. That was not the kind of love she wanted. "Why couldn't he be the kind of dad that she wanted?" was all she thought as she walked to the house. This damn beautiful house that would never be a real home. At least, she could be with her mother. Lillie always made the children feel happy and much loved.

Gradually, the story of the visit with their father came out to Lillie and Tom. The adults had been unhappy about Richard's lack of paying child support. Lillie's call to Richard regarding not allowing him to take the children to girlfriends' houses did not go well. Lillie asked for child support and Richard's response was only that he could see by her new house that she did not need his money to raise those kids. He refused to send support money. He refused to drive all the way up to Michigan to get them again. From now on, he would visit with the kids when they came to visit Ohio. Lillie was livid with Richard for a long time. This made Tom very happy and he reveled in it. The children and Lillie loved the new emotional support they felt from him, though they knew it would be short lived. Lillie contacted the court system regarding child support and it came to a point where Richard would go to jail if he did not begin making the ordered payments. At this point, Lillie gave Richard the choice to release Kimberly and Matthew for adoption to avoid jail and payments. She told him that Tom would adopt them and they would not press Richard for the child support he was behind in and this would then release him from any further obligations to the children. Richard agreed with this solution right away, even though he knew it would end his visitation and parental rights.

Tom and Lillie had discussed this adoption possibility in private for quite some time. Both of them liked the idea as it would provide them with legal papers and birth certificates with the name Rollins for the schools. Everyone in this small Michigan town believed that Tom and Lillie had been married only the one time and that the children were Tom's biological children. It was sad, if the truth had been told, but Tom liked the way Lillie's children looked more than his own biological children. Kim and Matthew fit the look of the executive family image he had in his twisted mind. They were beautiful little kids and Lillie was the perfect, beautiful wife that was involved in charitable functions. So all of the adults talked about the adoption, but no one at all asked the children. They were told that on next Thursday they were going as a family to the court to have their last name legally changed from Sullivan to Rollins. The poor kids had not realized that they were still legally Sullivan. They did not have a choice about this and did not even ask about it. Lillie explained the awkwardness of having different last names and that the school needed official paper work, but in order to make this happen they had to have Tom legally adopt them. She told the children that she thought it was wonderful that Tom wanted to adopt them. That the adoption was really an important step in fitting in as a family here in this small town. Without being told, the children knew they were never to speak of Richard or of the divorce. They knew they were always to act as though Tom was their biological dad and they always followed their mother's wishes. It did make them sad to keep this secret and to pretend that Tom was their real dad, but now he really would be their real dad. When Lillie told them that Richard would not be taking them for visits any more, she let them know how happy she was to not have to worry about them. She told the children that he was not fit to have the kids alone and they totally agreed on that point. They were rather relieved at the same time their hearts broke that he was giving up being their dad. They were young, but they felt the enormity of losing a dad. They sensed the awfulness of not being loved enough and having a parent give up for the sake of money and convenience. A father that would not fight for them was an awful thing. This was a parent that had held them and knew them. "How could he give them up after all of this time?", they wondered. Matthew and Kimberly felt different from other children in a kind of out of body numbness. They were not as sad as they should have been about being rejected by their dad as they were too consumed with the horror of the permanence of Tom becoming their father. They had hoped all along that their mother would get them away from Tom. They secretly wished and, at times, even told their mom that they wanted her to divorce Tom and move out. Now, he was becoming their dad for real.

Tom and Lillie went into a little room with a judge while Matthew and Kimberly sat in wooden chairs in the hall. They did not speak, they had no reason to as each child knew how their sibling felt. Tom and Lillie came out smiling and the judge asked to see the kids in chambers alone. They were surprised at how seriously the judge spoke to them. He appeared to be genuine and spoke of wanting only the very best for them. He explained the adoption process clearly and asked if they understood why they were there. Oh boy, did they ever know. The next thing he asked took both children by surprise. He asked them if they wanted to be adopted by Tom Rollins. No one ever asked them if they wanted things to happen, it just happened. Millions of things they could say ran through their minds. Kimberly wished she was brave enough to give an honest answer. She thought perhaps Tom could be taken away to jail if she told the judge how mean he was. Then she was afraid that would disappoint her mom, might make her mother angry. Obviously, her mother wanted Tom to be their dad or they wouldn't be here. In truth, she did not believe she had the choice to answer what she felt, but felt she could only answer in the way her mother expected. It was with all of this swirling through her mind that she finally said yes. Hearing the child's hesitation, the judge asked if she was sure. She said yes. He then turned to Matthew asking the same question, Matthew said yes. Kimberly felt angry, she felt the judge should know they were too young to answer such a big question. She felt the judge should ask about their lives with Tom and maybe ask them again if they wanted this. Maybe, if given enough chances to say no, she might get the courage to say she did not want this adoption. Kimberly wondered why this judge did not know that kids do what adults tell them to do, that kids do what they think will please their parents. Well, it was done. Matthew and Kimberly sat there and watched the judge sign the papers that sealed their fate. Tom and Lillie were pleased and took the kids out to eat. They went shopping for more new clothes that they did not need.

When Kimberly returned to school and wrote her name on the top of the paper, she signed it Kimberly Rollins as she had been doing since their arrival to Michigan, as her mother had practiced with her and her brother before sending them to this school. This time she wrote it with new understanding. She had been lying before, but now it was true. She decided it was alright.

Up On the Roof

Tom began to escalate the rules and expectations for the kids. Table manners were strictly enforced. No laughing or singing was allowed at the table. Dinner was a quiet somber affair. No leaning or elbows on the table. Potato chips had to be broken into small bite sized pieces, food being put into ones mouth should not touch the sides of the mouth or it was too big and needed to be cut. Now, many of these rules are good manners, but strictly enforcing all of them at all dinners made for a pretty stressful time. The house was always and forever kept totally immaculate. The children could not leave a play item or book out if they got up to use the restroom or leave for a short period. They could not work puzzles as they would need to be left out to complete over days. Their house always looked ready for a magazine photo shoot. That was stressful. Tom often had Kimberly walking around the room picking up fuzz or pieces of stuff even after the room was vacuumed. Often she could not even find the piece to pick up for quite a while. One particular time, when she could not locate the fuzz to be picked up, she gave up and pretended to pick up three pieces of fuzz. This satisfied Tom. She was shocked, but pretended to walk with the imaginary fuzz to the trash and throw it away. He was sending her all over the place to pick up stuff he didn't even see! What a revelation! This would make most people upset or angry, but for Kim in this tricky situation, she saw it only as an answer to more quickly relieve her agony in searching for stuff on the floor. She continued to pick up imaginary fuzz almost daily for the next nine to ten years. It shut Tom up, so it was a small price to pay to keep the peace for her mother. Kim, on the other hand, would have loved to confront Tom and make a ruckus, but she knew that would cause so much trouble for her mother.

Matthew found all of this quite stressful, but soon learned that no one would tell on him due to trying to "keep the peace". Matthew especially began to cause small trouble at home. It was a cry for freedom and a wish to escape the insanity of Tom. On several occasions, the first summer with Gerri, Matthew would be found climbing the antennae tower hooked to the side of the house. He would climb up to the roof and walk around. The roof being flat, made it a bit less dangerous, but he was only 7 the first summer he did this. Being on the roof was freeing and one way he could get back at Tom. It also brought him a great deal of attention. Gerri would hear something thumping on the roof and go out and about have a heart attack seeing the small boy walking around up there. She feared he would fall off or fall through. Kimberly would catch him climbing the tower to the roof and go into hysterics. She too was afraid her brother would get seriously hurt. The times he would stay on the roof for long periods to walk around or sit up there, Lillie would be called at work. She would tell Gerri what to say and sometimes it made him come down. He then began to do it when Tom was gone, but Lillie was home. Lillie also was very worried about him being up there. When he came down, she would talk to him and spank him. Matthew did not seem to mind the spankings and at times would laugh during them. He needed to get the anger out of his system and this worked to some degree. It helped him to stay sane in a very insane house. At the time, Lillie and

Kimberly thought he was just being very naughty, well that is what Matthew thought at the time too. As the years wore on, Lillie began to realize the stress Tom was causing her son. This made her heart ache, but she didn't want to go back to being a poor single mother. She absolutely did not want her children to experience the poverty she had, so she stuck it out. She tried to give Matthew extra attention and snuck him secret snacks at bedtime to attempt to make up for the anxiety he had due to Tom.

I Am Your Father

It was a breezy hot summer day in early August. The Rollins' family was visiting and boating at the little yellow cottage of Grandpa Walloon. School would resume soon, so Tom and Lillie decided to take the children clothes shopping in Toledo, Ohio. This was an annual trip that Kimberly looked forward to and that Matthew endured. It was one of Tom's favorite things to do, spend money in public and look like a big shot. Tom did not like to spend money that could not be seen, thus bills and food shopping were kept minimal. Kimberly had realized this love of public spending early on. Tom enjoyed paying with large bills as well. He would leave with several hundred dollar bills in his wallet and attempt to pay with them at each stop. Often the store clerks would comment on not really ever handling hundreds often or at all (a hundred dollar bill went much further in the 1960's and 70's). That was just the response Tom was waiting and hoping for. He would act very nonchalant, smile a little and perhaps make a sly comment like, "Oh, you get used to it". Lillie would never admit it and no one would ever suspect, but she thoroughly enjoyed it too.

As the "fashion family" paraded through the mall, Lillie was proud of how well they all looked and how wonderfully her children behaved. Other children got tired or hungry and whined, not the fashion family children. Other children begged for things or spoke loudly, not the fashion family children. They knew better and they tried so hard to be perfect. Other families would look with envy upon this wonderful family. They would ask their children, “Why can’t you be more like those children”? If those parents had known what it took to create children like this, they may not be so anxious to replicate it. Matthew and Kimberly did not want to upset Tom and hear the screaming in the car and at home. Screaming about one incident could last a week or a day, one never knew. There would be a lot of crying and they would see the sorrow on their mother’s face. They would do about anything to avoid the screaming and being put down and called names. Tom might even chase them through the house screaming and scaring the daylights out of them. Lillie would try to calm him and direct the children to their rooms, where they would run and cry. No, misbehaving and talking were not worth all of that sorrow. They were smart children and not about to bring on that wrath if it could be avoided, which it could often not be.

As the four of them walked through the large main foyer headed out with arms full of packages and bags, they heard someone say, “Hello there son”. Matthew felt a hand on his shoulder and he turned to look up at this man speaking to him. Tom, Lillie and Kimberly all turned and looked. They did not recognize this individual and Lillie thought he looked familiar and perhaps was one of Matthew’s coaches. So they stood waiting for clarification. Soon, this stranger said to Matthew, “I am your father”. Instantly, Lillie grabbed both children turned them back toward the doors and they all four walked out of that mall very quickly. As they walked, Lillie whispered, “Don’t look back” and they did not.

Once in the car, Lillie began to talk with Tom about how she had not even recognized Richard Sullivan. That is when the children knew for sure that it had been their father, Richard. They were a bit afraid of him anyway and this entire episode had been jarring to all of them. The thing is, it made for a wonderful trip home. Tom and Lillie were talking about how much he had changed. Richard had gained weight and his hair was quite a bit longer. They laughed together and talked about how inappropriate that was of him. Lillie and Tom were both amazed that they had not known it was Richard. The children found joy in their mother's happiness and in Tom's being like a normal human about the situation. This joy and comradery were extremely rare. Inside, both Matthew and Kimberly were pleased that their biological father had acknowledged them. Maybe he did care just a little. Kimberly was glad that he had reached out to Matthew as she understood how rejected her brother often felt.

More Perverted Than You Know

Tom lost his job as an accountant within the first few years. Lillie learned that he had been accused of embezzling and fired. He was fortunate that he was not prosecuted. He was able to get a job with another very good company in town as an executive in finances. This company believed Tom's lies and did not like the company that fired Tom. He was more careful and conscientious this time, for a while. Tom worked with this new company for two years before running into a bit of trouble. Tom had been visiting prostitutes in a larger town about an hours' drive away. He had told Lillie that he had some out of town meetings and she had believed him. When the prostitutes' pimps began calling the house and talking to Lillie, she asked him about it. He told her they had mixed him up with someone else. She knew better, but went along with it, until he was threatened at work. His boss found out that a self-identified "pimp" had called the office three times. He called Tom in. Tom received one more chance and was told to get his life in order. Lillie was horrified when Tom's boss called her personally to warn her. He told her that he was concerned for her health and safety and felt obligated to let her know. She knew it was no mistake. She was humiliated and worried about what disease she might have and what the community would say.

The next morning, she gathered up the children's things and packed up suitcases. It was November and she wanted to maintain her job and the kids' school while she worked out what to do. She took the kids right after school and before Tom was home from work. They left and drove an hour to get to the cottage, her father's house again. She and the kids had the cottage to themselves as her parents were back in town for the fall and winter. She promised herself that this was just until she found a nice apartment for herself and the kids. The kids knew only that she was mad at Tom and they were over the moon with joy to get out of that house, the house that had made them "rich" was not a joy anymore. She was able to hold back her tears and anger when she saw her children's excited faces. This was an adventure to them, she thought. She didn't realize that it was so much more than that to them. They felt like they had finally escaped to freedom. Their little hearts filled with hope.

It was dark when they stopped at the store for some groceries and then drove on to the little cottage. The children relished the musty mildew smell of the place. They adored the old beat up cottage furniture. The place had been closed up tight and needed heat turned up and the water turned on. Fortunately, her dad had driven out and set it all up before they got there. He left a key and a note saying to stay there for as long as she needed, even years. While she was in utter turmoil, terror and depression, her children sang, laughed and were full of joy. They were so happy that their mommy was mad at Tom. Lillie warned them that they had to go to bed earlier due to having to get up for the long drive to school and work in the morning. They didn't care and were more than happy to share a bed if it meant freedom. Lillie on the other hand, did not sleep. She dozed occasionally only to awake to the awful truth that not only had Tom been cheating on her, but that he had lost a lot of money in his pursuit of sex with prostitutes. Of course, she wondered what was wrong with her. This was a second husband that had cheated. She was beyond humiliated and devastated. The only thing that got her up and out that door in the morning was trying to keep things normal for her children. She was not going to jeopardize their education or her job. Above all, she loved her children dearly.

They got up and drove back to Michigan in the dark. They ate muffins in the car and drank hot chocolate from an old thermos. Fortunately, the weather was dry and little to no snow fell that November. They made good time and actually had to wait in the car out front for the school to open. Lillie then went on to work and was back out in front of the school to pick them up at the end of the day. This is how their days went for an entire week. Lillie had told her boss at the pharmacy a simplified version of her problem. He had heard things from others, thus he allowed her to work shorter days until she could straighten things out. In the meantime, Lillie had quietly and humbly been checked out by her doctor. The doctor immediately put her on some antibiotics. The minor symptoms of an STD went away quickly. All she could think was how dare he do this to her.

They stopped at the house once on the fifth day to pick up a few more items. Tom had left a letter on the counter for Lillie and she slipped it into her purse without the kids knowing. They hurried like thieves gathering only what they needed and got out fast. None of them wanted to get caught by Tom. In the children's minds, he would kill them if he caught them. They felt that he would not kill their mother, only them. So, they hurried and did not grieve over toys and things left behind. They hoped and prayed that this adventure would never end.

The adventure ended on the eighth day. Tom had written a very pitiful letter. He declared his love for Lillie and his deep regret. He blamed his horrible childhood and prayed and begged her forgiveness. He wrote of his terror of not knowing where she was and if she was ok. Her family would not speak to him, nor would her boss and friends at work. He had no clue that she was going to work until he saw her car there during a day he called in sick in order to try to find her. He had spotted her car in the hospital parking lot and had waited by it until he decided he was getting too much attention. Worried that someone would tell her he was there, he left and decided to return when it was the end of her work day. When he did return, her car was already gone. He had no idea that she was ending her days early to go pick up the children. In fact, he really had not considered the children in any of this. It was his dishonesty in this letter that convinced Lillie to return. He had promised to take better care of the children. To have more fun with them and to write up a will putting Kimberly and Matthew in as equal beneficiaries with his biological children. He also lied when he vowed to never have sex with any other woman again. He claimed to only want her, forever. Lillie buckled under his false promises and although she doubted his complete honesty, she decided to go back home and try again.

Her children cried quietly as she drove them back to the beautiful house full of false hopes and dreams. They knew that their life would not be any better. They knew Tom would not change, yet here was their adult mother falling for it all. This was one more instance when Kimberly felt that their mother was not taking proper precautions. She had questioned her mother, in her own little girl mind, in many small instances prior to this. There was the time when Tom took them all boating before they were married. He had thrown out some inner tubes and Lillie had taken the children out of the boat and put them in the large inner tubes to float in the middle of the lake. Kimberly had begged her mother politely to not put them in the tubes. Lillie had laughed and called her a "worry wart". Matthew was excited and went in first. Kimberly was lowered into the tube second. Tom was already swimming around the tubes and Lillie dove in from the boat. It was fun and Kimberly tried to enjoy it. The tube was big and slippery and both kids kept slipping down and having to pull back up. Kimberly was not as strong as her brother and soon her arms could not pull her up again and she slipped off the tube and went under the water. She had no idea what to do. She was seven at the time and did not know how to swim. Matthew was only five and could not swim either. She was scared and furious at the same time. How could her mommy not know this was a bad idea? Her mommy always thought that everything was going to be fine and that Kimmy needed to stop worrying. Tom found her and brought her up. After much sputtering and coughing, she was fine and worried that her mom might make fun of her. She could then see the utter fear in her mother's face. Lillie was white and shaking. No one made fun of Kim. They got Matthew in the boat and went back to shore. And so, the buildup of Kimberly's worries and slight distrust of her mother's judgement grew.

Back Home; Use Your Wits and Psychology

At first, things were better. Tom was very happy to see them all and had presents waiting for them. The children tried to forget the past and just be as happy as their mother appeared to be. The first week or two was good. Then small things came creeping back. Picking up imaginary fuzz was the first thing Kimberly noticed come back. Tom and her mother were arguing about something was the next thing. Then Tom came home with a puppy the next day. Lillie was not happy about it but did enjoy the pure bliss of her children with the new dog. The little dog brought much joy to Tom and seemed to relax him. All was well for another week or so. Soon, the house was never clean enough and the table manners never perfect enough. When Tom's car pulled into the drive after work, tensions in the house would sky rocket. He was grumpy and growly. His family tried to be perfect, they tried to keep the peace by doing what he wanted, but it was never good enough. This is when Kimberly, only in 5th grade with no training in psychology, began to realize that picking up imaginary fuzz may be only the beginning of keeping the peace. So the next time Tom came home and went off about Matthew eating four cookies instead of the allowed two, Kimberly piped up saying she had eaten her two cookies. Well, that shut him right up and he just went over and watched T.V. all night. Hmmmm, she was on to something here. When he began yelling about the driveway having pebbles on it and Matthew not sweeping, Kimberly said Matthew had swept, but that wind had picked up and blew more down. Matthew still had to go out and sweep, but Tom quit yelling. There were somethings one could not lie about or create a story about to shut him up and this psychological manipulation became a daily game for them all. Why were three Pepsi's gone, the floor needed vacuuming every day and "Get down and scrub that spot on the floor". Bring Tom more ketchup. Go get him some more chips. On and on it seemed to go.

Only Kimberly would ever dare to yell back at Tom. She had been manipulating him long enough that it made her feel a bit of power. Matthew just tried to ignore him and also knew that Tom flared up fastest around him. Lillie was busy trying to keep the peace and protect her children. She did not want another divorce and absolutely feared being poor again.

Thanksgiving and Christmas Whiplash and Uncle Ick

Family get togethers and holidays could not have been more opposite between the Walloons and the Tritch/de Sallowes. Norma Tritch was sister of Ellen de Sallowe. Ellen had married Ichabod de Sallowe many years ago and had stuck with him through the many ups, downs and horrors of living with the man. Ichabod was extremely intelligent and a self-made millionaire. Norma worked hard at being an excellent nurse and resented her sister's apparent easy wealth with Ichabod, known as Ich (Ick) and Ellen's own wealth in selling real estate. Norma knew that she would be limited on potential income with her chosen profession. She had never dreamed that her uneducated sister would someday make so much more money than she ever could with a four year nursing degree. Ellen was able to garner wealthy clients due to her connections to Ich's business friends. Norma did not envy her sister's marriage. Although Norma' first husband had been mean and very difficult to please, he had died young and tragically in a car accident. This left her a young widow with a small son. As she looked at her son, Tom, and his mannerisms, she would find herself amazed at the similarities between father and son both physically and emotionally. This made her a bit distant with the boy and also made it easier to give him over to her parents to raise when she met the large and tough Peter Tritch. Norma disliked how much Tom reminded her of his father. She did love her son, she just did not want to raise him.

The de Sallowes had three children that appeared to hate their father. The children were all grown adults living on their own when Lillie and her children met the family. They had a daughter that was openly gay, very unusual for the 1970's. Her name was Brenda and she was a wonderfully funny and loving person. She drank too much, like her father, but was always very fun to be around and always kind. The two boys were older than Brenda with the oldest son being the obvious favorite. When Kimberly and Matthew first met this side of Tom's family they were impressed with the immense wealth. Ichabod was basically a functioning alcoholic whose company put up with him due to his brilliance in business. Ich provided beautiful homes on lakes and fabulous cars for his wife and oldest son. The other children were given wonderful gifts and cars secretly by their mother. Ellen had always felt the need to compensate for Ich's meanness and abusiveness. No one would know the hell they went through as children at the hand of Ich, but Kimberly got a taste of "Uncle Ick's" perversion and wondered at what might have happened to Ich's children.

One Thanksgiving, when Kim was fourteen years old, the family had dinner at the de Sallowe's gorgeous home on the lake. Norma and Ellen were wonderful cooks and made everything from scratch. Nothing would dare land on a Thanksgiving or Christmas dinner table that had ever been in a box or can. Upon completion of the meal, the adults went to talk or watch the game on TV. The children, there were four including Tom's two biological children that were visiting and now two adopted, were sent to the basement to play. Ellen and Ich would never have grandchildren as all three of their children had made decisions to not become parents, another rarity in the 1970's. Thus, the only playthings were a pool table and a ping pong table. The kids loved these "toys" and began to play quite happily. Suddenly, the kids noticed that Uncle Ich had followed them down and was sitting on a chair in the shadows. It seemed creepy to all of them, but they went on to play figuring he was worried about his things being used by children. Aaron and Ann were from Tom's first marriage and were eleven and ten years old respectively. Matthew was twelve years old, but much taller and stronger than eleven year old Aaron.

The girls played pool while the boys played ping pong. Ich moved his chair over toward the pool table. Kim noticed, but said nothing even though her mind began to reason that he could not hurt them too much with parents upstairs. It was a large house and most likely an adult could not hear cries for help, but one of the four could certainly run for help. She began to chastise herself for having such bad thoughts and feelings toward this man. He had not done anything wrong and Kimberly did not know of his past. She had been taught to be nice to people and to be helpful. The only thing screaming trouble and caution was her gut instinct and it was warning her greatly. She wanted to run away, but worried that she would look stupid. She did not want to offend anyone so she continued to ignore the man and played pool with Ann. Ich began to give her advice on how to hit the ball and how to play angles. As her gut screamed warning signals and became nauseous, she reasoned in her head that he was really just being nice. She was so foolish for thinking he would hurt them. He was just a strange man that did not know how to behave with kids. Kimberly continued to reassure herself of this as Ich came up behind her and helped with the pool stick in her hand. “Odd”, she thought, when he placed his arm around her waist with his hand on her stomach. “Oh, no way!” her head screamed, when he moved his hand up over her small breast. Her stomach lurched with nausea as she pulled away from him. She thought that perhaps it was a mistake and she was not going to freak out. Then it happened again. This time he was even closer and she could smell the alcohol on his breath and hear him hum slightly. She pulled back and turned to look him in the eye. This was not a mistake and he gave her a very sober and direct look leaving no mistake about his intentions. Kimberly decided to give him a dead on stare right back. Having had to stand up to Tom gave her a bit of a backbone as she was always too submissive and respectful to any adult. Ich saw in her eyes that she was not the victim and submissive he had thought, so he turned and toddled upstairs.

Kimberly was much too embarrassed to say anything about it and the other kids were clueless as to what had just happened, so she kept quiet and went into a bit of denial mode as she had learned from her mother. Her mother came down a few seconds later and had sensed something wrong. Lillie could see a quiet fear in her daughter’s eyes and knew that something was not ok. She had seen Ich come up from the basement and had been surprised that he had even gone down with the kids. There was something very unsettling about Ich being alone with the kids. He was not a kid friendly kind of guy and Lillie did not like the way Ich’s adult children avoided him and only spoke with and went near their mother. She had a great uneasiness about this family and especially about

Ichabod de Sallowe. At first, she wrote it off to his excessive drinking, but her gut was feeling like it was so much more than just a drinking problem.

Lillie pulled Tom aside and told him that they probably should go. When she shared how Ich had come up from the basement where the children were, Tom actually turned a bit pale. Tom told her to get the kids and he went to gather their coats. Lillie noticed a menacing look pass between Tom and Ich and was surprised when Tom just announced that they were leaving and had the family walk to the car with no goodbyes and no hugs. Once home, Lillie put the kids to bed and went to speak with Tom. Tom admitted that Ich had physically and sexually abused his own children. He claimed that Ich physically was rough on the boys and sexually abused his own daughter for years. Tom claimed to never have witnessed it, but something in the way he spoke made Lillie feel that Tom had been included in some form of the abuse at the hands of his Uncle.

Future Christmas's found the de Sallowe's out of the country or just stopping by the Tritch house to celebrate briefly and then leaving. Kimberly never spoke of the incident to anyone, but felt that her parents knew what Ich was capable of and that is why they never returned to the mansion on the lake.

Christmases and Thanksgivings at Grandpa and Grandma Walloons were carefree and full of love. As soon as they walked into the home on a holiday, the air would be cigarette blue and every other adult was smoking. They would all land in the "front room" as the living room was referred to. Two couches and two chairs would be filled up with the remainder of adults and children on the floor. Talking, sharing and an abundance of laughter was the norm. Sometimes, the children would go to the second level and get into the closet that held Lillie's old prom dresses, ballet gowns and tutus. The little girls would dress up in them and parade around and play out a variety of pretend scenarios. Jerry and Sarah's third child had been born. There was now a blue eyed, red headed baby girl named Meghan. Every child was careful with the clothing as Lillie had explained to them how special and expensive each item had been. The girls all enjoyed hearing the story behind each outfit. Only God knew what the two boys were up to, but it usually ended in something needing to be cleaned up or the girls running away from them and screaming. All children stayed away from the bedroom with the small door in the wall that led to the attic. Their Uncle Babe's stories had been passed down from child to child and no one was about to try their luck.

When it came time to eat a holiday meal at the Walloons, it was great fun and required a lot of cooperation. Children went first and were helped by adults as needed. There was always plenty of food with many special homemade specialties and goodies. There was also canned or boxed food that had been added to or improved upon. This improvement was referred to as having been "fixed up" or "doctored". As in, "that potato salad over there has been doctored and those baked beans are real good, grandma fixed 'em up". The food was displayed on the dining room table. Now, the Walloon dining room was very large with a gorgeous dining room table, chairs and buffet that Lillie had purchased for her first home with her money from teaching dance; money she spent before Richard started taking it. After her divorce and remarriage, she never had room for it and it remained at her parents' home. So, all would fill their plates and most would return to the front room to eat while a few might stay at the dining room table to eat. Dessert was usually on the buffet and was grabbed randomly and frequently. The stories would fly around the room as everyone ate and listened. Even small children behaved well and were of no trouble as they received a lot of attention and love while the adults sat on the floor eating with them. Even the youngest child enjoyed the stories and laughing. At some point Grandpa Walloon would break into song or have someone come over and "flick" his thumb. He loved to have one of his children or grandchildren sit beside him and flick his thumb with their thumb or rub his thumbs. Later, all would realize that his hands worked so hard all day and all week that they were probably sore or arthritic. Some believed it was his way of getting attention. One knew that if they sat near grandpa, they were soon going to hear him say, "...flick my thumb will ya".

It was obvious that Tom enjoyed his time with the Walloon crew. They always stayed much longer at the Walloon home than at the Tritch home and usually chose to spend the night at the meager home instead of in the lovely guest rooms at the Tritch house on the lake. Kimberly and Matthew were always relieved when they were able to spend most of their visit with Lillie's side of the family.

The Fashion Family

The Rollins family had gained some notoriety around the small town. They were all considered good looking and such young looking parents. Tom had gotten involved in local activities and Lillie was in a sorority for local upper class women. She had been voted the Queen of the sorority one year and that brought local news to their new home in town. Lillie was to share about the charities that the sorority sponsored. The Rollins now lived in a large historic brick house with a beautiful stone wrap around porch and a huge stained glass window at the curving staircase's landing. They were on the local news and in the paper as the "Fashion Family". The children looked very somber in all of the pictures as they had just been screamed at the entire day by Tom. The house was scrubbed and the kids were scrubbed, but not well enough in Tom's opinion. It was a stressful disaster to be the Fashion Family. By the time the news crew arrived, only Tom was happy and in his glory. The rest of the family was sad, drained and utterly depressed. Fake smiles and short answers from the kids made it through the interview. Lillie did well and was able to fake it better than the children had. Tom tried to be the show stopper and did gain some admiration, he could be charming and so friendly. Lillie went on that year as the Queen and representative of her sorority and was even offered a job at a T.V. news station as a local anchor woman. The kids begged her to take it as it would be over an hour's drive and they told her she could divorce Tom and the three of them could make a clean start. The children never knew how seriously she had considered that job and move, but they did know she thought about it. She ended up turning it down and staying, yet again, with Tom.

The last summer they would spend in the beautiful old house, Sarah and Jerry came for a visit and then left Brian and Renee to stay on for a week. Meghan was too young to stay for that long. Lillie loved her niece and nephew and enjoyed their stay, but had to walk on even more egg shells around Tom to keep any type of harmony. Kimberly helped by being extra observant about cleaning and Matthew helped by keeping Brian out of the house most of the day.

Mid-visit, Brian and Matthew had been out hitting golf balls at the high school. Matthew and Brian were 13 and 11 years old respectively. Matthew kept warning Brian to watch out and wait until he was out of the way before swinging. After about 15 minutes of hitting balls, Matthew and Brian walked to the other side of the field to retrieve the golf balls. Brian decided to begin hitting the balls back randomly just as Matthew bent to retrieve a ball. As one might have expected, Brian's golf club whacked Matthew in the head causing an explosion of blood that had both boys screaming and sure that Matthew was going to die. They could not stop the flow of blood, so Matthew hopped on his bike and peddled the two miles home. Brian followed, all the while in utter terror that Matthew would die at any moment. Matthew was sure he would die soon. The blood was dripping off of him and onto the ground as he peddled for home. His head hurt like no pain he had ever felt. Once home, the girls began screaming, crying and running for Lillie. Lillie was scared, but the children could not tell as she put on her calm face and gathered Matthew into the car and headed for the emergency room. He was promptly stitched up, given aspirin and sent home. All were relieved to see that Matthew would live.

The days with Brian were always filled with adventure and often some horror to be covered up before Tom got home. Renee and Kimberly had a fun visit and Renee would go with Kimberly to "help" babysit. On the last day of the cousin's visit, Brian and Matthew were in the garage while the girls played around on the big porch. The girls heard a large boom and whoosh sound. Now that could not be ok. They ran to the garage to find Matthew with the garden hose trying to spray out a huge fire running up the inside of the garage wall. Brian was running to get Aunt Lillie and the girls just stood there and screamed. Lillie came out and grabbed the hose from Matthew and told the kids to back up. She said they would call the fire department if she couldn't stop it. Well, the fire department needed to be called and one of the neighbors called while Lillie battled the blaze. The fire department quickly extinguished the fire and talked to the two little boys about safety and not ever using gasoline. They had realized from the odor that gas had been used and the boys confessed to trying to start small fires, thus the readiness of the garden hose. They had gotten away with it all week, but used the gas on that day to create a better fire. Once the firemen left, Lillie began to try to clean up the garage, hoping to lessen Tom's impending rage. The entire north wall was charred. As she climbed a ladder to scrub the wall, she noticed a coat on a high shelf. "How odd", she thought. She pulled the coat down. The pockets were bulging with some type of objects. Lillie climbed down the ladder and reached into the pockets and pulled out books and a magazine of utter pornography. It was very perverted pornography like she had never known existed. Unfortunately, the kids caught a glimpse of the pictures and were groaning with being "grossed out". Lillie told them that this was a neighbor's old coat that she was supposed to sell at a garage sale. She said, "I guess George forgot this stuff was in his coat". The children believed her and this led to them being very afraid of poor, kind, old George when they should have been even more afraid of their strict and angry "dad". The kids were shocked when Lillie told them to leave the mess and that Tom would clean it up as she walked into the house. They were pleasantly surprised that she was so calm about the fire and the mess now. They were even more shocked to see Tom come out of the house, after he had run in yelling about the garage, and begin to quietly clean. He never became angry with the kids. How did their mother change his mood and diffuse that anger today when she normally could do nothing. They were relieved and awestruck. They seriously had no clue that the horrid, perverted pornography had been Tom's, but Lillie knew. She was in her bathroom vomiting and crying. Tom was pretty shook up at the sight of her. She had put up with his running around and had believed the counseling had worked. She had willed herself to trust Tom again and he had begun to fail. He promised her it was just books and not women. Lillie said nothing, but he knew it was bad. These books were not just pictures of woman and stories of sex, but of people with animals and things unknown and unbelievable to Lillie. This stuff was sick and also violent. She threw up again.

She led everyone to believe that she had gotten the flu. She looked awful. She was so thankful that Sarah and Jerry would be picking up the kids this afternoon. She would be unfit to continue caring for them. Tom could not have been more “dear”. The nicer he was, the sicker Lillie became. Yet, she stayed with him. When next she found pornographic books hidden in Matthew’s bedroom’s dropped ceiling, he told her they were Matthew’s, not his. Well, that did not add up at all. How would a boy his age get such books? Even if he had, it was Matthew that had summoned his mother to check out what was in his ceiling. He had been a bit concerned when he noticed an odd shape near the light of the lowered ceiling tiles and together Matthew and his mother pulled the books down. Tom’s explanation did not make sense. Tom was perverted, a cheat and a liar. Still Lillie stayed. He blamed her son, lost jobs, cheated on her, broke her trust and his promises, bullied her children and made everyone uneasy. Lillie stayed.

She stayed hoping for things to be better at first. Then she stayed thinking things could change with counselling and her challenging him. Perhaps, he would change if she kept praying harder, made the kids clean more and be quieter. Lillie had to make this work. She did not want a second divorce. It would be a failure and an embarrassment. It would mean lack of money and prestige. She had Tom sleep in the guest room and threatened to leave again as she had before. He promised to change and be better. Tom loved Lillie like he had never loved anyone before, but he was a sick man and his love was dark and sick. Lillie waited for the normal to come back. When it did, she just went on as though nothing was wrong. The ability to deny her reality became Lillie's strongest skill. A skill her children also began to learn. A dangerous and hurtful skill. And so, they stayed.

Then a few months later, she discovered that she was pregnant. Lillie hoped that this might help Tom to feel joy or contentment. Tom was thrilled to be having another child. He and Lillie painted the large guest room blue with white trim. If the baby was a girl, they would decorate with more pink. Matthew and Kim thought it was a bit creepy, but they both looked forward to a baby to hold and love. At the same time the neighbor lady, older than Lillie, learned that she too was pregnant, but with twins. Much happy conversation centered on these new babies to come and plans were made for them to cover for each other when it came time to give birth. When Lillie hit her third month, she became even more nauseous. Every day she became more ill. At first no one was too concerned, then her illness became violent. Lillie's doctor had her taken to the emergency room where it was discovered that the baby had died and was now causing an infection. Lillie was very ill. It was possible that she would not survive this.

Tom was with her much of the time, but when he came home he was so nice to the children that they knew something awful must be happening. The neighbors watched them during the night and Aunt Sarah was on her way up to stay for a while. Kimberly was scared that if her mother were to die, she and Matthew would have to stay with Tom. She decided to beg Sarah to take them if something happened to her mother and she was angry for even thinking like that, but her survival mode had kicked in. Kimberly did not say anything to Matthew about her fear, she did not want to worry him. For her part, Lillie was feeling her life ebb away. Her doctor had told her she would be fine, but she could see the worry on his face. A nurse friend of hers did explain the dangers so that Lillie could be prepared if death came. Lillie was amazed at how weak she was and also at how she was not panicked about dying. During one of the worst times, she knew she could have let go and she was very tempted to do so. Death appeared as a much needed escape from this illness and pain as well as from her emotional drama with Tom. Death was preferred by Lillie except for one important factor, she needed to live for her children. So she fought to survive when letting go was so tempting.

When Sarah arrived, she did not have her three children with her, not even new baby Meghan. Kimberly was surprised, but soon realized that Sarah planned to be ready for anything and to spend time nursing her sister back to health. Lillie was far more ill than Sarah had been informed of. Sarah shook with fear for her sister's life when she saw her in the hospital bed looking so small and helpless. Lillie was pale and weak. She struggled to feed herself. This infection was vicious. On top of this was Lillie's sorrow at losing the infant. She did confide in Sarah that she felt it was a blessing as Tom was so difficult to live with. She had been worried about how she was going to maintain emotionally with the addition of a baby. That, in turn, made her feel guilty about the loss, as though it were her fault due to her thoughts. Sarah was a blessing and such a relief for Lillie. She had worried so much about her children as she lay there. She told Sarah that she and Jerry were to take the kids if she didn't make it through this. She did not think Tom would fight to keep them. Sarah promised to take care of the children, but told Lillie that she would not have to worry about it. She promised her sister that she would soon be well enough to go home. Lillie was with Sarah when the doctor came in with results from the fetus and infection. The doctor informed Lillie that the fetus never had a chance. The baby was not formed correctly and it was a boy was all he would say. She should not try again he advised. This brought some comfort to her heart. It took another week, but Lillie did survive and go home to her children. She was not able to get out of bed much and Sarah was a help the first two days, then it was time for her to get back to her children. Kimberly was able to help out after she got home from school. Matthew would run errands around the house for his mother and Tom brought home supper every night. Lillie gradually got back her strength and healed, but not before Kimberly, ever listening and eavesdropping, heard her mother confide to a close friend that she had feared that the infant might have been born with Tom's personality. Lillie wondered if this was God's way of protecting her. Her friend had agreed and thought that would have been more than anyone should have to bear. Kimberly thought they already had to bear more than anyone should.

The Pool Will Not Fit! God Damn Flies...

Tom always had a speed boat and that brought a little joy to the family's life. The kids and Lillie were good water skiers and enjoyed the water. Tom only yelled until he got the boat running, then there was peace and joy. The boat also gave them fun at Grandpa Walloon's cottage and they went to Ohio almost every week-end. Being with their grandparents is most likely what saved the children's sanity. Tom behaved better in front of others and only criticized the kids in private. One day, while at the cottage, all of the family was gathered and enjoying the boat. Tom loved that he was the speed boat's owner even if he could often not get it started without help from someone else. He usually flooded it or something. As evening arrived, the boat was put up and dinner consumed picnic style on the lawn, Tom began talking about the swimming pool he was having put in. That was the first anyone, including Lillie, had heard about a pool. Jerry piped up that there was not enough room for a pool at their new house. Where did Tom think he was going to put it? Well, Tom said there was plenty of room in the side yard. The kids were so excited to hear that they were getting a pool, they did not question Tom's ability to get what he wanted. Lillie was concerned about how that would look, right in the side yard along a sidewalk. He assured her that a big privacy fence was all that was needed and it would look great. Knowing how fastidious Tom could be, Lillie began imagining having to vacuum the pool everyday too.

When the children got up several mornings later, they found men measuring their side yard. They began dancing around and talking about the new pool. They could not understand why their mother was not happy. She said it would make the house look bad to have a large fence right up at the sidewalk. She said she was not sure it was legal to put a pool there. The children then became more cautious in their joy. They knew their mother was most likely correct, but they still had hope, until they heard Tom come in saying, “God damn flies”! Well, that was certainly a bad sign for the pool. There was absolutely not enough room for a pool of any type according to these men. Tom then had had another company come out that afternoon and received the same answer. “God damn flies”! Whatever that meant, the children knew the pool was not going to happen.

Lillie and Tom talked for a long time that evening. She loved that house and did not ever want to move. She had had draperies custom made for every window. She had helped Tom paint every wall. She loved that house. Tom wanted a pool and if it meant leaving this beautiful house, well then so be it. He began looking at houses with pools. Lillie refused to go look at any other house. It took a lot of courage and back bone to say no to Thomas Rollins, but she was staying in that house. Fall came and Tom stopped looking at houses. She had won a battle. She was thrilled to be in her home. She adored watching her children run down the curving stairs. The stairs were wide, the dark stained woodwork was original and perfect. She loved the beveled glass in the windows and the gorgeous entry with dark wood, marble flooring and double set of heavy wooden doors. The house actually had a vestibule to enter through and keep the cold and heat at bay. The fire place was huge and like none she had ever seen. They had just had all new carpeting put in that spring. She would not leave.

There was no more talk or mention of a pool until the next spring when Tom broke the news that he had purchased land to build a house. This house would be a ranch style and would have a large yard with a brand new pool. Everything was going to be brand new and Lillie could pick out everything thus getting exactly what she wanted. What she wanted was that old beautiful house she already had. She knew that it was a done deal and that she was not going to win after all. Land had been purchased with money from the recent deaths of Thomas' grandparents. These were grandparents that had raised Tom when his mother remarried after his mean father had died and Peter Tritch did not want any children around. His mother and Aunt had received large amounts of money in inheritance from the deaths of their parents, the Howards. Tom had been left a lesser amount, but enough to live a lifetime on if one was careful, but he was not a careful man with money or people. He was careful with objects and material things. Lillie put on a brave front for herself and the children. She reasoned that it would be fun selecting items and designing a new house. The kids would love a pool she thought. Perhaps it was for the best. Good bye old house and good bye more opinions and desires. They all lived under Tom's Thumb.

The new house was coming along well. Lillie did get to pick out many things, but if Tom had a strong opinion about a thing or two, well so be it. He had deemed it best to have the same carpet run throughout the house, which was fine with Lillie, except that he wanted shag carpet and he wanted it to run through the kitchen too. He reasoned that the family room and dining room connected with the kitchen in the big open space and he wanted the same flooring to run all the way through and he wanted shag carpet because it was so popular at the time. A bit of discussion and arguing ensued, but in the end, Tom got his way. He also demanded that the pool be put as close to the house as possible. Lillie pointed out that if people splashed, the windows would get spotted from the water. He did not care. They just could not splash near the windows. All three of them felt their hearts drop. More rules, more worry, another thing to get yelled at about. How could one swim, use the diving board and be sure not to get water on the windows? The pool was built as close to the house as possible. Tom demanded that the pool pump be put in the basement of the house. He did not want to see pool equipment or to build a surround as was suggested. The pool people recommended against that, but Tom got his way. Lillie did enjoy decorating and designing some things and was able to move out of her gorgeous brick home with a minimum of tears. Tom bought two more brand new cars and then was fired from his job. New house, new pool, new furniture, new cars, no job. Well, he still had some inheritance left.

The Walloons Are in the Pool

To celebrate the new house and pool, Tom told Lillie to invite all of her family up for a cook-out and swimming. Ol' Scrappy and Thelma rode up with Uncle Babe and family. Uncle Jerry and family drove up from Union City Ohio/Indiana. Union City was on the state line and time change was a nightmare for citizens that lived on one side and worked or went to school on the other side. As family arrived, Tom's mood improved; he was anxious to show off and knew that he had the best home in the Walloon family. Eleven relatives plus the four Rollins made for fifteen people and the new house and pool were ready for the commotion.

After the greetings, hugs, kisses and food; all were ready to swim. Now Thelma did not own a bathing suit and Scrappy just brought extra shorts, all others donned their suits and hopped in. There was so much laughing, talking and fun that soon someone had talked Thelma into just going in with her bra and underwear. There was a privacy fence and Lillie promised to dry her clothes later, so I'll be darned if Thelma didn't go straight into that house and come out in her undies. Everyone there, except for Tom, had hooked her bra and seen her in her underclothing at one time or another, thus no one was shocked. The family did hoot, cheer and encourage Thelma to get in the pool. She could not swim and was typically fearful of water, but she stepped into the shallow end. Soon, Uncle Babe brought her a large inner tube and helped her into it. The pool water splashed and swished as Thelma was slurped into that tube. Thelma squealed, hooted and covered her face as she laughed and jostled in that tube. Most family members were red with laughter at the vision of Thelma's plump legs sticking up out of the tube and Boyd swimming around her with a lit cigarette in his mouth. "Come on momma, you can do this," her husband encouraged. This brought more laughter and cheers. Soon, people were gently rocking her tube just to hear her yell, Babe swam under her and goosed her. She declared that she had not had this much fun in many years. She loved the water, the family and all of the attention. Kim was surprised to look over at Tom and see a relaxed smile on his face. Water was splashing everywhere and getting on the house windows, but he was laughing right along with the family. She enjoyed these small glimpses into the humanity of Tom. They were rare.

Then, out came the vacuum cleaner late that afternoon. Tom was vacuuming the room where all of the Walloons sat talking. They took it as the cue to go, everyone always did. Tom professed over and over to Lillie that he did not do it to make people leave, but they always did leave. Tom could only stand a "mess" for just so long and then he had to get it all cleaned and in order. He was a driven man full of madness. His obsessive compulsive disorder was just a small irritating part of his undiagnosed illnesses. Matthew and Kimberly knew that window cleaning would be their next task. He had had to have that pool so close to the house against everyone's recommendation; windows were often being cleaned.

The Pimps Are Calling

A few months after the house was built, Tom began going on a lot of business trips again. These were buying trips for items and stock for the new clothing and gift store Tom was starting up, but Lillie knew that was most likely trouble again. The kids believed he was going on business trips and did not care where or why. They were glad he was gone once in a while. He had become angry again as the house was completed. He yelled, as was normal for him, about things from breaking potato chips small enough before you ate them to Matthew wearing "dirty" socks. The socks had come straight from the dryer and were simply stained. Tom began yelling about Matthew traipsing dirt all over the brand new house and carpet. Matthew ignored him and then just took off the socks. Tom kept raging, going on and on about how Matthew ruined everything and had no respect for anything or anyone. Lillie had tried to calm Tom, but it was no use. Kimberly had had enough and, as she increasingly had begun to do, began yelling back at Tom. "What do you expect? Socks get stained, just buy us new socks everyday then..." and so on. Tom eventually stopped. His rage was over. Kimberly yelled back for a little longer this time. Tom shut up and took it. Wow, all were surprised!

Tom respected Kim in his own very sick way. He thought she was pretty and liked that she was popular and smart. Matthew was also very popular, smart and extremely handsome, but that just enraged Thomas even more as he felt that Matthew was everything he himself had wanted to be in school. Matthew was kind, he was called, "the friend of the friendless", but he reminded Tom of the guys in school that laughed at him when he was young. Matthew reminded him of the guys that spread the story of Tom peeping in windows. Tom had been caught doing numerous creepy things during his high school years. Tom often roamed the city not wanting to go back to his grandfather's house. He was found wandering neighborhoods, peeking in windows and masturbating. Tom did things that if Lillie had known were true, would have kept her from dating him. It also drove Tom crazy that Lillie loved Matthew so much, even though he was her own son. Tom was a very sick and perverted man and this is why children and dogs shied away from him. They sensed something very wrong with this man. Adults were just charmed by him and took a long while to figure out his sickness. For reasons that Kimberly could not put into words or thought, she always locked her bedroom door if she was ever left alone with Tom. She had started doing that when she hit puberty. Fortunately, it was very rare that she was ever alone with Tom. If she or Lillie had known what he was capable of or what he thought, they would have left in a heartbeat, screaming with fear. From childhood, she and Matthew had known something was not right with this man, but they had no words for it and no power.

The first call came to the house when Kimberly was home alone. They had barely been in the new home for a year. It was summer and Kim was going into her sophomore year in high school. She answered the phone to a deep voice with a heavy southern, urban dialect, a voice she did not recognize. The caller asked if she was Thomas Rollins' daughter. She confirmed that she was. The man laughed a mean rumbling laugh and began to tell her to let her father know that he had Tom's wallet. He said her father had been with a pretty little prostitute and that she had taken the wallet when she left. He wanted Tom to call him back that night after he got home from work. He said Tom had his number and hung up. Kimberly shook with the knowledge that had just been thrown at her. She had never been told of any of the past issues, but was not surprised about the call and did not doubt the caller's words. This is something she would not doubt Tom capable of. She knew he was capable of this against her mother and so much more. She told her mother about the call when she got home. Lillie told Kim there was a mix up, that the caller had the wrong number or the wrong idea. Lillie left and went to talk to Tom at work. Tom reassured Lillie and then Kimberly that night that it was a prank to blackmail him. That someone had stolen his wallet when he was in Detroit on business and they were trying to get money from him. A week went by and no sign of any more trouble. Kimberly and Matthew wondered how their mother could keep sleeping with Tom after all of this, but Lillie had convinced herself that Tom was telling the truth. He had worked his charm yet again on the sweet and somewhat gullible by choice, Lillie.

The Fight

Tom came home the next Monday in a rage about Matthew eating pizza in the family room. No mess had been made. They all often ate pizza in the family room. Kimberly and her boyfriend were in the basement watching T.V. when they heard Lillie screaming for Tom to stop. Lillie never screamed at Tom, or anyone. Kimberly knew it was something very bad. She grabbed her boyfriend, Nick and yelled for him to come and help her. She could hear the panic in her mother's voice like never before. As she ran upstairs with Nick close behind, she worried that she might be getting Nick into something too big and dangerous for him to handle. Nick was only beginning his senior year and not a fighter. He was tall and strong, but was he a match for an angry man with adrenalin flowing? She could hear banging and thudding and had no idea if Tom was hurting her brother, her mother or both. She was going to call the cops as soon as she got upstairs to a phone. As they reached the top of the basement stairs, they could see Tom tussling with Matthew while Lillie was holding onto Tom's shirt. Matthew was not hitting Tom, but just holding onto Tom's arms to try to stop the attack. Tom had hit Matthew and was attempting to shove him around. Pizza was smashed on the floor and on the wall. They were huffing and puffing, but made no vocalizations. It was an eerie silence except for the thudding and banging. Kimberly had never witnessed anything like this and she screamed repeatedly for Tom to stop. Tom rammed Matthew's head into the wall just as Nick jumped in and grabbed Tom's arms. Tom immediately stopped when he realized that Nick was there and felt the boy's strength against him.

Kimberly had the phone and was dialing the number to the police station when Lillie told her to stop. She held the phone and dialed another number, knowing she shouldn't stop, but not ever wanting to disobey or hurt her mother. She felt that maybe Lillie knew best what to do, but in her head she knew her mother made bad choices. She dialed another number while Tom sat down on the floor and Nick stood some kind of awkward guard and Matthew walked outside rubbing his head. Lillie said, "I promise to take you kids and leave if you will just not call the police". Kimberly had presence of mind to tell Tom to not stop them and to not talk to them or she and Nick would be sure to contact the police instantly. He shook his head in compliance and complained about his hand hurting. Really, he complained about hurting his hand from attacking her brother, what a sick demented man. He wanted pity and help from the very people he was hurting! They gathered up some overnight things and headed out the door to the car in the garage.

Nick told Lillie that she should take Tom's fancy car. That she deserved that at the least, but Lillie piled them all into the new yet simple Ford Maverick. She drove Nick home and begged him to not tell his parents. She then drove to the cottage at the lake. Again, this was her safe haven. Years ago when she had left and come to this little cottage, Tom had never thought she was there and she never told him where she went. He had always assumed that she had stayed with one of her friends in town. He never dreamed that she drove two hours a day round trip to keep her job. So, she realized that he would not figure it out now, five years later. She had endured so much from this man. She had put her children through so much for the sake of her marriage and a middle class existence. This time the children were not as joyous about the leaving as they had been five years ago. They were not as hopeful for a change. They had seen their mother put up with ridiculous behavior from Tom and had no illusions left. Being older, they also had begun to develop a life and friendships outside of their family. They had connections with friends and school that had helped them to stay somewhat normal. They grieved at the thought of leaving them, but they knew they would leave all of that behind if their mother really left Tom and wanted to move away. This leaving was bittersweet for the children. Kimberly was 16 and loved her boyfriend, friends and school. Matthew was 14, had close friends and also enjoyed school.

Three days later, Tom had worked his magic on Lillie to make her return. He promised to go to counseling with her. They attended several sessions and then all was supposedly good. Tom had received more inheritance money from his mother's share to help him out since he had lost his job due to the prostitution blackmail. The pimps had repeatedly called Tom's boss and that had ended his employment and forced him to start up his own business. This was also the stress that caused Tom to be violent with Matthew earlier. Lillie told Tom that she wanted to go to nursing school as part of the deal for her return. She knew in her head that she needed a better job to depend on. The way Tom handled jobs and money was not going to keep the family safe at times, even though he had inherited enough money for two life times. She was mentally preparing for a time when she might really leave him and never come back. The children were thrilled when she explained this to them and they made her promise them that she would leave once she had her degree. Lillie promised that she would leave if things ever got that bad again.

With this new money, Tom had decided to start up a clothing store in town. He bought and remodeled a store. He and Lillie worked together and he actually listened to her about the need for an infant and children's clothing store in the town. Lillie decorated the store and it was lovely. It was a very classy children's store. People in the small town were excited to have this store and it filled a need. That is how the store began, but Tom soon tired of the infant and children's line and began shifting to young junior and teen girls clothing. Lillie had warned him that there was too much competition in that area. Tom did what Tom wanted. A small thought of Tom's perverse behaviors crossed both Lillie and Kimberly's minds. They would not speak of it to each other until many years later. Now, Tom was surrounded by young women and teen girls, it was gross and sick to see him running clothes to them and helping them select outfits as though he were some sort of designer and expert and not just a sick perverted man getting his jollies. He would often tell a young skinny teenager that she had a, "good teen build". It would completely gross out Kim and the other employees and sometimes even the teen would be disturbed and end up leaving quickly. Tom would even compliment some of the mother's that came in, often coming across as creepy. Kimberly was working there during the summer and Lillie often helped out on week-ends, thus they witnessed firsthand his odd behavior and poor business skills. Even Kim, with no business training, knew he was running this business into the ground. He would keep money in envelopes for dress clubs and lay-a-ways and then dip into it for cash for himself. He loved to lavish cash on Kim and Lillie and even Matthew if people were around. If someone came into the store that he wanted to impress, he would often turn to Kim and tell her to pick out an outfit or offer her cash for her shopping or movie outings.

Tom had run for and been elected for several school board positions and had been a trustee for 3 years. He then ran for school board president and had won, placing him in the lead position for the last two years. His family loved it as it was another meeting that kept him away from them. He loved to be recognized and greeted with the new respect that this position brought him. Kimberly even had several teachers talk about her father with renewed interest and respect since his election. Lillie had helped him with his campaign and was a great boon to his popularity. She also enjoyed this attention and liked the way it made her family appear to the people of this small community. Outwardly, they were still the "Fashion Family" and were often admired for this false facade. The children never talked about the reality of their lives to anyone, even rarely speaking about it to each other as they lived it daily. Often, Kim's friends would tell her how lucky she was to have a dad like Tom. She would smile and cringe, but say nothing. The one time she had tried to confide in a friend, they did not believe her and thought she was trying to get attention so that sealed her lips even more. Very little was ever said to their close relatives as they did not want to bring dishonor to their mother or disappoint her.

Matthew and Kimberly lived most of their lives trying not to disappoint their mother and to not bring her any more heartache. Tom was on a high when Kimberly became a cheerleader and was praised by her teachers for doing well. Tom did not take much pride in Matthew other than the fact that Matthew was extremely handsome, like his Uncle Jack and Uncle Boyd, but Tom often received credit for the boy's good looks and was told how much Matthew resembled him. Tom did not approve of any of Lillie's attention toward the boy. He became jealous and found reason to pick on Matthew. Tom did not approve of Matthew's desire to dress in the "cool" fashions of the 1970's and certainly became upset when Matthew began to grow his hair longer. It did not fit the image that Tom sought to portray and added more conflict to an already volatile relationship. Tom felt jealous of Matthew's easy popularity and athletic abilities. He often saw Matthew as the high school boys he had always wished to be and never fit in with. He saw the growing teenager as an enemy, as competition for Lillie's affection. Lillie and the children did not realize this perception of Tom's and if they had, they would have realized that obtaining peace was a losing effort. They also did not realize how mentally ill Thomas Rollins was. He was seen as "difficult" or "spoiled". He did love them in his own unsettling way, the only way he knew to love anything. It was far from a nurturing love.

After intense arguments and screaming sessions, often beginning as soon as Tom walked in the door from work, he would feel guilty or scared of losing them and would come home with gifts. He would usually bring records for the kids and sometimes candy or flowers for Lillie. One could truly have done all of their chores and be sitting quietly reading or watching the T.V. and have Tom arrive home and begin screaming before the door was completely open. Tom would often bang on the bathroom door when Kim was in there and tell her she was taking too long, even though another restroom was available. He then would begin to call her "poopie" as a nickname. He might begin yelling about where all the Pepsi went or why the driveway was not swept, even though no Pepsi had been consumed and the driveway was quite clear, a hang up he had left over from when they had pebbles on the roof from the first house and then became an obsession forever, one that Matthew could never do correctly. At times even Kimberly and Lillie had gone out to help Matthew sweep to be sure it was completely clear, only to have Tom come home enraged about the dirty driveway. Once he was told that all three had swept, he would often shut up and stop complaining. They had all learned that they could tell Tom whatever he wanted to hear, even an out and out lie, and it would settle him down and shut him up for a while. If he caught Kimberly eating chips out of the bag, a no no, she found she could simply say she had eaten them from a bowl and was just putting the bag away. It was an obvious lie, but he did not challenge her on it. The same was true of Lillie, but there was no winning or shutting Tom up for Matthew. The teenager stayed away from home as much as possible when Tom was around. That was his way of staying sane. Sometimes

God throws you a life line and that life line for Kimberly was Nick.

Several of Kim's friends attended the same church as Nick and his family. These friends reassured her that he was a good guy after Nick had called and asked Kim to go to a local high school band concert. He had called two weeks ago to invite her to go sledding with a group of friends, but she had said no as she did not even know who he was. She was a bit amazed that he knew her. Nick was two grades above her in school and she did not know all of the upperclassmen. Although she was young, she too found herself being attracted by people of wealth, power and with big egos. Nick was the total opposite of that. He was very good looking and reminded her a bit of a Native American Indian warrior. Nick was kind and friendly. He was the complete opposite of her fathers, both biological and adoptive. He was persistent in his pursuit of dating Kimberly and that was a good thing for her. She was too distracted with trying to put up a good social front, keep up with school activities and homework to be able to think straight about dating and "guy selection". If she had been left to her own inclinations in the boy department, she would have stuck with some of her earlier attractions, boys more self-centered and wealthy. Nick was God's life line away from repeating her mother's mistakes and continued bad choices.

Her mother adored Nick and his kindness. By now, her mother had realized the wonderful value of a kind and loving man like her own father, but she could not stop her own self-destructive choices. She could not change her value of money and status as a definition of success. She was attracted to confident men with large egos. Lillie clung to what she felt would maintain that feeling of being "good enough" in society. She needed respect from others and cringed at the thought of being pitied. Her daughter was forming those same those attitudes and values against her own will. At some level of awareness, Lillie saw this tendency in Kim and did her best to guide and encourage her daughter away from guys and people like Richard and Tom. She did not, however, realize this tendency in her son. Lillie had no idea that the girls Matthew was attracted to were very controlling and self-centered. She was unable to recognize that same personality in the female version. The girls Matthew dated were all socially accepted as pretty girls. They chased after Matthew and called him. He never had to call to ask a girl out. If he liked someone, he could mention it to a friend and that girl would call. Matthew was quiet and rather laid back so he did not mind when the girl he was with called the shots. He often did not care about what they wanted to do or where they wanted to go, he would be happy to go along. This was a dangerous path for a guy with his tendencies and without a good natured woman with good values, Matthew would be led down a miserable path with no skills on how to change that course. Even Matthew's friends called on him and knew that it was rare to receive a call from Matthew. Matthew just never needed to reach out to others, they always came to him.

The Violence Escalates

Nick was visiting and hanging out with Kimberly by the pool. It was a beautiful day with a warm and constant breeze. It smelled of summer plants, tanning lotion and chlorine. Matthew had just arrived home and parked his mini bike in the drive by the house. He intended to grab something to eat and drink and then take off again. Tom decided to stop at home earlier than his usual arrival time. He could not handle the sight of Matthew's mini bike sitting out by the house. It should be in the shed. He flipped out with rage and stormed into the house where he found Matthew making a sandwich with Lillie. They were talking and laughing. Their closeness and joy undid Tom. This added fire to his already out of control fury. With his mental illness in full form, Tom lunged for and grabbed Matthew by the shirt. Matthew was as tall as Tom but was still quite thin compared to the enraged man. Matthew was taken by surprise and pulled off balance, he stumbled and fell to the floor. Lillie raced to Matthew and was stopped by a slam of a fist to her ribs. She screamed in pain and yelled for Nick. She kept screaming for Nick to come help them. Nick ran in as fast as he could. He was shocked to see a form of Tom that he did not recognize. In the seconds that it took for him to cross the room he registered a twisted, pale face with bulging eyes. Red streaks ran up Tom's face over the pale skin. The eyes were tortured and wicked. Nick shook with fear inside at the face of pure evil. He had never seen such a malevolent face, even in the horror movies.

Nick ran for Tom and grabbed him by the upper arms. He used all of his strength to shake Tom as he pushed him away from the family. Matthew was rising to help, but Lillie grabbed him and pulled him down. Tom was a large man, but Nick was taller and had the strength of youth and tennis in his arms. He was able to push Tom to the couch. Then Tom began grunting and rocking as he swore repeatedly, he looked every bit possessed by a demon. That demon was his very sick mind and it was a dangerous and frightening thing. Nick was confused as to what the next step should be, who does one call for help in this type of situation? He knew that Lillie had stopped Kimberly from calling the police before, so he hesitated and looked to her for directions. Lillie had always known how she had wanted something handled before yet now he noticed that she was in a lot of pain along with a great deal of fear. She only sat on the floor with her son and daughter and cried. Matthew was getting up again and starting toward Tom. Nick knew this could go bad fast. Without thought other than a “God help me”, he grabbed Matthew and pushed him toward the garage door.

Fortunately, they always left their keys in the cars and Nick directed Matthew to the backseat. He ran back in, grabbed Kim and Lillie’s arms and led them to the garage as well. He could hear the growling and swearing from the couch getting louder and something was being banged on. Nick did not have time to look and see what was happening, he heard Lillie moan with pain as he shoved the two women to the car. He hopped in and heard Tom running through the hall toward the garage causing a fear in him he had never known. This was a real life nightmare, one where you feel you cannot move fast enough, where your limbs are jelly and you are in slow motion while the danger moves in quickly. He screamed for everyone to lock their doors as there was no power lock. He prayed that they all heard him in their own states of shock. Tom now had the house door to the garage open and banged on the car and tried to open Lillie's back car door. Thankfully she had heard Nick and the door was locked. Nick had the car started and in gear when Tom pushed the button to shut the garage door. No way was he going to stop for a garage door. Nick hit the gas and shot out of the garage as the door came down on the hood of the car. He drove around town and let Lillie decide if she needed to see a doctor. She could barely get her breath and was wondering if a rib was cracked or bruised. She was very frightened as Tom had never hit her before. She also had never seen this level of insanity in him and she did not even recognize it as such. Her studies of mental illness in the nursing program that she had just begun were very basic. It is very different to read about the illness in a book than to live with it in a family member.

Lillie told the kids that they would drive to their Uncle Babe and Aunt Janet's house and stay there for the night. Lillie was too frightened to be alone at the cottage and was also concerned that her ribs might really be broken. She did not want to let her parents know what Tom had done. Nick drove to his house and was relieved that there was a plan for them to leave town. He hated to let them go alone, but knew they had to. Lillie took the driver's seat when Nick got out. They waved goodbyes and took off for Ohio. Lillie had to pull off the road before they were even out of town, she could not drive with the level of pain she was having. They had nothing with them, not even their purses with their driver's licenses, but that did not even cross their minds. Kimberly took the wheel and drove longer than she ever had before, a straight hour and a half with no stopping. They pulled up to Uncle Babe's house and were relieved to see his truck in the drive meaning he was home and not on a long haul. Having him there made them all feel a lot safer.

Lillie went to the door, leaving the kids in the car, so she could explain what was going on to Babe and Jane. Then she motioned for the kids. They all went in and sat around the dining room table and spoke quietly. Lillie downplayed the entire situation and said that she hurt herself trying to keep Matthew and Tom apart. Jane saw through the lies and later spoke to Babe about her fear of this situation for Lillie. They stayed just one night and headed back the next afternoon. Lillie went in a laid down on Kim's extra twin bed and fell asleep. They all changed clothes and the kids began to pack when Lillie awoke and told them to put their things away, they were not leaving Tom was going to leave this time. She told them that she had called him and told him to pack and get a hotel room. She told the kids that Tom had agreed to a divorce and promised to be gone. Such relief had never been felt before. That night, Tom did not come home and yet Lillie still slept in Kimberly's twin bed. Kim liked having her mother near, she felt she could keep an eye on her and help her due to the continued pain. Lillie took a lot of aspirin over the next few days and slept a lot. The kids decided that she must have called in to work, but were shocked when she missed her nursing class. She never would do that unless she was really feeling horrible! That scared them both, but Lillie told them she just needed time to get better and things were fine. Not one of them knew that Lillie was suffering from cracked ribs, depression and a state of shock.

After a week, Lillie told the kids that she was going with Tom to counseling. When they began to debate with her on why she would do that again, she explained that she had to help him even if they were getting a divorce, he needed her help to get to the counseling to heal. Both kids knew at that point that he was working his way back and they were sick at heart about it. Tom moved back home about three days after that first meeting with a psychologist. Lillie continued to sleep in Kim's room for a week and then everything went back to the horrid state of "normal". Lillie had been told by this psychologist that Tom was very mentally unstable and that most people with his type of illness cannot maintain relationships for more than a year. The fact that they were still together all this time later was amazing. Lillie took that a badge of honor and Tom convinced her that it was all because he just loved her so very much. The counselor had explained that she should not continue to put up with any abusive behavior and to leave before any physical violence erupted again. He felt a divorce was in order, but Lillie felt really loved and also plain worn out. She was exhausted and suffering from undiagnosed depression herself. So she stayed with Tom yet again.

Babe

Boyd Walloon Jr. was his father's son in personality and his mother's side with height and build. He was the largest of all of the Walloons and appeared giant when next to his family members. Boyd Jr. was a gentle giant and was filled with love for his family. He was ten years older than his niece, Kimberly. His wife, Jane was the absolute love of his life. She had long dark hair, deep blue eyes and was tiny and thin. He and Jane were the parents of two darling little girls. Melanie was dark haired, blue eyed and outgoing, full of spunk and opinions to be shared. Carrie was blond haired, blue eyed with a sweet shy smile and a sensitive old soul. Both little girls were beautiful and the youngest of all the Walloon cousins. They adored their father the way Boyd Sr. was adored by his children. Jane was the backbone of the family as Boyd Jr. was a semi-driver and would be gone for days at a time. Jane was intelligent having been the top student in her graduating class, but more than that, she was very independent and able to handle the family and finances. Both Boyds could play and joke with abandon and both Boyds were diligent workers and providers. Oh, and could they tell stories! They could tell a story in such a way that would have friends and family laughing and gasping for air with tears streaming down cheeks. Boyd Jr. was called "Babe" by his family members due to being baby Boyd when he was born. Baby Boyd then had morphed over the years into "Babe". As young boy, Boyd had disliked being referred to as "Baby Boyd". As a truck driver, he had many stories and when he would start to tell one, everyone would scurry to gather near to listen. One could never retell a "Babe" story as well, so listening to them first hand was a priority.

One story was about a truck driver that had not been following the rules of the road well. At that time, truck drivers were often first responders and helpers on the highways; they followed an unwritten code of ethics and were always there to help each other. Well, Babe had been frustrated by this guy for many miles. He watched this guy cut in and out of traffic and almost cause an accident. Babe got on his CB radio and got this truck driver's attention and asked him to stop at the next truck stop. He offered to buy the guy lunch with the intention of finding out if he was a new driver or just a jerk. The driver accepted Babe's offer and as they pulled into the next stop, it became clear to Babe that this guy was a newbie. Well, he thought he would hop out and show this kid the ropes, give him some professional truck driving etiquette tips and rules. He was pretty distracted thinking about what to say and how to be kind about it. He pulled up next to this guy and as the kid hopped out and turned toward Babe's truck, Babe began to hop out and got his boot stuck on the door. He turned to loosen his foot only to end up losing his balance. He fell out of the door with his head hanging upside down, his foot was still caught in the door and he was hanging there, trying to right himself, all the while mumbling under his breath and fully embarrassed. He thought to himself to just calm down and pull himself up. Try as he may, he could not pull himself up and fell back still stuck and still hanging upside down. Now he looked over to the young guy and saw the kid trying hard not to laugh. The kid walked toward him and asked if he needed any help. So here was this big, seasoned truck driver hanging upside down, arms a flailing with a beet red face. The guy kept walking over to help, stopping occasionally to turn away and shudder with laughter. The guy finally helped Babe up and loosened his foot from the door. The young trucker says, "Maybe I should be buyin' you lunch", and begins laughing all over again. Throughout the lunch they talked and then just randomly cracked up at the very thought of the incident.

Then there was the trip through the mountains when the weather had been so bad and the curvy roads were icy. Babe fought his big rig all the way up that mountain and back down. When he finally got on a straight highway, he began to realize that he had been driving for a long time and that mountain had worn him out. He was afraid that he was going to fall asleep and it was a pitch black night. He did not have time to stop and sleep, but knew he was in danger, thus he decided to pull off the road onto the wide shoulder of this highway and take a very short nap. He had no idea what time it was, but suddenly awoke with a start. He had not turned off the truck's engine as it was just to be a quick nap. So as he awoke, he heard the engine and looked up to see the big truck was off the road. Well, he grabbed that steering wheel for all it was worth and tried to coax the truck back onto the highway as he screamed and broke instantly into a sweat. A few seconds later, he remembered that he had pulled off and realized that his truck was still in park and not moving at all. As he told these stories he was laughing and cracking up all the way through, this would cause even more laughter as his family imagined this huge man going through such stuff. Boyd Jr.'s laugh was one of those gasping for air, beet red face laughs, so infectious. His stories were self-depreciating and showed his true humbleness.

When all or most of the Walloons were together, Tom would be a totally relaxed and happy person. He could lose himself in their stories and humor. He could feel the love of a normal family and be a part of it for a moment in time. The kids and Lillie all saw the possibility of a good person, they had no idea how forcefully mental illness had a grasp on Tom. They had very little knowledge of mental illness at all. This is why when Babe would tell stories or joke around all would see a "what could have been" version of Tom. They had no idea that this glimpse into a normal happy family would later torture Tom and make his insane thinking worse.

The IRS Takes Everything Away

Lillie had felt that Tom was keeping another dark secret on top of his continued cheating with other women. She saw a darkness in his spirit that she could not put into words or explanation. He was shifty and quiet. He was not starting trouble or complaining at home. Kimberly was in her freshman year at University and Matthew was in his junior year at the local high school. At first, Lillie had thought that having Kimberly away had depressed Tom or maybe he was having financial woes. They were paying for college now on top of their normal expenses. While it was a huge relief to have Tom come home and be silent, it really felt like the quiet before a storm. Lillie did not know how right she was.

One evening, Lillie heard Tom speaking inside their bedroom. She could tell he was on the phone. Lillie usually avoided listening in as she attempted to stay in her world of denial, but she knew something large was brewing and felt compelled to listen in. She went to the family room phone and carefully lifted the receiver being careful to cover the voice piece. She could hear what sounded like a child's sobs and Tom's mother's voice. Norma was talking about getting money together and assuring Tom that it would all work out. In the background, Peter Tritch was griping about having to, "...bail that bastard out again". Norma screamed at Peter, "Just shut up! This is too big a deal and it is MY parents' money! I will do what the hell I want"! Tom finally found his voice and explained very quietly that they were coming tomorrow to take everything. That he was losing the house, cars and even the golf clubs. Lillie thought he was referring to loan sharks or black mailers, but she wondered how they could get everything. Tom began to moan, sob and then in a high-pitched voice he explained that he had ignored them for too long and that he was going to prison. He had a court appearance scheduled for next week and was completely freaking out. Norma told Tom to calm down and that she would hire a wonderful attorney they knew, that she would pay his back taxes and fines. That she would save him and all would be just fine is how Norma ended that conversation.

Tom called to Lillie through the bedroom door and asked when Matthew would be home. Finding out that the boy would not be home that night was a great relief to Tom. He pulled himself together with the reassurances from his mother and her money and told Lillie the story of his tax evasion. Of course he did not see it as his fault. The IRS did not know what they were talking about and had made mistakes that he now would have to pay for. Lillie did get him to admit that he had not really paid all of the taxes he should have. He cried, he begged and bargained with promises of fidelity for her to stay with him. Lillie knew she could not leave Tom when he was this down and depressed. It would be coldhearted to walk away at this time as far as she was concerned. She had put up with far worse than this. Tom's lack of values and morality were far worse than this tax evasion for her to stomach. She assured him that she would help him through this. She reminded him that her car was in her name since her father had purchased it for her a few months back when money was tight. Her father had had the wisdom to put it in her name as he too had felt something was very wrong with Tom's finances. So, at least they would have a car.

The court date arrived and true to her word, Norma had an attorney for Tom. The attorney had also been provided with funds to bail Tom out of as much trouble as possible. In the end, Norma could only provide damage control. Her money kept Tom out of prison, but it did not protect him from losing his house and car. Tom should have been embarrassed, but he was indignant. No one understood what all was going on with Tom financially. He was able to keep his business with close monitoring of his taxes for the next year. Norma helped Tom buy another very nice home with a pool in the same town. Somehow, he was able to get a loan for a brand new car and Tom came out looking pretty good to his fellow citizens. No townsperson knew of Tom's tax issues except a business pal of his that he had confided in years ago when it all began. That businessman kept quiet about the issue and Tom was able to continue on as though nothing had happened. Both Lillie and the local business man were shocked that it all turned out so well.

Scrappy's New, Old Cottage

Boyd and Thelma had purchased his father's old cottage and sold the house in town and the other cottage. This put them in better position for their retirement. This was the cottage Boyd's dad had died in. He had collapsed in the kitchen right by the stove and passed away. Scrappy was in his glory to have his dad's old home. His family members visited frequently. Tom had another new boat and that continued to add to the enjoyment of the little home.

The family had all gotten together one beautiful summer day in 1976. Cousins were talking, laughing and running around everywhere. Tom spent the day in the boat giving people rides and turns to water ski. Fortunately, Jerry was there to help get the boat running. When the big lunch break came, food was served in the very small kitchen and carried out on paper plates to the various tables and blankets spread around the large yard. Thelma relished sitting among her children and grandchildren, talking and laughing. People ate, yelled and hooted at the stories being shared. As people finished eating, they began to slowly take care of their mess. Too slowly for Tom's comfort. As he knew better than to approach the adults and try to boss them around, he walked over to four girl cousins sitting and talking on a blanket.

Melinda, Meghan, Renee and Carrie were enjoying being together and sharing stories. They were teenagers and young pre-teen in ages. A brunette, blonds and a redhead; they were beautiful, sweet and independent minded. These girls had been raised by Sarah and Jane. They were raised to speak their minds with grace, to a point. They were not intimidated by adults. Tom told these little darlings, "If you loved your grandma and grandpa, you would stop talking, get up and clean up this messy yard". All four were surprised at his comment, of course they adored their grandparents! How dare he question that! It was brunette haired Melinda that spoke up first. She said, "Well, if you loved Boyd and Thelma, you would pick up this mess!" They all stared up at him without moving and without fear. Tom walked away. When he was out of hearing distance they quietly congratulated Melinda, snickered and made comments about how rude and bossy Tom was. They felt badly for Kim, Matthew and Lillie for having to put up with him, but they knew nothing about the depths of the awfulness. They also decided to not let Tom see them helping out for the rest of the day. They would sneak in and help with the dishes or empty the trash when he was not looking. They would not give him any satisfaction. They were not about to have him control them in such a rude and condescending way. Once, when he was walking back from the lake and into the yard, Carrie had to run in and warn the girls he was coming. They had all been putting their grandma and grandpa's laundry away. They put down everything, turned on the T.V. and sat on the couch together. Thelma could barely contain her smirk when she saw what they were up to. They had filled her in about his comment.

I'll Have Me the Chilla

Kimberly had been dating Nick for three and a half years now, yet she was still nervous about going to visit her grandparents with him. They went down for the day and Grandma Thelma Walloon decided that they would take the young couple to eat at one of her favorite spots. Crawling into the backseat of Grandpa Boyd Walloon's car, Kim told Nick to be sure to buckle up tight. Grandpa Walloon was known to drive down the middle of those old country roads even when going uphill. He was also known to take the long country way around to anywhere and drive by points of interest. For Boyd Walloon those points of interest included where old friends had lived and where they were buried. As they neared the restaurant where they were promised "all the smelt you can eat", Kim was confused as they seemed to be in farmland with only a gas station ahead. She quietly prayed that they were not going to pick up food at a gas station. Thelma said, "Well, here we are"! Kimberly questioned her grandparents about where in the world one would eat at a gas station. "Oh, they have a real nice place in there with tables and all" replied Boyd.

So, the four proceeded to enter the gas station that reeked of gasoline with a hint of greasy burger and fish. Sure enough, there were two tables that would seat four each and a small counter with three red vinyl covered stools. Paper menus gave quite a long selection of food choices. After all that talk about the smelt and how delicious it was and how you could get as much as you wanted, Boyd says, "Guess I'll have the chilla." Thelma gives him a dirty look that she saved for rude and bad men. She then told Boyd that he could not have the chilla as it will give him heartburn and keep him up all night. Well, then he gripes and moans that he will just get the smelt. Nick and Kim thought that is what the big deal was, the reason they were there, but old Boyd look dejected about not getting chili. When the waitress/gas station attendant comes to get their order, they all ordered a variety of things and then Thelma piped up, "Well, I guess I'll get me the chilla". What?! Poor Boyd.

A Wedding

Kimberly and Nick had grown very much in love. They had a fun and devoted relationship. They knew that they were meant to be together forever and had decided that they would be married eventually. As they attended college together, they began to realize that they could get married and continue their educations if they were careful and worked part-time. They began to see other couples successfully attending college and living in married housing and thought that they could do that as well. Nick had snuck away one night using Kimberly's car (a car that had been her mother's until Tom had purchased a new one for himself, giving Lillie his other brand new car). Nick drove to a nearby town where he knew a jeweler that would give him a good deal on a diamond ring set. Then he returned Kim's car with her assuming he had just used it to get some groceries. Living in the dormitories gave them very little privacy so Nick planned a nice outing with dinner at a Chinese restaurant that they both enjoyed. It was there that he asked Kimberly to marry him. Although they had made plans about what to do if they were to marry, they were only plans, so Kimberly was truly taken by surprise when he asked and gave her a very pretty diamond engagement ring.

Nick and Kim were not aware of the situation with Tom, not completely. He had also started a coat business with a local friend that made the coats and Tom promised he could sell them in Kalamazoo. Tom used money from his mother yet again and bought a small store to set up the coat shop. He hired a full time manager and a full time sales person. Nick and Kim worked at the shop part-time. They both wondered at the business sense of the store, its product and its poor location. Sometimes their paychecks did not clear the bank. They knew trouble was brewing, but had only a small idea of the tax trouble Tom had been in. They had been told only as much as Lillie had strength to tell. They knew a house and car were lost to the Internal Revenue Service due to tax evasion. They did not know how awful things had been back at home nor how much Lillie had suffered. Matthew knew a bit more, but had become good at denial and avoidance, much like his mother. When Nick and Kim would come home to visit, Matthew and Lillie did not share all they knew because to live in true denial is a full time thing. They both tried to live in the moment.

When Kimberly announced her engagement to Nick, her mother cried. This was not at all the reaction she had expected. Her mother loved Nick and had encouraged the relationship. Lillie was extremely worried that Kim would not finish college. Secretly, she was anxious about the money a wedding would cost, but she never troubled her children about having enough money as she never wanted them to question their financial security as she had. Lillie had wanted her daughter to have wonderful college experiences and to be free and happy. She desired for Kimberly to live the carefree life that she had always wanted for herself. She worried a marriage at such a young age would result in babies and a divorce and she wanted so much more than for her children to end up living the way she had. Kim reassured her mother that she and Nick had planned out their life together and that it included both of them getting their college degrees. Lillie resigned herself to their plan and hoped that it would work out the way Kimberly had reassured her it would. So Lillie threw herself into planning a wedding and it was a very good distraction from Tom and his problems.

Kimberly knew that her grandparents paid for her wedding dress and believed her mother when she told her it was because they wanted to do so and had insisted on it. Lillie would never let on to her daughter that she did not have enough money to pull off the simple wedding. It was obvious that the wedding planning began to bring a lot of joy to Lillie as she was planning and designing the wedding that she never had. The plans for the wedding were common for that time and called for a church wedding followed by a reception with cake, punch, mints and nuts. There would be some pretty great music for the wedding and reception due to Nick being in a Christian rock band and having great musical friends that would play for free. It was a pretty wedding and the love and music made it very special to many attendees. Nick and Kim went on to live their life in their college town, they both worked and attended college. Money was tight and they lived very simply and with complete joy.

Descent into Madness

They had been married for only a few months when they received a strange call from Matthew. Matthew never called them, so fear instantly ran through Kim when she heard her brother's voice on the phone. He did not sound at all like himself and began to describe a strange occurrence and to beg for them to come down as soon as they could. He went on to describe how he had come home from school finding the house empty as usual at that time, but hearing an odd humming and buzzing noise. He followed the sound through the house and into Kimberly's old room. Upon reaching the doorway, he could tell that the humming and buzzing was interspersed with whispering. He was frightened and ran out and to the garage to see if anyone was home. There he saw Tom's car parked and running with the garage door up. Matthew could not have seen this from where he parked when he got home. So now, Matthew surmised that the noise in the closet was most likely being produced by his dad. Tom should not be home at this time of day. Matthew began to wonder if Tom had been robbed and was tied up in the closet. He worried that the burglars might still be around. He called his mother and asked Lillie what to do after describing the scary situation to her. She told him to leave the phone off the hook and to go check the closet. He was terrified, but did as she told him. Slowly approaching the closet, Matthew could hear more whispering and a soft banging. He called out Tom's name as he stood frozen in the doorway wondering what in the world had happened.

Tom began to weep for help. He urgently whispered to Matthew, "I need your help. Help me, please. Stay away from the windows so they do not see you and whisper so no one can hear". Tom's voice was quivering and filled with fear. He repeatedly told Matthew to stay away from the windows and to not turn on any lights. Matthew opened the closet door to see Tom in a fetal position on the floor, shivering and with his hands over his head. Tom whispered, "Did they see you?" over and over. Matthew said no one saw him and that he was going to get Lillie. Tom said, "Yes, yes, yes, get her, get her…" Tom made some unintelligible noises along with his speaking. He wanted Matthew to instruct her to park at a corner and to walk through the back yards. To tell her that she had to sneak in the back of the house. To tell her to come fast. His speech became garbled and made no more sense. Then Tom began to rock and weep as he lay on that closet floor in full mental break down. Matthew was completely creeped out and shivers ran through his body to see a human being in such horrible shape. It was beyond frightening to see this man reduced to a babbling paranoid heap.

Matthew closed the closet door and ran back to the phone, but the line was dead. He began to dial his mother's work number when he heard her car in the driveway. She had rushed home suspecting that Tom was having a mental crises. She knew things she had not shared nor known how to deal with. She had called Tom's mother on several occasions to ask advice as he was her son and Norma was a well-trained nurse. Norma had spoken with Tom and had given Lillie a name and phone number of a psychiatrist in a town about an hours' drive away. Lillie had heard that people had seen Tom walking around town in a very strange manner. She had seen Tom sit in the darkened bedroom for hours until it was time to get up and go to work. She knew he was losing his business, that he was bankrupt and had lost all of the money he had been given and inherited. She had only told his mother and Peter Tritch. Lillie knew that Tom was losing what little bit of sanity he had.

Lillie dashed into the house and spoke quickly with Matthew to get the few details and then ran to the closet. Tom screamed an awful, blood curdling, scream when Lillie opened the closet door. Matthew grabbed his mother and pulled her back wondering if Tom might come out and attack her. Then they heard the babbling again and the bang, bang of him rocking back and forth on the floor. Still in the fetal position, Tom tried to talk but made even less sense than he had earlier. They could make out that he thought people had surrounded the house and were shouting for him to give them their money back, they were shouting to have Tom hung in the tree that stood in the front of the house. He knew a rope was tied and they were waiting to hang him. He would say, "Can't you hear them chanting?" That made both Lillie and Matthew's spines tingle. Tom was so spooky that Matthew's legs felt like jelly. Lillie explained to Tom that she and Matthew were going to get him help and take him to a hospital. He shook his head violently and whisper screamed, "Noooo, noooo". Again, he babbled and talked about how they would get him and hurt him. Lillie talked and talked until she really became quite fed up with all of this. She looked at Matthew and said right in front of Tom, "We are going to humor him and play along. You go see which car has the most gas. We are going to tell him that we are sneaking him past the people to get him away and to safety." Matthew saw that his mother's car had the most gas. He pulled it into the garage and turned off Tom's car. He ran back to the closet, all the time harboring a fear that Tom would snap and kill Lillie. Then he thought that most likely Tom would snap and kill the both of them. Matthew grabbed a large knife as he ran through the kitchen. Matthew was only 18 years old, but he knew he could take Tom if he had to.

Once, when Matthew was 17, Tom had gone crazy mad over something and had barreled down the stairs running for Matthew. Matthew had had enough. He simply stood up and when Tom got to him, he grabbed Tom in a big bear like hug and held him in the air. Now, Tom had a couple of inches on Matthew, but Matthew was stronger. Tom had begun to yell for Lillie. She had come to the top of the stairs, looked down and saw Matthew holding Tom in the air and had heard him yelling, "Look what your son is doing to me. See what he is like?" At that moment, it was so pathetic and yet so hilarious to see Tom up in the air struggling to get free, that she burst out laughing and said, "Put him down Matthew". Matthew put him down, ready to grab again if he needed to, but Tom just walked back upstairs mumbling to Lillie how bad that kid was. Tom totally left Matthew alone after that. Matthew was relieved to find out that he had enough strength and now power too.

So, as Lillie wrapped a blanket over Tom, Matthew closed all of the draperies in the house. Lillie convinced Tom that they had to get him out of the house and to a place where no one could find him. He opened his eyes for the first time, looked at Lillie and then Matthew and nodded yes. He could see they were prepared. He shook his head yes and pointed to the knife in Matthew's hand mistakenly thinking it was to keep the people away from Tom. To protect Tom! Matthew just told Tom it would keep them safe. Tom slowly stood up and with Lillie at his side and Matthew following with the knife, he slowly crept down the hall. He was hunched down low and still trying to keep out of sight. It was slow progress as he would stop from time to time and wonder if the people had gotten into the house. It was all so real to Tom that it almost made Matthew wonder if people were in the house after this mad man. Tom was terrified to go into the garage. Matthew told him that he had just checked out the garage and had made sure the doors were all closed and locked. Tom babbled, flinched and moaned when Matthew went to the garage door and opened it. Lillie told Tom to move to the backseat of the car quickly and he did so. Tom laid down on the floor of the backseat and Matthew moved to sit in the passenger seat. Lillie told Matthew that he should probably get in back with Tom in case he tried to jump out or something. Matthew really did not want to do that, but he did it. Lillie started the car and Tom pulled the blanket over his head and around himself very tightly. He mumbled something about the knife and found comfort in repeating it. They backed out of the garage and both Lillie and Matthew half expected to see angry people in the yard even though they knew better. One can get so sucked into the world of the mentally ill.

They drove for a time and then notified Tom that they were out of the town so he could sit up. He absolutely refused because he was sure they were now following him in cars and helicopters. He began to mumble and rock on the floor of the car, all covered in a blanket trying to take solace in the knife held by an 18 year old boy. Matthew asked where they were going and Lillie was a bit concerned that Tom might freak out if he heard, but she quietly said, "The psychiatric ward at a hospital an hour from here". Matthew was blown away. He thought for sure that they would go to Ohio and hide him at Grandma and Grandpa Tritches' house. He was very relieved and scared at the same time. He began to wonder if Tom would be like this forever now. Lillie assured him that they had medicine and counseling to help Tom. Matthew knew he would be leaving home at the end of this school year and really hoped that Tom would never get out of the hospital. He felt a relief in thinking that Tom would be kept away from his mother and the family. He did not want to move and leave her with him. That had always felt like a bit of a burden that he should not have to bear, yet he did. Matthew felt very alone out here on the highway with his mother and a totally lost and broken dad. He did feel sorry for Tom right now, but he also kept that knife in his hand for the entire trip. Lillie was very relieved to have Matthew with her. He had made this all possible; for if she had been alone with Tom, she did not know if she would have had the mental strength to do this. She might have just crawled into her bed, gone to sleep and ignored the whole thing. She could do that. Lillie often would go to bed and sleep away her worry, sorrow and depression. It was all a part of her "avoid and deny" skill set.

The hospital admittance was all a blur. Men had to go to the car and haul a screaming and insane Tom out of the backseat of the car. They then watched as he was sedated and taken away. Matthew and Lillie huddled together on a mustard colored couch. A very kind nurse had brought Lillie some coffee and Matthew a Pepsi. It was then that they both realized how long they had been dealing with Tom's melt down. Matthew had found him after school around 3:00. The drive was a bit over an hour and it was now almost 8:00 p.m. They were both exhausted and still had some paperwork to fill out and doctors to talk to. Just before midnight they hit the highway to head home. Tomorrow was Friday and they both had to get up early and go on about their "normal" lives. Once back at the house though, they both had a second wind. They were starving and decided to grill out burgers. They sat on the back porch eating burgers, potato salad, and crunching potato chips without breaking them into bite sized pieces, drinking as many Pepsi's as they pleased. The talking and laughing was healing and they went to bed and fell fast asleep. In the morning, Lillie got up and went into work. Matthew skipped school and slept in, she wished he wouldn't have and yet was glad he was resting. When he woke up, he called his sister and begged her to come down. He knew having Nick around would help a lot too. Lillie was thrilled to hear they were coming and even happier to know that Matthew had filled them in so that she would not have to relive the story.

Tom signed himself out of the hospital a week into treatment. It was against doctor advice, but he felt much stronger and in control of his thought process. His new medication seemed to calm him and he decided it was time to get home. In the meantime, his store had been locked by creditors and all was lost. They had allowed Lillie and several former employees to return to the store to retrieve some personal items. Then they were locked out. Lillie had advised Tom to stay at the hospital to follow the treatment plan and to get some rest, but he refused. He called his mother to come and get him as Lillie told him that he needed to stay for at least another week. Norma called to inform Lillie that she and Peter were going up to visit Tom and would be bringing him home to her this Friday. Both Norma and Peter agreed that Tom should stay longer, but that if he didn't want to he shouldn't have to. Lillie informed Norma that the house was up for sale and that it might be too much for Tom to come home to, but they brought him home anyway. Tom pulled it together for a bit and spent his days looking in the newspapers for jobs and sending out resumes. Lillie had found a job in Toledo, Ohio that paid much better than her job here in Michigan and she needed to get away from this town and all the embarrassment. One day, a woman that was a very close friend to Lillie pulled her aside and told her about strange sightings of Tom around town. She informed Lillie that many had reported seeing someone in a bad woman's wig and long trench coat walking around town and in particular past the store that Tom had once owned. New owners were working in the store to set it up for themselves and were rather alarmed at his lurking around. It was fairly obvious who he was if one had known him before. Lillie knew this was most likely true and confronted Tom on this. She calmly told him that everyone knew it was him with a wig on and that he had to stop, so he did. Lillie then knew that she needed to speed up their departure from this town.

Lillie informed Tom of the needed move to Toledo and he agreed, changing his job search to that area. Matthew graduated from high school and got a job in a nearby town and vowed to stay in the area. Before Tom and Lillie moved away, Matthew decided to marry his high school sweetheart, even though he did not want to get married. Julianna wanted him to move to Florida where her brother worked and she now lived, but her parents insisted they get married, so Matthew gave in and did. Julianna's brother got him a job and Matthew worked hard during the day and strived to please Julianna, but things were never good enough for her. He was never good enough, fun enough or rich enough. He sometimes had similar feelings when dealing with her as he had had when dealing with Tom. In this way, Lillie's predispositions were carried on in her son. Matthew and Julianna made it for little less than a year before he moved back north and they were divorced. Julianna was a good person and very beautiful. She was just very young and found Matthew easy to control, yet she was unaware of the sorrow and misery it caused him. Her parents were also very critical of Matthew and demanding of his time and help. For his part, Matthew was looking for freedom and happiness, not for a wife and family, so this was unfair to Julianna.

Back Home in Ohio

Lillie loved the anonymity that the larger city brought her. She was unknown to the area and her new job was interesting. She was learning to run a doctor's office as well as prepare and attend to patients. Tom eventually got a job selling used cars and seemed content. He had stopped taking his medicine for his mental illness when they moved and she was concerned, but he seemed to be doing well. Christmas was coming and she was excited to have the children all visit their new apartment in the city. She was the primary bread winner and provider of insurance now. She did not mind this at all and found great satisfaction in the realization that she could make enough money to provide for herself if she ever needed to.

Tom lost his job about 16 months into the move. Lillie did not want to leave her job, but knew that Tom was restless and looking at jobs in Michigan. She decided to head him toward the Kalamazoo/Battle Creek area as that would bring her closer to Kimberly and Nick. Matthew was now driving semi-trucks in Ohio and living near his beloved grandparents. He had a girlfriend that drove Thelma Walloon crazy. Matthew's girlfriend came from problem people and to top it off she was pregnant with another man's baby. Matthew did not set out to make her his girlfriend, as he often had girlfriends that had chased him down until he gave in. This was the case with Lynn. He had tried on several occasions to get rid of her, but she often came back crying and now her mother had thrown her out of the house. Department of Human Services had placed her into a motel room and given her food stamps to provide for her. Matthew found himself taking her to the store and feeling awfully sorry for this girl but especially for this poor unfortunate baby. His taking care of her, led to her sleeping on his couch and Matthew driving her to her doctor appointments. He would be gone for long stretches driving his semi only to come back to a filthy house and Lynn. It was maddening.

Goodbye Ohio and Hello Kalamazoo

Lillie found a wonderful job in a doctor's office in Kalamazoo, Michigan. Right before they moved, Tom had found a dog that needed a home and took Lillie to see it. The old lady that owned it said she could not take good care of it anymore and her grandchildren were abusive to the dog. Tom took the dog over Lillie's concern about finding an apartment that would allow dogs. Tom said they would just buy a house then, but there was absolutely no money for that. He made no sense. Fortunately, Nick heard of some condominiums for rent that did allow small dogs and this dog, named Bandit, was on the small to middle size. Tom moved with Lillie and Bandit to a small two bedroom condominium and was able to find a job with a small business that made custom car parts. He was in the position of finances/accounting again. A position he was not qualified for nor had been successful in previously. He was happy and appeared to have a great deal of power with this company. Kimberly and Nick were thrilled to have Lillie closer where they could see if she was ok and keep an eye on Tom's mental health.

They all often felt that once the children grew up and moved out, that Tom would do better with his emotions. That he would have less to be angry and disturbed about. This proved to not be the case. Tom would get very agitated at unexpected times. He would scream at Lillie and she would try to appease and then end up ignoring his rant and let it run its course. Lillie took up knitting and crocheting when the kids left and she became excellent at it. She was able to use that and her love of reading to keep her distracted from Tom's ranting. Nick and Kim marveled at all she was able to make and Lillie was thankful to have the distraction. Tom continued with his neat freak ways. One time, when he had a day off and Lillie had to work, she came home to find that he had ruined the carpet in the living room and dining room by scrubbing it to get it clean. The carpet had not even shown any stains or marks, but Tom had been convinced that it was filthy. Lillie was just sick about the ruined carpet and asked how he had cleaned it and why he didn't call a carpet cleaning company. He said that he just wanted it cleaned right away. Tom had used dish washing detergent, water and a hard scrub brush. It was the brush that had ruined the carpet fibers and the carpet fibers had rubbed Tom's knuckles raw and bloody. His hands were a mess and now they would need to purchase new carpet before they left the rental of the condominium. He never apologized for his actions, never acted sheepish or like it was an odd thing to do. It was reasonable to him. He then picked up a new habit, perhaps because of Lillie's ability to ignore his insanity. Tom began to rub at and pick out his eyebrow hairs. The only thing that kept him from pulling out too many hairs was his vanity. He did not like the way he appeared with sparse eye brows, so he did more rubbing and less picking.

Mr. Clean

Tom took great pride in his appearance. He loved certain clothes and they always had to be clean and pressed. Lillie did not mind doing this as she too enjoyed very pressed clothes that looked like new. Once, on a trip to Uncle Jack's farm in Missouri, Tom had been coaxed onto a wagon ride. Tom sat on a bale of hay in his light blue polyester knit pants and his white knit golf shirt. He also was wearing his white leather slip-ons (penny loafers). The rest of the family was in much more casual clothing wearing jeans, tennis shoes or boots. Everyone got off of the wagon ride at one point due some minor flooding that had crossed the path. Uncle Jack drove the tractor and wagon across and then the wagon riders had to try to jump over or wade through the water resulting in everyone getting wet or muddy. Tom was the last to cross and was none too happy as he stood there smoking his Benson and Hedges non-mentholated cigarette. The family on the other side included most of the Walloons, minus Thelma and little Carrie. Oh my how they chuckled and pleaded with Tom to jump. They relished seeing him get dirty as no one had ever seen Thomas F. Rollins with any type of dirt or stain on him. Well, Tom took a few steps back and trotted out, with a small leap he landed in the middle of the water but continued the jump onto the dry land. Everyone stood in stunned amazement to see Tom without one single drop of water on his shoes or pants. He had no mud on him and was the only one without a dirty butt from the hay. The screaming and laughing increased with everyone asking how he did that. Remember, no one ever felt laughed at by Walloons and that included the mentally unstable Tom. He enjoyed this notoriety among the family and smiled broadly. He tried to explain how one could jump into water and pull their foot out quickly and at the correct angle to not get wet. Everyone just rang it up to dirt and water knowing better than to mess with Tom. They laughed all the way back to the farm. This story lived on in infamy among family members and was often retold at get-togethers. Tom was then referred to as "Mr. Clean" on and off for the rest of the trip and occasionally after that as well.

Tom enjoyed this family and did admire Jack for his bravery and having received many medals. He appreciated Boyd Jr. for his sense of humor and love of his family.

During that trip, some of the family took turns riding a couple of horses that Jack had. One horse fell in love with Lillie and would follow her everywhere. It got so that she could walk and the horse would follow her with whomever was on its back. Well, Thelma decided that she would like to try to get on a horse. Jack got a step stool for her and helped her up. It took quite a bit of time to get her on the horse and a lot of laughter ensued. Thelma got to laughing so hard that it made her have to stop and just stand on the stool while her two sons held her up. Finally, she got on a horse, but the horse refused to move. Jack pulled on its reins and coaxed it with food, the horse rejected taking any steps with all of Thelma's weight on its back. They called Lillie over, as this was the horse that followed her, and still the horse would not take a step, it knew better than to even try. Pictures were snapped of Thelma on the horse wearing a cowboy hat and then she was helped down. Jack gave the poor horse some sugar lumps and a carrot. The trip was a wonderful time with all of the Walloons together. These were times when Tom acted more normal and the Walloons had little clue as to how disturbed he was, how awful being "Mr. Clean" was for Tom and his family. Boyd Walloon Senior knew he was one messed up "wack-o" as he referred to him privately, but honored his Lillie Sue Baby and never told what little he knew.

Destroyed Again

Lillie knew that she could weather this marriage, whatever it brought. Now that the children were grown and on their own, she could focus on taking care of herself, or so she thought. Tom's need to clean everything was escalating now that the kids were gone, which confused Lillie. He would empty cupboards, dressers and closets to scrub them and reorganize. He began to shower at least twice a day, emerging from the bathroom red as a sunburn from washing so hard. Lillie was trying to get him back into counseling and knew he needed to be back on his medication, but Tom was now too suspicious of it all.

Matthew, Kimberly and Nick knew of some of these occurrences, but were kept in the dark about any that Lillie could hide from them. Nick was shocked late one night when Lillie arrived at their townhouse. She was angry at Tom and wanted to stay in their guest room. She had the little dog with her, which led them to believe that perhaps Tom was not at home. She said only that he was making her upset and she needed to get away. In truth, she was lonely and quite scared. Tom had begun to act strangely again. He would pace the house and question her extensively, repeatedly asking about where she would be during the work day. At first she thought he was becoming paranoid again, but she soon began to find evidence that he had been home during the day. She surmised that he had lost his job yet again and was pretending to go to work each morning. Upon calling his place of employment in pretense of needing to speak with him, she had discovered that he was still employed with the company. Lillie questioned him to no avail, so the next afternoon she drove home during her lunch and saw his car in the garage. She got out and snuck into her own house. Lillie was very afraid of what she might find and her mind was reeling with many possibilities. What she found rocked her to her core. Tom, his boss and two women, probably prostitutes, were in their bedroom having sex. Drug paraphernalia was strewn about and not one of these people even noticed her. This was a scenario that she hadn't even dreamed of. She snuck to her car, cried a bit, then drove back to work and finished her day with patients never letting on that she had been destroyed yet again.

Tom's Great Epiphany

Tom had known that he was committing sins against himself and Lillie. He knew that his soul was damned and he was desperate to save it. He came to the conclusion that he needed to attend church where Nick and Kimberly attended. He had been going with Lillie to that church for just shy a year when he finally gave in to his baser instincts. Tom had decided that it would be ok to do whatever he wanted as long as he was not married. He felt that his soul would be saved. He needed to distance himself from the church and all that he had held dear in order to live the sexual life he had always desired. These thoughts and opinions had been helped to form by his new acquaintances at work and on the streets. He had suffered his entire life trying to be something he was not. He would be happy and his soul would be fine if he would just become his true self. He was not sure that was completely right though as he still desired to be the wealthy executive with a wonderful family. He often bragged about his family and was very proud of how beautiful and wonderful his wife was. He bragged about his son's hard work and his daughter becoming a teacher. These things he truly did value. This struggle had resulted in Tom feeling dirty and out of control, which led to his escalating cleaning behaviors and some paranoia. Eventually, he decided that he needed a clean break and to start over with a different life of total freedom. After a little over twenty years of marriage, he needed to get out.

When Lillie met him at home the next day, after staying with the kids, she and Tom had a serious talk. She thought it would lead him back to counseling and she had planned to move out until he was better and back on his medication, also following another check for STDs. He followed her suggestions with the announcement that he had decided that the two of them had completely different values. Lillie thought to herself, "Well, yeah. He is just figuring this out now"? He went on to tell her that he wanted a divorce. Lillie went livid. How dare **he** want a divorce, how dare **he** leave her. It should certainly be the other way around. She should be the one telling him to get out and never come back. Lillie agreed that they had different values. She grabbed her purse and left. She drove back to the townhouse, where she now had a key, and let herself in. She shook as she silently screamed at herself for having put up with all of Tom's atrocious and wicked behavior only to be left by him.

Nick and Kim were astounded by what she told them. She told them everything, but left out the part about Tom's boss and another prostitute joining Tom. They knew only that he had had another woman in Lillie's own home and bed. They knew only that Tom had asked for a divorce citing differences in values. Nick and Kim told Lillie to go get some sleep and then began calling friends and gathering a truck to get their precious mother moved out of that monster's house. Lillie had not asked them to get anything from the house. She only said that she would gather her things while Tom was at work. As devastated as Kim was over her mother's sorrow, she was equally rejoicing that perhaps this time Tom would be out of her mother's life for good. It was then that she remembered an unusual conversation with her dad a few weeks ago.

Tom had said, right out of the blue, "I have always worried that if something ever happened to your mother, that none of you kids would ever come to visit me." At the time, Kimberly had found it quite sad and had reassured Tom that they would visit him. He had known then what he was about to do. Well, this was a game changer, you do not dump someone that had saved you time and again, had sacrificed over and over for your well-being and then expect that everything will be pleasant and friendly.

Lillie was so humiliated and sad that at forty five years of age she was moving into her twenty eight year old daughter's guest room. Nick and Kim would be teaching during the day and Lillie would continue to go to work as though nothing had changed. In the evenings, she would look for apartments, stay in the guest room out of the way and knit. It would be ok she decided and then cried hysterically with great sobs at all she had done and not done with her life. She gasped for air and sounded like a small child. Then she allowed herself to sleep.

The next morning was a Friday and Lillie was shocked to see that Kim and Nick were still home as she got ready for work. They told her that she needed to go to work and to give them the condo key. She asked what they were up to. They informed her that they along with a couple of friends were going to get her things with a truck. Lillie told them to only take the clothes, dog supplies and her marble top table. She said she wanted nothing else and Tom could have it all. She really did not want that dog, but was worried about how it would be cared for with Tom. She was torn about the dog as she knew that Tom loved it and would really miss it. In the end she confirmed that the dog should not be left there. Nick reassured her that he and Kim would help care for it whenever she needed them to help out. The other major problem with taking the dog was that she would have a more difficult time finding an apartment and Nick and Kim's townhouse association did not allow animals. She wanted to take the day off, but they all knew she would be better not going back there yet.

Nick and his friends insisted on taking all of the furniture. Lillie did show up at the condo during her lunch break and told them to leave Tom the TV, the mattress and his Lazy boy chair at the least. She also begged them to not take so much. He needed things, but they told her that if they did not take it now, they might not ever be able to. Later, if she so chose, she could always give him stuff back, but for now the wise thing was to get as much as she would need to live on as she would be on one income now. She knew they were right and went back to work. The entire time they moved the furniture out, Kim was frightened that Tom would return and cause a problem. Nick and his friends were hoping he would show up, which worried Kim even more. She knew none of them were violent men, but they were angry men right now. Kim thanked God for friends like this. They had your back and jumped right in to help. Lillie was overwhelmed with the care and concern these friends had for her. Chuck, one of Nick's friends, had helped her come to terms with the taking of the furniture and kitchen ware. He promised to leave enough for Tom to survive, but told her that she needed to learn to start standing up for herself and to take better care of herself.

She had really needed to hear that from someone outside of the family. She was always partial to Chuck after that.

On Her Own

Here she was, forty five and on her own for the first time ever. She was so glad to have found an apartment only a mile from Kimberly's place. The little dog, Bandit, had been a very good thing to have with her. Bandit kept her focused on day to day needs and kept her company at night. Nick and Kim came over almost every day to check on her and to make sure she ate. Lillie often forgot to eat or just was too sad to be able to swallow. They had seen her lose weight and had noticed that she had only popsicles, bread, coffee and dogfood in her kitchen. She claimed popsicles and toast were the only foods she could tolerate right now. Both Nick and Kim were glad that summer was coming as they could be there a lot more for her. She needed her family. Every week end, Lillie drove to Ohio to visit her parents, brother and family and her son, Matthew.

It was after one of these visits, when her car had acted up all the way back to Kalamazoo, that she asked Nick and Kim if she should fix it or buy a new car. Yes, she had to ask someone as she had never been allowed to make decisions on her own. She had done the same thing with renting an apartment, asking over and over if she was doing the right thing. Nick and Kim sat down with her and went over her budget to show her that she did indeed have enough money for a brand new car if she kept it in the medium price range. She was very excited and had them go with her to look at several cars. Once they all decided that she had found a couple of good ones and had discussed a good price for them, she made herself go back to the dealership alone to buy the car of her choice. She was so proud when she drove that shiny red Grand Am off of the car lot. She began to feel a little bit more confident. More than she had felt in many years. She drove that car right past her old condo, knowing that Tom would not recognize it. She actually still had the key to that condo and seeing that he was not home, let herself in to walk around. She was very surprised to feel relief at not having to go back to that place or to Tom ever again. She thought that perhaps going back there would be a bad idea and if anyone had known, they would have counseled her to not do that. Yet, that going back, seeing the place, his things, feeling that familiar sorrow and claustrophobia was the best healing she had. This made her more sure and happy then any of the counseling she had received, counseling that she did value and continued with for a year.

She began to eat on her own and take the little epileptic dog for walks. Bandit had always had seizures and since he was older when they got him, they never knew if he was born that way or if it was from an injury. It all just made him even dearer to Lillie, which was really something as she was not an animal lover. Her daughter had always loved animals, so she was there to help out with the dog and his needs. Lillie began to lengthen her stays in Ohio on the week-ends as her parents were failing in their health. Family visited them often and usually ended up pitching in to be sure chores were done and groceries were purchased. When family was not around this all fell on Lillie's shoulders.

The Devil You Know is Better Than the One You Don't

Tom began to call Lillie immediately after the divorce was finalized. He wanted to talk, have dinner and just see her. Her entire family begged her to not fall for this sickness of Tom's. She needed to stay away from that ongoing pain and they all tried to convince her that she was too special and good for this type of relationship. Lillie decided to "date" Tom anyway. She explained that she had invested most of her life into this relationship and that he was familiar. Nick and Kim worked diligently to keep an eye on her.

Lillie was visiting Tom at the old condominium when the phone rang and she answered it while Tom was making some sandwiches. He had attempted to get to the phone, but she had beat him to it. The voice on the other end was instantly angry upon hearing Lillie's voice. She screamed, "Who are you? You are a whore! Let me speak to Tom right now"! Lillie hung up the phone and quietly walked to her car. Tom asked where she was headed and her response was, "I am headed absolutely nowhere". She drove to her apartment and began to complete the applications for nursing positions in Ohio as she cried and cursed herself out. How could she keep falling for the same lies and false promises over and over? She decided a part of her must be seriously defective, a part that contained good judgement and trust.

Tom disappeared shortly after that episode. No one knew where he had gone, but no one really tried too hard to find him either. Nick and Kim had gone by his condo and saw that a new couple lived there now. Tom never called or wrote and in this way made sure his "fear" of not being visited came true. Lillie and her family went on with their lives, only occasionally wondering where Tom had gone off to. It would be six years before any word of him would reach Kim's ears. When that time came, Kimberly and Nick's lives had moved on and their family had grown. They had little Amanda and were in their second new home.

Infertility

Kimberly and Nick had been trying for a baby for two years. They had gone to many medical interventions and had decided to draw the line at risking a pregnancy of multiples. It was still in the early stages of infertility advancement and horror stories of pregnancies with 7 or more fetuses was not unheard of. They had decided that raising a child and creating a family was what they wanted and it did not matter if they did that biologically or through adoption. It had been a long and often devastating journey, but once they changed their focus to adoption there was a definite relief. They both knew that the adoption choice would most likely bring other struggles and challenges, but they were determined to follow through to build their family. It had been a long and often devastating journey, but once they changed their focus to adoption there was a definite relief.

Some people assumed that being around babies and pregnant women would be too difficult for them, especially for Kim, but that just was not the case. They often found themselves battling and explaining away emotions and thoughts that others assigned them. Most people were just trying to be sensitive and this was understood by Nick and Kim. Fortunately, their family understood their feelings and did not hesitate to have them babysit the various nieces and nephews. One time, a woman approached Nick's sister, Chris, and told her to not have Kim watch her little boy. She told Chris that Kim would most likely run away with him and hide. She felt the fact that Kim and Nick loved the little boy and could not have a baby would only lead to that type of trouble.

Chris approached Kim and Nick and asked them if they were comfortable babysitting the child the two times a week that they had been. They both said that they enjoyed their time with their nephew. Chris then went on to explain what she had been told and that she knew they would not kidnap the boy, but wondered if it made them feel bad. They assured her that it did not bother them and thanked her for checking on them. It was frustrating to realize that people talked about them and their situation behind their backs, but that was the truth of some people.

Kimberly had been pregnant for a short time and had miscarried, but she never thought that she would never have children. She knew, one way or another that she would be a mommy to someone and of course it would be through a legal avenue of parenthood. She did not waste her time with crazy schemes and was upset that people would assume that all women having difficulty conceiving would be made crazy. She was sad and disappointed, she cried frequently about her situation, yes, but she was not out of her mind. She and Nick had redirected their energy toward adoption and house hunting. They had saved enough for a down payment on a home as well as put some aside for adoption costs and that took a lot of their time and attention.

Soon, they bought a house and asked Lillie to move in with them so they would not be too far away. There was a master suite in the walk out level for Lillie and that would give everyone their privacy. This also was a great money saver for them all. Lillie paid a little rent, but far less than she had been paying, which helped her to start a savings account and helped cut costs for Nick and Kim. They used this extra money to save toward adoption costs. Ten months after moving into the cute bungalow Lillie was falling in love with a man in Ohio and Nick and Kim received notice of a baby soon to be born whose birth mother had selected them to be this miracle's parents.

Nick and Kim were called one cold December day by the adoption agency. The baby had been born and the birth mother wanted them to have the little boy before the New Year. What an amazing Christmas present! They were overjoyed to receive this child into their family. The drive to the adoption agency took a little over an hour and they both worried that they had forgotten something essential. As it was Christmas break, the agency was closed and they were to meet the social worker in the front office. They could barely believe the instant love they felt when they were handed the almost 9 pound bundle of blankets and boy. They spoke with the social worker for about an hour, reviewing directions and rules, then they put the precious child into the car seat to begin the drive home. The bottle of formula they had brought was not needed until they brought the little guy into the house, he had slept the entire drive home. He was a large and contented baby that loved to eat and sleep. He rarely cried and his cries were answered with great speed and love. They had waited too long to even begin to entertain the idea of resenting or resisting his demands.

As they had promised, Nick and Kimberly took pictures of this precious baby and sent them to the adoption agency along with a letter describing his home and his progress. In turn, the agency would forward this package to the birth mother. Birth mothers were guaranteed to receive updates daily for the first couple of weeks and then monthly for the rest of the year. After the first year, the adoptive couple was required to send annual updates at Christmas. A birth parent could opt out of receiving these, but an adoptive couple would need to continue to send these updates so they could be filed in case a birth parent changed their mind. Kimberly had taken a maternity/adoption leave from teaching and was able to stay home full time for the next few months, with the intention of taking a yearlong unpaid leave following this. She was thrilled with this role change and looked forward to investing time into raising this child. Still she found herself confused as to why she was unable to kiss this darling baby. She could cuddle him and adore him. She held, rocked and enjoyed him, but never felt the desire to kiss him. It began to really bother her after the third day. She was a person who found it easy to love, snuggle and kiss her nieces and nephews, the fact that she felt a barrier to kissing this infant bothered her. She decided that it would happen once the adoption was final. She felt some concern as to the finalization of this adoption, but was pretty confident that it would work out. Horror stories abounded on TV and from person to person about failed adoptions, birth mothers and families changing their minds after months to years and finding loop holes to get a child back or regarding biological fathers coming back to gain custody of a child they had not known about. These thoughts flitted across both of their minds, but seemed a rare and distant threat.

One rule the adoption agency had was that you were not supposed to take the infant out in public or out of state for the first month and not out of the house for the first two weeks. So, whenever the phone would ring, Kimberly felt the need to run to answer it to assure the agency that they were following the rule. It was much too cold to be outside anyway, so she or someone should be home with the baby. So on the one morning she was home alone and finally able to take a bath, she did not want to shower due to trying to keep an eye on the baby and listen for the phone, the phone rang. Of course, she had just rinsed her hair and was dripping wet when it rang. This ringing made her feel jumpy and empty. It felt like something was wrong. She wrapped up in towels and ran. It was indeed the adoption agencies' social worker. The birth mother wanted her baby back. After this wonderful week of being parents, they were losing this bundle, their son. He felt like theirs and they wanted him. The social worker asked them to bring him into the adoption agency today or tomorrow. Kimberly was shaken to the core and had just enough presence of mind and breath left to say that she could not ever do that. They would need to come and get him, she could not bring him back and give him away. Without any thought, she called her husband, her mother and her boss. She explained what was happening to them and told her boss that she wanted to get back to work as soon as possible. She could barely make herself walk into that bathroom to get the sweet baby boy. Her legs shook as she lifted him and walked with him into her bedroom to get dressed. They were coming for him and would be there in two hours. He would be gone in two hours. The nursery would have no purpose and be empty in two hours.

Once dressed, she began to pack up his little things. As she did this, there was a knock at the door with a wonderful friend from work. She had been told by the principal that Kim had called with the news about the birth mother changing her mind. This dear woman had asked to leave early and they had allowed it as she told them she was going over to help Kim out. So here stood Kathy in the door asking what needed to be done. Kim was so shocked and grateful to have her there. She gave the baby to Kathy and asked her to clean him up and feed him as she could barely bring herself to hold him, the pain of losing him was too great. In her mind, she had actually considered just leaving with the baby. If she had been wealthy enough to leave the country, she might have tried it. That was how desperate and on the edge she was. Deep inside, though, she knew she would never really be able to do that. She just wanted to change this horrible future and keep this little boy that she had named, loved and cared for. She had had a doctor's appointment for him just yesterday. She wondered if this birth mother could care for him as well as she had. Would she love him as much? Would this tiny being miss the routines and smells of his home and mommy? So she wrote out some notes, included his newborn diary and calendar. She lightly sprayed her cologne on his little clothes and blankets hoping it would help him transition.

Nick and Lillie arrived shortly after Kathy and began their own grieving. Kathy was the anchor, but she was angry that this could happen in this way. Most people do not realize how adoption works in this country and it is important that the correct decisions are made, but when it is you and your family going through it, one really does not care at that time. You just worry about yourselves and dear God in Heaven, you worry and pray for that baby. Nick and Kim would pray for many, many years for this boy. Kimberly always remembered his birthday and sent up special prayers.

The birth mother, in this case, had tried to hide the entire event from her parents. They had no idea that she had been pregnant and given birth. The birth mother had left out the pictures and update from Nick and Kim and that had triggered the entire course of events. They made her call and get him back. They pledged their love to her and the baby. The birth mother, bless her, had sent pictures and an update to Nick and Kim through the agency. Nick and Kim asked the agency to hold onto the letter and pictures for a while as they were not ready to see that. When they did finally ask for the letter, they were relieved to see a family that looked like it loved and could care for this little guy. They even kept the first and middle name that Nick and Kim had given him. The birth mother thanked them profusely for taking such good care of him and for all of the items they sent with the baby.

They decided to wait a month before putting their names back on the adoption waiting list. They knew they needed time to grieve and heal a little bit before trying this procedure again. Knowing that domestic adoptions can really be difficult, they decided to catch their breath before moving on. They both knew that they would move on with adoption and that somehow, they would become parents. It was an even more frightening endeavor now that the nightmare side of adoption had happened to them. Kim had a difficult time eating and was losing weight from the sorrow, Nick had a difficult time coming to terms with putting them at risk for this type of loss and pain again. They continued with prayer and discussion until they came to the point of being brave enough to try again and they had the adoption agency put their names back on the active list a little over a month from the loss of their first baby.

"My God, Woman!"

Lillie brought her parents for a visit to Kalamazoo. Matthew, his two children, Lillie, Boyd and Thelma all drove up to visit Kim and Nick for the day. After visiting for the morning, they all decided to go out to eat for lunch. Taking two cars they all drove to a local restaurant. Lillie rode with Nick and Kim and the others all rode with Boyd. After parking side by side, all hopped out except for Thelma. She had been in the back seat and it took a while for her to exit a vehicle. Ol' Boyd was all shook up about a noise he heard coming from under his car. He walked to the passenger side and got down on all fours, placing his head low to the ground to peer under his Buick. Just about then the family spied Thelma, backside first, scooching out of the backseat. Some family members yelled warnings to Boyd while others screamed at Thelma to stop. Neither one of them understood what the yelling was about, so Thelma kept scooching and Boyd kept inspecting. "No Grandma stop, Grandpa is on the ground behind you!" they yelled. "Get up Grandpa, move out of the way!" they screamed. She just kept a backin' out and he stayed right where he was and the entire family watched with horror as Thelma stepped right on Boyd's head with all her weight directly on his right cheek. Then she continued on backing out still not knowing what the commotion was for. Boyd hopped up, rubbing his head and face screaming, "My God woman!!!" Thelma figures it out just as the family erupts with laughter. What a scene, what a riot in that parking lot. Boyd's left cheek is embedded with small stones and gravel, this results in more laughter as they help him clean up.

True to form, Boyd pretends to not let it bother him and walks toward the restaurant. The family moves slowly talking about what just happened, laughing so hard and trying to calm down. They know Thelma does not want to cause a scene, they need to enter the place with some dignity. They gather themselves and follow Boyd in and are seated at booths. Soon, Boyd and several others decide that they do not want to eat here. They want to go to a restaurant that serves breakfast all-day. Leaving their waters and napkins, they all up and leave. Once again cracking up in the parking lot. This time, even Boyd laughs with them.

"Do You Know a Thomas Rollins?"

Kimberly was working part-time, job sharing a position with another teacher. She loved her students, but was very happy to be "mommy" most of the time to her daughter. Nick was teaching art at the high school level and life was peaceful for the three of them in their quiet little neighborhood. As Kimberly had been getting a lunch ready for Amanda that afternoon, the phone rang. When she answered, she was surprised to hear that it was a call coming from a hospital in the St. Joe/Benton Harbor area. Her mind raced to think who she knew that might be travelling in that area and have been hurt. She did not know anyone that lived near there. Carefully and a little timidly, the voice on the other end asked if she knew a Thomas Rollins. Kimberly was shocked and a little angry to be getting contacted by Tom in this way. Her dad leaves her mom, disappears and now that he is ill and hospitalized, he wants her help and attention. Her mind was racing on how and if she should or could help this man out. The voice went on to explain that she was the hospital's social worker and that they had had a very difficult time getting a hold of any of Tom's family. She went on to say that Tom had suffered a massive heart attack, did Kim understand that. Well, yes she did. She said that the heart attack had been so great that it had killed Tom. What?! Tom was still quite young for death, he was barely 48 years old. This was not a call she would ever expect to get. The social worker went on to say that they had found a folded paper in Tom's wallet that had a "girlfriends" name and phone number on it. This woman had told them that she knew of Tom's daughter and that she knew she was a teacher because she was a principal in another building in the same district where Kim taught.

That was another huge shocker! The woman had given the hospital Kim's phone number so that she could be notified. She explained that she was no longer in any type of relationship with Tom and would most definitely not come to identify the body. At this time, Tom's mother had died. When the hospital had called to try to find relatives from another number Tom had, they had reached his step-father, Peter Tritch. Peter was none too kind and spoke horribly about Tom. He had told the social worker, "That son of a bitch can go to hell. I want nothing to do with him" and then hung up on the poor startled woman. She then explained to Kim that she had not been able to get any other contacts. Kim gave her the names and cities of his biological children and then agreed, against her better judgement, to go to the hospital to make final arrangements.

When Nick and Kim arrived, the social worker met them and said in a bewildered voice, "You are the only person I contacted that was civil and not full of hate for this man. What did he do? Even murderers have people to grieve for them and that loved them. This man has no one, but you". Kim explained Tom's bizarre relationships and how he used people and then would move on. He had abandoned his own biological children and was cruel to his adopted children. He did not know how to build relationships and nurture anyone. His dead mother would be the only one that would have truly still loved him even though he had caused her immense grief and was not kind to her. As they sat there, the office phone rang. After a brief conversation, the social worker looked shocked. She explained that the biological son had called her back. She had spoken with him after Kim had given his name to her and he had cussed her out and called Tom horrible names.

She wondered why in the word he had called her back and said he was coming to the hospital to see Tom. Kimberly smiled sadly, and said that she knew exactly why he had had a change of heart. Eric had most likely changed his mind after calling his mother to tell her the news of Tom's death. Eric's mother, Patty, had always thought that Tom had a lot of money that she and her children had been barred from. Indeed, Tom had inherited a great deal of money, what Patty never believed were the stories of bankruptcy and that at times, her child support had been paid from Lillie's small salary. These were facts that would be difficult for anyone who knew of the Howard's wealth to believe. Kim went on to share how meagerly they had all lived while Tom spent all of his inherited money on stores, cars, boats, clothing and prostitutes with their pimps bribing much of the money as well.

Kim felt really badly that Eric was hurrying up to Michigan, most likely with his mother in tow, hoping to cash in before Matthew and Kim did. Kim knew there would be no big money and most likely there would just be huge unpaid debt left behind. She told the social worker to give Eric the money in Tom's wallet, money she had offered Kim at first. She said it might help make up for the gas money. She told the woman to let Eric know that he could go to Tom's apartment and take what he wanted. Kim was not ever going to go there and did not want anything more to do with Thomas Rollins. She arranged for his basic burial and left.

Once home, she soon received a call from Eric. He was in Tom's apartment with his mother and they wanted to know if there was anything she wanted. She said absolutely not. She briefly explained that Tom had always lost all of his money and that she had paid her own way through college. It was also explained to Eric that Tom had gone through half of his mother's inheritance in addition to his own. She wanted him to know that they had not lead the golden life that Patty had thought. She told him to take everything and that if he found a million dollars, he had her permission to take it all. He did not need to share with her or her brother. Eric laughed and said that a lot of the stuff was rental furniture. There was very little there, a bit of cash and a cat; the apartment was sad and creepy. Did she want the cat he wondered? Kim felt awful at the thought of Tom consoling himself with a cat. She felt bad for the cat, but said she could not take it. Eric sounded as though he was beginning to understand the emptiness of being Tom's family all around.

It was a deep coldness of spirit and soul that blocked Thomas Rollins from loving and being loved. Kim understood this, but was glad he had disappeared and kept to himself. She explained that they had moved twice since his disappearing and had an unlisted number due to some of the difficult students that Nick worked with. The woman had been surprised that Kim and Nick had not seen Tom in over 6 years. The woman Tom had dated, that knew Kim, had mentioned that he visited his daughter and had driven her past Nick and Kim's house in Portage on his was to his new condo. When the hospital social worker repeated an address that Tom had lived at only two years ago, both Nick and Kim went cold and numb. They were shocked and horrified to learn that he had lived only three blocks behind them in a condominium! Kim instantly remembered hearing stories from her relatives' friends about Tom being a "peeping Tom" while growing up in Delta, Ohio. Had he spied on her? How had he known her address? Had those noises and bumps in the night that were "nothing" really been Tom roaming around their house and yard? Kim was becoming nauseous at the possibility of that. It was horrifying at the same time it was so pathetic.

A Forever Family

It was the middle of March, Nick and Kimberly had just completed a week of teaching. Nick was doing paperwork in the basement office area and Kim was cleaning the kitchen floor when the phone rang that Saturday morning. It was the adoption agency letting them know that a birth mother and her mother had already selected them as potential adoptive parents for an unborn baby. The baby was due sometime toward the middle of April, so there would not be much waiting time. The birth mother and birth father were both involved in the decision and wanted to meet Nick and Kim at the hospital once the baby was born. That was so scary to them both, but the agency informed them that this was a much more stable situation with a couple that agreed on the choice of an adoption plan for their unborn baby. They told only immediate family and their bosses. Fortunately, Kim's boss was very supportive and happy for her. This would be the second time in only a few months that Kim would be applying for adoption leave, but the entire school community was interested and on her side. She had little idea at the time how rare this support was from an employer, yet she was very appreciative and relieved that it all was working out well for her career. She loved being a teacher and working with children that had a variety of learning needs and differences. Being a mother was even more important to her though and she hoped to be able to have both worlds.

It was a cold, windy and sunny March 23rd day when the phone rang that afternoon. Kim was met with a surprising statement and question upon answering the call. "Your baby girl has been born! What is her name?" It took her just a second to register the voice of the adoption agency's owner, Deb. She wanted a name and Nick and Kim had kicked around many girl names and had only settled on a boy's name at this point. Her mind was racing as fast as her heart. Her joy put on hold as she tried to sound prepared. It felt like admitting that they were unsure of a girl name would not be appropriate or appreciated by the agency. Although the agency was professional, they made it known that they represented the birth parents and were designed to be a service to them and for them. Nick and Kimberly had no problem with that philosophy at all, but it just made them feel like they needed to be always correct and perfect. They were used to being questioned repeatedly and having to provide answers and documentations. They had taken personality and compatibility tests. They had been fingerprinted and lectured to. They had attended parenting classes and had their friends and pastor questioned about them. So, to not have a name ready seemed too unprepared after all they had gone through. Kim gave them the name that Nick and Lillie had said they loved the last time the three of them had discussed it, Amanda. Kimberly was still thinking about naming a daughter after her mother, but without confirmation, she gave the agency the last agreed upon name. The second she spoke it out loud, she knew she loved the name for her little girl. Next they wanted to know a middle name, so Kim gave them one of her favorite contenders for a first name, Nichole. In this manner, Nick and Kim's daughter was christened with a name that would be placed on the birth certificate and adoption paperwork. This would be the name that would be presented to the birth parents. As she hung up the phone, she prayed that everyone would love this name as much as she did. She was also hoping that she had sounded confident enough to Deb. That there would be no misgivings or changing of hearts and minds.

Deb had informed her that the infant was premature and very tiny. At 5 pounds, little Amanda had developed jaundice and would need to stay 4 or 5 days in the hospital in Detroit. That is where she had been born, the birth family was from the Detroit area. That was all Kim knew. That and she was to get prepared and be ready for the next phone call. Kim and Nick would need to rush out that night and buy blankets, onesies and diapers to replace those sent with their first baby. Then they would get baby girl clothes in extremely small sizes. The cost of clothes for a 5 pound premature infant were almost double the regular newborn size. They purchased a couple of outfits as the agency had told them to get appropriate sized clothing and not newborn size yet. Baby Amanda would use the family heirloom bassinette with the new mattress that had been used by their first little guy. They would eventually purchase a crib. Both of them hoped that the adoption would be finalized quickly, but agreed to try to see this as just a foster placement to try to avoid the awful heart ache that had happened just a few months ago.

When the time arrived for them to travel to Detroit to pick up infant Amanda, they were materially and physically prepared and hoped and prayed that they were emotionally prepared. Deb had informed them that the birth parents wanted to meet them at the hospital before they received the baby. The birth mother wanted to hand the baby over to Nick and Kim herself. Kim found that very brave and admired the woman's courage and determination. She hoped that the birth parents would not have a change of heart once they all met. She prayed that she could give them some measure of comfort and healing; mostly, she just wanted to get that baby home and start her family, her forever family.

Entering the small hospital where they were directed to was surreal. The hospital was much smaller than they had expected and, as they were the first to arrive, the attending nurse was unsure what to do with them. It made them feel awkward and they could see that the hospital staff was both curious and a bit nervous. This was a first for this small hospital. They had been informed by the adoption agency beforehand, but it was so new that there was no protocol for them to rely on. Deb and the agency social worker, Pat, arrived minutes later. They were well versed in these situations and that put the staff at a bit more ease. Everyone was escorted into a smaller waiting room once Deb asked for a more private space. Now they all waited for the arrival of the birth parents. A half an hour passed so Deb went to call the birth mother's home. Deb was informed that they had gotten a late start and should be arriving shortly. Another long thirty minutes passes and still they had not arrived. Fears and concerns were escalating for the waiting couple as well as for Deb and Pat. There was no way they would be able to move ahead with taking the infant home without following the plan that the birth mother had outlined. It was becoming apparent that they may need to leave without the baby and drive home only to wait for another arrangement. It was also on everyone's mind that the young couple may have changed their minds about the adoption. Deb said they could give them another twenty minutes and then the meeting would be tabled. As the infant was to be released from the hospital that evening, the adoption agency may have to make arrangements to take the baby to a foster home until further notice from the birth family. What a horror to Nick and Kim. They were there, they could care for the baby, but they would not be allowed to do so.

A nurse walked in with a huge smile on her face. She announced that the mother and father had just arrived. She then escorted in a darling young couple that appeared happy and rather clueless about the wait they had just put everyone through. They explained something about stopping for gas and food when questioned by Deb as to their tardiness. The birth mother was relaxed and curious. She enjoyed talking with the future adoptive couple and asked a lot of questions. The birth father was quiet spoken and Kimberly thought that she sensed a hesitation from him. He was very polite and spoke when spoken to, but he did not venture any question. After getting to know each other a bit, Deb then suggested that they go check in on little Amanda. It was then that the birth father smiled with pleasure and said, "Amanda is my little sister's name". It seemed a perfect design, a perfect destiny.

They took the diaper bag of supplies and clothes that Kim and Nick had brought; Deb went with the couple and a nurse while they changed the baby and got ready to bring her in to the anxious couple. Kim and Nick sat with Pat and tried to relax. Pat gave them some more information and had them sign some more paperwork. Soon, Deb walked back into the room, crooning over the darling preemie outfits and saying the baby looked like a small monkey. She went on to explain that the baby's head was the size of a small grapefruit and that she had a lot of hair. Kim tried to picture this baby, but it sounded a bit frightening. Deb explained that a nurse was changing the baby. The hospital staff insisted on doing this until all papers were copied and given to them. They would release the baby to the birth mother and father and then the agency could take it from there. Now, the four of them waited together again.

Kimberly and Nick then saw a beautiful sight. The birth mother came in carrying a small bundle with a beautiful face. Both birthparents stood side by side and they handed the baby to Kim. Deb and Pat were snapping pictures. Pat had the agency camera and said she would make and send copies for both couples. Deb had Nick and Kim's camera and was flashing away. It was then that the birth father said that this felt right and good. When Kim handed Amanda to Nick, he sat and began to rock the baby. Then the birthmother said, "She's at home. This is where she belongs". At that point everyone began to tear up or cry except the birth mother. It was as though she had come to terms with it or as though she was numb. The plan was that the birth parents would leave first. The social worker had said that would be best for the birth parents. Watching that young mother walking down the hospital corridor, leaving with empty arms made Kimberly and Pat actually sob. Kim was holding her dream come true in her arms and watching a woman/child make the hardest decision ever and walk away. Letters and pictures would be sent, but that was hardly a substitute for your baby. Kimberly knew that this was the right thing. She and the birth mother had discussed at length the situation and reasons for their decision and everyone knew this was right for the baby, but Kim's heart broke hard for that birth mother.

This adoption was set up to be a partially open adoption. First names were shared, but no last names and no addresses. This was mostly due to the slow change in adoption practice and due to the comfort level of the agency. Everything would go through the agency before being shared with the other party. The hospital nurses had been informed of this and had been coached by Deb and Pat what to share and what could not be shared. So it was with great interest and pleasure that Kimberly noticed a small pink ankle bracelet on Amanda's tiny ankle when she changed her diaper in the car half way home. The bracelet was left, most likely, by the nurse that had changed the infant's clothing. She had wanted information to be available for the child. This gave them the birth mother's full name as well as the delivering doctor's name. It was a nice piece of information for them to have and they appreciated it.

Lillie was on a vacation with friends out of the country when the news of the infant's arrival occurred. She would arrive back home four days after Nick and Kimberly brought Amanda home. Lillie would not know about the baby until she was back in the states as she was cruising from tropical island to tropical island and was difficult to catch on any phone service at that time. Kim was excited to let her mother in on the news. She knew Lillie would fall hard for this sweet baby girl. What Kimberly and her brother, Matthew, did not know was that Lillie was falling in love again. She had met an old high school friend and they had started up their friendship; that had led to an on ship romance. So, Lillie came home floating on air in love times two. She loved William Marshall, Bill, and her new little granddaughter, Amanda Nichole. Life was good.

It took three long months before the birth parents were able to get into court to sign their official release papers before the adoption could even be started. Until that time, Nick and Kim were legally considered foster parents. They knew that it was too late for their hearts the minute they had Amanda in her car-seat in the car between them, before they even left the hospital parking lot. She had let out a little cry that sounded like, "Naaaa-naaaa" and Nick looked at Kim and said, "It's already too late isn't it"; she knew exactly what he meant. It was too late for their hearts. They were in love with her. They did not feel like foster parents. So, those three months of waiting were long and awful. The stress was high and when the phone rang it brought great anxiety. The phone always rang with the echo of that bad news they had received in January. The haunting of the birth family changing their mind. Then the phone did ring one day, but this time it washed away the haunting with the wonderful news of a birth family that had signed court papers. With two families that were sure of their decision, one to release a baby and one to adopt. The interesting thing was that Kimberly had found herself able to kiss this baby right away, unlike with her first baby. In spite of the fear and worry about another adoption failure, she was able to kiss this baby. Perhaps, the spirit just knew this baby was here to stay.

Ol' Billbert and the Smoky Head

Lillie had enjoyed the first six months of living with baby Amanda and being there for Nick and Kim, but she knew that it was time to move ahead with her life. She decided to look for a job in Ohio near the Delta area. In this way she could be there for her aging parents and be closer to William Marshall. They had dated almost every week-end. One or the other would drive the hour and a half back and forth. Often, it was Lillie as she wanted to visit with her family as well. William went by Bill, but for some reason Scrappy called him Ol' Billbert.

Scrappy had just been diagnosed with cancer, most likely from years of smoking. The cancer had spread and was in most of his internal organs. He was very weak. Thelma kept a good eye on him, but her diabetes was taking a toll on her. Lillie's move back to Ohio came at a good time for them. She was hired as a nurse in a doctor's office not too far away. The office was close to Bill's house on a lake and she would stop by after work on certain days and they would go for a sail, weather permitting. Scrappy and Thelma had moved to a small lake cottage a few years back. Boyd just had to buy the cottage his dad had lived and died in when it came up for sale. Thelma had not minded and she enjoyed lake life. The cottage was quite a bit too small to accommodate everyone for holidays, so those celebrations were moved to Jan and Babe's house in town. Come summer though, everyone was to be found hanging out at the cottage. Old Poke's shed was still there, but now just used as a shed. The restroom had been torn out of it by a previous owner. The grandchildren that had visited their great grandparents and Old Poke there, loved the memories the shed brought back.

Bill often had Lillie invite her family to his house for family get togethers. He had a larger home on another lake that better accommodated the Walloon clan. One day, the air conditioner was acting up. It was an air conditioner that had been installed through a wall. Bill thought he could fix most anything and he began to work on the thing right there. Nick and Kim had brought Amanda, who was now crawling and rolling everywhere. As Bill worked and the family visited all in the same room, Nick noticed that there was a slight buzzing noise. He looked toward the sound, saw smoke coming from the wires and Bill's fingers; with his right thumb and pointer finger being black from the burning electricity. Nick shouted to Bill asking if he was alright. Bill turned, smiled and nodded that he was ok, but his face appeared quite stunned and pale. It was fairly obvious to all nearby that he had received an electrical shock when they witnessed smoke coming from the top of the bald spot on his head. No one thought that smoke coming from a head could be real. It was something for cartoons, not real life. Yet, here it was, grey smoke curling up from the top of Bill's head. Once they all realized he was going to be alright, the Walloons began to laugh and gasp for air. For his part, Bill was relieved to have survived intact as it had been quite a jolt to his system. He could only imagine how it must have looked to see smoke coming from his hand and head; he, too, began to laugh.

Bill enjoyed having Lillie's family over and it encouraged him to have his teenaged daughter over for visits more often. He had become rather reclusive and drank quite heavily at times. With Lillie, he was becoming his old social self again. He had always enjoyed friends and parties, but that had been lost a bit as the pressures from his last divorce and job stress increased. Bill was also quite vain about his looks. He had been considered handsome in his youth, a bit of a Humphrey Bogart in actions and personality with some "Bogie"/Sinatra looks. His balding spot had bothered him as he aged, but he kept very fit and tanned to compensate. Bill could be a bit of a braggart, but was also kind when it served his purpose or when he was in the mood, which was often. One did not need to know Bill for long to realize that Bill was first and best in his own mind. This was something that all of Lillie's men had in common.

Bill always did whatever he wanted and getting married again was not what he wanted. Lillie felt that if they were in love, they should follow through and marry. It was a sore point between them, but by now Lillie was used to losing and not getting what she wanted or valued. She was too used to giving in to the head strong men in her life. Lillie stayed with Bill through this disagreement and put up with his occasional drunkenness. She hated certain attributes about Bill, but he was by far saner than Richard or Tom had been. He was truthful, even if it hurt. Lillie had thought Bill to be totally honest about everything until he began to tell her about how he cheated the company he worked for. He was angry as his father had lost ownership of the company years ago, thus he felt entitled to a little extra money, items or time off. He said that he had increased his life insurance through the company and had purchased extra from another company as he felt his family was owed a more comfortable life upon his death. Lillie thought that was odd. His daughter would be the only one to inherit from Bill and she had quite a bit of money on her mother's side. Then Bill informed Lillie that he had left his money to his mother and that his daughter would only get the money if his mother passed away. At this time, Bill's mother was 72 years old and married to a very wealthy man, but Lillie reasoned that Bill just wanted to be sure his mother was cared for. Lillie loved Bill in such a deep way and was attracted to him in a way she had never been to any other man. Her family found her love for Bill hard to understand. He was so vain and self-centered and yet Lillie loved him with great devotion. Bill was the first of Lillie's men to love to dance. He was a good dancer and that brought Lillie a great deal of joy. The pattern of attraction continued. If one had asked Lillie if any of her boyfriends or husbands had any common traits, she would not have connected the destructive traits that they all shared. She was unaware of the pattern and in denial about the depth of the pain these men caused her and her children.

Bill was home alone and drinking heavily when he decided to kill the weeds that were growing up alongside his garage. In typical Bill fashion, he went for the big blow torch approach to kill the weeds with fire. As he began burning the weeds, he quickly realized his error in not accounting for how dry and tall they were and in not having a water supply within quick reach. Bill was halfway through when the flames from the burning weeds became out of control. He was surrounded by smoke and ran for the driveway. Coughing and with eyes watering, he looked up to see his garage in flames. He was not about to let his classic pale yellow Cadillac go up in flames. He raced into the house to get the keys only to remember that he had left them in the car. Frantically, he raced into a garage that was covered with flames and filled with smoke. He got that Cadillac out just before the roof collapsed. He still had not called the fire department when he realized that the flames had jumped from the detached garage and were now on his beautiful A-framed cottage. He ran to a neighbor and called for help. By the time the fire engines arrived, the entire back of the house was gone. They were able to save only the front living room and most of the contents that were not burned were ruined by smoke and water. Lillie had stored some of her furniture in his home as her apartment had not been large enough for it all. She was absolutely sick at all she had lost and for such a dumb reason. Bill had everything rebuilt with his insurance money and then had the place put on the market to sell. He had been deeply embarrassed at the incident and could never bring himself to confront the stupidity and his drinking problem. Bill found the new cottage a reminder of how out of control of his life he was. He was uncomfortable and haunted by Lillie's grief every time he opened the door to the new and beautiful cottage. These were feelings and thoughts he would never share. It shattered his own "tough guy who does everything in a cool fashion" persona. Everyone was confused when he sold the cottage since he had never shared his feelings and thoughts. He had loved living at the lake and had vowed to stay there until he died. He spoke of dying at the lake or in Antigua. His friends and family wondered what had changed.

Lillie was devastated when Bill announced a two month long vacation to Antigua upon the sale of the cottage. He was taking this vacation without even buying or securing another place to live before he left. Bill said he would just rent someplace when he got back into town. He said Lillie could come along to Antigua if she wanted, but that she would need to pay her own way. He had always been more generous than that. Bill also had not shared any of the insurance money with Lillie to help her recoup what she had lost in the fire. She would be able to join him for a week and then would need to return to work. The week she spent in Antigua was glorious and she hated to leave. Bill was oddly sad at her leaving and actually cried. This was not like him, but he had not acted like himself since the fire. Instead of slowing down on the drinking, since it had caused such devastation, he actually began to drink a bit more heavily. Lillie decided that his emotions had been heightened by the alcohol. She flew back to the states feeling a bit strange about Bill. She had such an ominous feeling that he would not come back to her and that when he did return, their relationship would be over. She cried most of the flight back.

Two weeks after arriving home, Lillie received a bouquet of flowers and a postcard from Bill. The post card was light hearted and had a picture of the barefoot cruise ship they had been on together in the past. He had written simply that he missed her and wished she could have stayed. He had signed it “Love Always, William”. Lillie usually referred to Bill as William, so she was touched by his gesture. Perhaps she had been wrong about him all along and that he would still be hers when he returned. Then she heard that he had sent his daughter and mother similar bouquets and messages. Well, at least he had included her. Bill had six more weeks of vacation left and would not return home before that time was up. He had made that clear to everyone. He loved the islands and planned to retire there. That was now his new dream and goal. This new goal of Bill's bothered Lillie as she knew she would not want to be that far from her family when she retired, but she knew she would probably follow him there to live if he still wanted her.

Then some very awful news arrived a week later. Bill had been in a bus that had crashed and tumbled from the side of a cliff. All were pronounced dead. It had been a fiery crash with mostly locals on the bus. Bill was the only tourist/visitor on board. There was not a body to ship back to the states due to the massiveness of the fire and the lack of extensive follow through by the island government, but Bill had left a request with his mother in writing explaining that he wanted to be buried on the island when he died. Even if he died in the United States, she was to ship him to Antigua to be buried. Thus, a memorial service was held for his friends and family and it was all done. Over. Lillie was in shock from how alive he still felt to her. She framed the postcard and kept it by her bedside. Her grief was deep, but she knew how to grieve and keep going, to live in denial and keep going. That is what she did. Just kept going.

Bill's insurance money was given to his mother a few months later. A week after receiving the money, Bill's mother went to Antigua alone to visit the site of his death and to retrieve a few of his belongings. She stayed only two days and was back in the U.S.A. before many knew she had even gone. It was Lillie's youngest sibling, Babe (Boyd Jr.) that brought up the oddness of the situation. He was skeptical of the death and wondered if Bill had found a way to collect his own life insurance money and live out his life in Antigua. That amount of money would go very far on the small island and would easily be enough to live out the rest of his life comfortably. Bill's mother went once or twice a year to visit the death site and to visit with Bill's friends in Antigua. This only added fuel to the imaginations of those who believed that Bill was still alive, well and laughing all the way to the bank. The insurance company checked on the death, but it was difficult working with the authorities in Antigua. Bill's mother always had a lot of money in her account that she claimed was the inheritance money and that she was saving as much as she could for his daughter, yet his daughter never received a penny, another oddity that had many believing that Bill had gotten away with faking his death. Bill would have been fifty five years old the month following this incident. Lillie always held William in her heart, she was totally taken with the man and the idea of him.

The Devastating Loss of Scrappy

On top of this grief, Lillie could see her precious father drifting away. His cancer was slowly and cruelly killing him. The scrappiness was leaving him. Boyd Sr. was now mostly quiet and no longer quick to laugh. He still had joy in his eyes when family and friends came to visit and that joy shone brightest when he saw his grandchildren and great grandchildren. He adored little Amanda, the youngest of the great grandchildren at that time, and called her "Ol' Blue Eyes" and "Smidget". Amanda running around and laughing would bring a smile to him. When he saw a video of the little two year old playing with her kitten and giggling, it brought laughter to his lips. The most common thing, his laughter, was now the most rare. Thelma would have family members help her to occasionally play that video of Amanda and the kitten for Boyd to cheer him up. And then, as so often happens, Boyd left his earthly self for Heaven with his children and wife by his side telling him they loved him and that he could leave now.

Nick wrote a moving eulogy that perfectly encapsulated Boyd Walloon Sr.'s loving and fun nature. It was impossible to breathe during that eulogy, it was so real and included the thoughts, stories and love of his family. The obituary had to be written with "Scrappy" after Boyd's name due to the fact that many of his friends only knew him as "Scrappy Walloon". Family members now turned to Boyd Jr. as their patriarchal example. Jack was still living so far away and he and Vera did not visit often. He was still such a quiet and withdrawn man, yet all could see the brokenness he felt upon the loss of this wonderful man, his father. Scrappy had been the silver thread of joy that ran through the Walloon family. He brought a sense of peace, love and truth to the world that few humans ever do. His legacy loomed large among those that knew him. He was never a wealthy or powerful man by earthly standards, but by the standards of the soul there was none above him. His humble sense of self and joy in his family made all right with the world. His sense of fun and humor made being with him a delight. Boyd Walloon Sr. knew how to love and to make you know your importance, not just feel it, but to know it. His son and namesake was the same.

It always brought great delight to Boyd senior's grandchildren and great grandchildren to know that he had given them a nickname, no matter how silly. They heard the descriptions of the man and heard family members sing his old songs and knew they were a part of someone special. The older great grandchildren had some memories of him, but the younger felt connected just by listening to the stories about him. Videos and pictures captured Scrappy's twinkling eyes and beautiful laugh. He was usually shown with a cigarette in hand and later those pictures and his health were used as a cautionary example to his loved ones. Scrappy without his coffee and cigarettes was difficult to imagine.

"My Life is About to Change Forever!"

Nick and Kim had seriously considered raising Amanda as an only child. Adoption was a difficult and sometimes painful road and they were not about to put their daughter through having and then possibly losing a baby. It had been traumatizing for them and they could not imagine explaining such a thing to a small child. Amanda was four years old when they decided to attempt an international adoption. In this way, Amanda would have a sibling. The adoption agency reassured them that once the plane lifted from Korean soil, the child was theirs. They even had to have insurance ready to cover the baby once the plane landed in the U.S.A. That made them much relieved, thus they followed through on adopting a baby boy from South Korea.

One day in August of 1993, Nick and Kim received notice that they had been selected for a little boy that had been born June 3rd of that year. The social worker made an appointment to bring over information regarding the child and to set up the flight. Papers needed to be filled out and money needed to be sent. Nick had a wonderful grandmother that had loaned them the full amount of cash (a bit over $10,000). They would then be able to pay her back monthly without any interest being charged. It felt good to be able to make the payments to the adoption agency without worrying about getting a bank loan. They decided the baby's name would be "David" in honor of Nick's grandma's husband. The baby boy selected for them was named, Yung-Tae Yoon by hospital staff in Taegu (now spelled Daegu). He had lived with a foster mother for the first six weeks of life. She had then taken him by train to Soule, South Korea to be held at the reception center until his flight to the United States. Infants released for adoption often are processed through the reception center before going overseas to their forever families. These babies may be going to many different countries, but most go to families in the U.S.A. At the reception center, infants are held in something similar to an orphanage. Soldiers are often brought in to rock the babies, talk and sing to the infants in the language of the country they are going to, often in English. Efforts are made to keep the babies held, played with and stimulated. Doctors check the children out thoroughly and send reports to the adoption agency in the appropriate country. Nurses and social workers in South Korea work diligently to select the infant's forever family from all the reports sent to them. Once a child is paired with a family, that family is notified by their adoption agency worker. Medical records and available information is sent as well.

The end of September brought an interesting question for Nick and Kim. The medical records for Yung-Tae came with a letter of rejection that they could fill out and send back if they changed their minds about wanting this baby! It was unfathomable to them that they would reject a baby, what in the word could be so wrong with him. Sight unseen, letter of a significant problem, they knew they would take, keep and love this infant no matter what was in that letter. Their social worker brought it over to read with them. They sat there dumbfounded when the "problem" turned out to be "more than the normal amount of Mongolian Spots that were also on the infant's arms and legs. Mongolian Spots are quite normal on darker skinned infants and they fade with time. Until they fade, they look like bruises, bluish/blackish spots of varying sizes. Adoptive couples are warned about these and they in turn must warn Caucasian day care workers and babysitters as they sometimes are reported for abuse. Many doctors and nurses can be unaware as well, so the adoption agency does a wonderful job preparing adoptive families for this. This social worker told Nick and Kim that due to this infant having so many and that they were larger than normal, they were being given the chance to wait for an infant with a normal amount of Mongolian Spots. She said that it was very important to the Korean adoption workers that a child be completely accepted and wanted. They did not want the adoptive couple to have any surprises that might result in their not loving and wanting the baby. Nick and Kim were so surprised and relieved. They wrote a letter explaining that they very much wanted this child. The social worker included an updated picture of the couple with Amanda, holding Yung-Tae's picture and smiling. That night they gave their son the official name of David Yung-Tae. They readied the nursery, bought some boy clothes and sent more money for his vaccinations and doctor care. Then they waited for all to be processed. What usually took four months took five due to so many adoptions being processed to the U.S.A.

Word of David's arrival came in mid- November. David would arrive just days before Thanksgiving. He would fly in with child care workers and five other babies. David was the only infant being dropped off in Detroit as the plane re-fueled. The other infants would get off and change planes to get to different places. Nick, Kim and Amanda along with Aunt Sophia, her two children; Eric, 6 years old and Elizabeth, 4 years old, Grandma Lillie and Nick's parents would all go to greet the new baby and bring him home. A lot of video and picture taking occurred. Kim and Nick laughed to tears when little Amanda, 5 years old, said, "My life is about to change forever", when the plane holding her new brother flew into the airport. The social worker had pointed it out and told everyone, "Your baby is on that plane." She said that it would be the largest plane to come in and would taxi to the international airport side where they all waited. Once the jet docked, they all went back inside to await the deplaning. Then came the infant, wrapped in the blanket that they gave the social worker. She had said that way they could see right away which baby of the six was theirs. And here he was, in their arms. They all laughed and cried and were so surprised at how beautiful he was. He was theirs and they shook with the joy of it all.

Jack's Revelation and Salvation

Jack and Vera had divorced after seventeen years of marriage. Jack had met a wonderful woman named Eleanor. Eleanor was a committed Christian woman who taught Jack about God's forgiveness of sins. Jack listened, went to church with her and fell in love with Eleanor and her God. Jack found that he could speak of the sins and fears of his soul with this woman. She is the only earthly being he ever confided his full life with. Eleanor is the only person that knew of Jack's trials and loves in Korea. She loved him and healed him; Jack was a change man.

Jack's entire family was amazed when he brought Eleanor home to meet the family. While they did adore her, they were most amazed at the new happy, smiling and carefree Jack. His family had never seen this part of Jack because it had not existed. Jack was relieved of the weight of his sins and sorrows. He was enjoying life like never before. Eleanor was very much in love with Jack in a true selfless way and together they created a warm glow.

When family gathered for the next Christmas, Jack and Eleanor made the trip from Missouri to Ohio for the celebration. The entire Walloon family was together to meet the new addition to Lillie's grandchildren, little David Yung-Tae, just seven months old. When Nick and Kim brought their children in, Jack and Eleanor were already seated in the living room of the Walloon's home. Amanda delighted them with her smile and then took off to play with her cousins. As Nick unwrapped the new baby from his blanket, Kimberly noticed her Uncle Jack's riveted attention to the baby. Jack had been informed that his niece and her husband were adopting an infant from Korea. He and Eleanor had talked about this and she had told Jack that God moved in mysterious ways. This may be God following through on the healing of Jack's soul and lost family. When Jack saw the chubby baby boy, he felt a tug and joy from God. He looked at Eleanor and Kimberly saw her return Jack's amazed look with a beautiful smile as she said, "See how wonderful God is". Kim had no idea the depth of this meaning and thought that they were acknowledging God's creation. Jack knew this child meant a completion of a circle for him. His extended family now had a connection to his lost biological family from Korea. It was God nodding his forgiveness.

Lillie's Choices/Matthew's Choices

Everyone knew that life had been difficult for Lillie lately. Her children knew most of her hardships and even they did not know all of them. Nick and Kimberly were busy with their careers and their beloved children. Matthew was busy working hard and raising two children on his own now. Matthew had made several bad relationship choices and had been married twice by this time. He had become entangled with a woman named Lynn. Lynn had been pregnant with another man's child when they met. She was young and cute. Matthew, friend of the friendless, had taken her under his wing occasionally when her mother would throw her out of the house. He felt sorry for her at first, but soon she began to overstay her welcome and to just show up uninvited. One time, after a long cross country semi trip for his employer, Matthew came home to find Lynn in his house. He had never given her a key and knew he had double checked the doors and windows before he left. There sat Lynn, surrounded by filth that she had accumulated while he was away. His food was gone and his house was a stinking disaster.

Lynn had broken a back window and climbed her seven month pregnant self through. She cried about being kicked out of her house again. When Matthew confronted Lynn's mother about it, she denied kicking her out this time. Matthew was laid back, not a trouble maker and great at denial just like his mother, so he ignored the problem. He just worked, came home and dealt with the issue. When his house had become unbearably filthy and unhealthy, he told Lynn to get out. He told her he would not live this way. Lynn called the police and told them that he was pushing her around and hitting her. Then as the officers began to haul off a shocked Matthew, she said to never mind. She said she was not pressing charges. The officers told her that they were locking him up for the night anyway to give her a chance to pack and get out. Matthew was shocked and stunned. He had a run to make the next morning and did not want to lose his job. The police officer told Matthew to get rid of Lynn as soon as he could if not sooner. He explained that Lynn and her family had a reputation for this type of behavior. They took him to his grandparent's home and told him to think about what she had just done to him. She was just like her mother, who had ruined several men financially and worse. They hoped this was a wakeup call.

Lynn did move out for a bit, but once her little boy was born, she came right back. Matthew's heart broke for the baby. Lynn loved her baby the way one might care about a new toy. She did not take proper care of him. Dirty diapers, dirty clothes, unwashed bottles being re-used, even Matthew knew this was not how to care for a baby. He tried to teach her. Lillie came over and worked with Lynn intensely on proper infant and child care. Lynn would appear to understand and be happy for the attention. She would do better when supervised, but get "lazy" when left alone with the baby. Lynn thought the infant slept through the night, Matthew knew that was not true as he got up to care for the boy when Lynn could not be awakened enough to care. Rocking the baby, feeding the baby and looking at this tiny little boy, had Matthew falling in love. He married Lynn, adopted the child and went on with this relationship and his denial. Soon, Lynn was pregnant again. This time a daughter was born and she tested positive as his biological child. Matthew had this done to be sure that he had legal hold on the children. He knew Lynn was unstable by now. Lynn was worse than he ever dreamed, she had no clue how to be a responsible parent, and she would not even make an adequate babysitter. Several times he let her borrow the car and drive him to work only to come home and not know where she and the babies were all night. Lynn would be gone with his car and his money. He then might have to hitch a ride from a friend or call his grandad to take him to work the next day. He would then worry all day as he drove his semi. Thelma and Boyd would be so angry, but they could do nothing except continue to help Matthew.

Snapped

Matthew's situation brought out great anger and sadness for Boyd and Thelma. Thelma let it eat away at her. She would not tell anyone about this awful situation. Thelma and Lillie discussed what to do for Matthew and the babies. One day, Matthew and Lynn had gone to visit Thelma and Boyd at the lake. Thelma was so upset she could hardly bare it. Matthew did everything while Lynn sat and ate. Lynn ignored her brand new infant's cries and her toddler son's hunger. It was Matthew doing everything for those kids and Thelma was beside herself with a rage she had never experienced before. Lynn and Matthew took the kids outside to walk them around while Thelma got ready to go get her hair done at the salon. Thelma rarely drove, but with her husband feeling poorly she often drove to the salon or grocery store. She backed the car out of the garage as she yelled out the window at Lynn. Thelma was telling Lynn what a "dirty trick" she had played on Matthew and how unfit a mother she was as Lynn yelled back at Thelma to mind her own business. Then she began to swear at Thelma. Without thinking, Thelma threw that car into drive and aimed toward Lynn. She gunned the car and Matthew ran to the open window and yelled at her to stop. Thankfully, she heard him and came to her senses. Here sat that devastated great-grandmother, shaking and close to a nervous break-down due to her love and concern for Matthew and those babies being abused and neglected. Matthew had her get out of the car and re-schedule her hair appointment. He called his mother, Lillie, to let her know how upset grandma Thelma was. Lillie came over after work to check on Thelma. Thelma had calmed down and was a little bit pleased with herself. "I guess I showed that good for nothin' trollop what I thought of her." Trollop was a word used in this family to indicate a bad mannered woman that ran around with a lot of different men. She and Lillie then laughed and cried together.

Then came the awful day that Matthew came home to his two and half year old son and one year old daughter alone and crying in the house. The children were in dirty diapers and hungry. Lynn was nowhere in the home or the neighborhood. He had driven to work, so she did not have the car. He reasoned that she must not be too far away, but this was beyond unacceptable, this was a crime. Matthew, for the sake of his children, called the police and filed a report against Lynn. She could not be found. It turned out that she had fled the state with some guy and went to live with him. Thelma's exact definition of a "trollop". She then stayed out of state, for fear of the court system and having to pay child support, for the next eighteen years. She would call the children occasionally and usually ended up crushing their small spirits and hopes. She claimed her love, but forgot their birthdays. She claimed her devotion and made promises, but rarely followed through. Her son and daughter had been known to wait by the front door for hours because she said she would stop by to see them. Matthew could not reason with them. Lynn had told them to stay there so they would not miss her and those poor broken hearted children would sit there and wait for their mommy that had abandoned them so badly. Lynn was mentally ill, but that means nothing to a child wanting their mommy to hold and love them like other mommies do. Waiting for her, afraid to leave to go potty in case they missed her arrival and she left all because they were not waiting as she had told them to do. With large brown and blue eyes, the children stared down the horizon with hope that rose and fell every time a car passed. Small bottoms sitting on hard cement with pointy knees pulled up to chests. Tiny shoulders, heavy with adult problems and sorrows sat dutifully, waiting for a mother that sat two states away in her crumbling house trailer with no real intention of going to see her babies.

The Daddy Mommy

Matthew became his children's mother and father. It was a horribly difficult situation that always left him feeling as though he was failing them. One person cannot fill both roles, but damn if he did not try. Both children did relate to him and find comfort in him as though he were a mother. He had to fill that role most of the time, especially when they were so little, so young. The bond between father and children was extremely close and they brought each other much joy. This then would lead to future difficulty for any woman trying to fill a step-mother role. They had their mother and father rolled into one and did not want anyone disrupting the three of them. They also had their grandmother, Lillie. Lillie, who would do anything to help these babies feel loved and happy. She paid for their day care and often bought them food and clothing. She loved them and rocked them to sleep. She took a small part of the "mommy" role in addition to the grandma role. Aunt Kim also wanted to help, but being a few hours away made it difficult. She would buy groceries and diapers occasionally, take the kids for a week-end here and there and for a week or more during the summers, but she was not enough support for Matthew and the kids. Single parenthood is tough, being a single dad was tricky when time needed to be taken off work due to childhood illnesses. Companies were often surprised and not forgiving when a dad wanted to take a day off for his sick children. Matthew's supervisors knew and understood about his situation, but the higher ups did not. He was called in on several occasions to explain why he took time off for his children. Day care would not keep a sick child.

Thus, they often stayed with a neighbor lady that was too old for watching children, but just wanted to help poor Matthew out, whenever the kids were sick.

I Must Have Cancer

Kimberly enjoyed her children so much. It had been a long road to obtaining the dream of children. Everything seemed delightful and she wanted to experience it all. Even when the baby cried a lot or Amanda became grumpy from wanting more attention, Kim loved having it all. After about a year, adoptions are finalized forever by the courts if all has gone well. Kim and Nick felt so much better about this adoption. It was far less stressful than the domestic adoption situations they had gone through. So, Kimberly was very concerned when she began to feel more tired than usual and then discovered a lump on her breast. She feared her joy at being a parent was going to be tempered with dealing with breast cancer. She explained her symptoms to a close friend at work; her exhaustion, occasional nausea and now this lump on her breast. Her co-teacher said that if she did not know better, she would think Kim was pregnant. All knew that was not possible, so Kim stood in the shower the next morning before her doctor's appointment, crying hard and praying with all her might to just be able to live and raise her kids.

She went to her gynecologist for the exam and to be given a plan on what to do next. The crying had left her weak and emotionless. She was grateful that she would not be a basket case in the doctor's office. The calm she felt was from God, the fear was gone, but she was not accepting this cancer. She would fight it like everyone fought cancer. She thanked God for feeling numb when the nurse insisted that she pee in a cup for a pregnancy test. This nurse knew her and knew her history of infertility. Kim asked why that was even necessary, but the nurse said they needed to rule it out before any treatment could be prescribed. So, Kim gave her urine sample and sat in the back room waiting for what would come next.

She was shocked to see that nurse walk in grinning and almost laughing. She felt that whatever had made that nurse laugh should have been saved for when her patient was out of sight. How rude this woman was. Then the nurse came close, took Kim's arm and claimed, "You are pregnant my dear"! Two other nurses now came in and looked so pleased and happy. The three of them gaped at Kimberly and said, "Aren't you happy? You are finally pregnant"! Her first thought was, "What if I have cancer and am pregnant, this could be worse". Her next thought was fear that being pregnant would jeopardize the finalization of David's adoption. Domestic adoptions were doomed by becoming pregnant before finalization, but she was unsure how an international adoption would be affected. All of this was running in less than a second through her mind along with, "I should be happy and screaming for joy…"! So, Kimberly plastered on a big smile and faked a laugh for the nurses. She explained that she was in a state of shock and that this may take a while to sink in. Once the doctor examined her, he reassured her that the lump was most likely fine, but did need to be looked at and surgically removed at just the right time of the pregnancy. In a daze, she went to pick up baby David from his daycare. The daycare worker knew something was up and got her to tell her about the pregnancy. Next, her husband called and wanted to know how the doctor appointment went. "Wow, how do I explain this?" Kim wondered. Nick too was shocked and concerned. This was a lot to deal with for them both.

New Relationships/Same Old Patterns

Matthew had begun dating a woman from work. He had dated several before her and that caused some work drama. Matthew was usually being pursued by some woman. He was still a very handsome man, but barely getting by financially. He was single, sweet and kind, but had two children he was raising one hundred percent of the time. This did not dissuade woman from chasing him down in hopes of marriage. The current woman, Gwyneth, was one of the prettiest woman at work. They both had positions in the cereal kitchen and saw each other frequently. She was a strong country type of woman with a gorgeous body, pretty blue eyes, curly blond hair and a great laugh. Matthew was quite taken with her. She had a child from a previous marriage and was now on her own to raise the boy. Her son was older than Matthew's children by a few years. Matthew was concerned about forming a serious relationship with Gwyneth as she had strong ideas about raising children that conflicted greatly with how he was raising his children. He thought about these concerns, but did not discuss them with her as that was his way to avoid conflict. However, most woman would take that as agreement. Gwyneth could obviously see how casually Matthew raised his kids. How hands on and loving he was. She saw him work with them to be nice little humans and she knew he was not big on punishment. Here is where her strong disciplinary raising of kids ideas bull dozed over Matthew. They were soon married and she was calling the shots about housing, furniture and time management. Matthew was glad to have her take care of all of these things. When she started becoming angry at the way he handled his children, he felt very much like he was in his mother's role with Tom.

Gwen also controlled the finances of the family as well. She had Matthew put his money into a joint account with her money and from there she handled the bills and the shopping. At first, it was a great relief to him to not have that financial worry hanging over him. Matthew never wanted material things much and his mother always bought his children school clothes and items as they needed them, so he was not concerned when Gwyneth would come home with doo dads and cheap furniture from a variety of low end department stores. She always had new clothes and looked nice. She had a newer truck that she took good care of. Matthew was content with this situation until he began to get calls from various credit cards that were past due. He contacted the bank and found that there was no savings and very little money in checking. When he asked Gwen how she was going to buy the groceries they needed with not enough money, she replied that she would just charge it. This had obviously been going on longer than he realized. It was obvious that they were about to lose the house and Gwen's truck would be repossessed soon as well. This brought flashbacks of Tom and Lillie. He had watched his parents go through this and now his role with Gwen was reversed and playing this sad story all over again.

He knew in his mind that this was past time to leave this relationship, but he kept hoping it would work out. He began to no longer enjoy Gwyneth and to get that old pang of dread when she was coming home or when he was driving home to her. His feelings were reminiscent of growing up with Tom. He began to see himself in his mother's role. He was frustrated at his children's behaviors and had to admit that they were easier to deal with when Gwen was around. It made it easier for him to hang in there for longer than he should have. Matthew knew how his children felt when Gwen would go after them and yell and punish them, he saw it in their little faces and he relived his childhood dread in his heart at these times. He did not want his kids to feel the way he had, but was also often in denial and a bit relieved that Gwyneth would take care of everything. He simply needed to go to work, come home and stay out of the way. He began to realize how his mother had felt especially when he considered going back to one paycheck to survive. So, Matthew stuck it out with his marriage far longer than he should have. He put up with Gwen's strong outspoken behavior and realized that she loved him the only way she could. She did favor her son a bit, but was also strict with him. Oh, but it hurt to see her be so mean to his children. He wondered if some of their whiny and naughty behavior was due to her strictness or was it just their age. Matthew struggled greatly with these thoughts and hated the way he felt controlled and bossed around again, just as though Gwen were Tom governing him all over again. When the relationship was over after ten years of marriage, Matthew vowed to never get into that type of relationship again. He had discussed with his mother about the bad choices both of them always made in spouses and she agreed that he was just like her. She herself was now into another marriage, her third, that was a replica of the first two and of the relationship she had had with Bill.

Matthew made a vow to never marry again. He told his mother and sister that he did not trust himself to make better choices and was afraid he would continue the self-destructive pattern he and his mother seemed to follow.

Matthew's children were finishing high school when he began raising them alone again. The judge had declared that the debt should be split 50/50 regardless of who accrued that debt. Matthew was frustrated as he felt again manipulated by a partner. He knew he had not run up any of that debt. Gwen immediately filed for bankruptcy. Matthew was tempted to do so as well, but did not want all of the consequences that came with having declared bankruptcy. So he struggled along, paycheck to paycheck. When his car broke down, he had to go further into debt to pay for repairs due to living expenses and paying off debt took all he made and then some. Matthew and his children lived carefully and frugally, but he could feel the losing battle of finances creeping up on him. He looked for a better paying job, but none was available that paid what he was making and included insurance coverage that he needed. The help he received from his mother kept the finances going like a bandage on a broken arm. This financial help his mother was able to give was due to her marriage to a wealthy business man. Lillie Sue (Walloon) Rollins had married Devin Norman Blaine and that had freed up the little money she made as a nurse in a doctor's office. It was this money that Lillie used to help Matthew through the tough times. She then began to help out his children by purchasing them each a car; paying for the insurance and licensing for them. In turn, she had made them each promise to do better in school and to help their dad out. Of course, those promises were quickly forgotten.

The Marriage Curse Continues

Lillie's family members were all happy for her in this new relationship. She appeared happy and relieved to be married again. Devin was approachable, charming and so thoughtful. He was not a handsome man at all and in these ways was far different from men Lillie had been with before. Devin had been born in England and raised in Italy. This resulted in a very unique accent. At 18 years of age, Devin had come to the United States of America for college. He came from a very wealthy family and used his trust money and wits to build a small empire in Ohio. Kimberly and Matthew thought that their mother had finally broken her self-destructive pattern. The more they observed Lillie and Devin together, the more they could see the big difference in this relationship and they were pleased for the difference. Matthew and Kimberly saw a glimpse of Devin's ego and pride, but were relieved that he kept it in check.

Before this marriage to Devin Blaine, Lillie had flown to South Carolina where her sister, Sarah had moved years ago. Sarah and Jerry were still married and now lived in a beautiful ranch home near the ocean. Sarah went walking along the ocean every day that she could. Lillie always loved being with Sarah and when the two of them were at the ocean, she felt the most at peace. It was walking along the Atlantic Ocean beach in South Carolina where Lillie seriously and honestly talked with her sister. Sarah was not surprised when Lillie told her that she was hesitating marrying Devin as she was not sure she really loved him.

She was frightened due to all of her past mistakes and miseries. She told Sarah that she was not at all attracted to Devin and thought it unfair to him. Lillie had also heard some unflattering rumors about Devin. But what really surprised Sarah was to hear Lillie express the deep love she still felt for Bill Marshall. Bill had been "dead" for a little over a year now and had been separated from Lillie for two years. Lillie admitted to feeling as though Bill had been her one true love. She still ached for him and cried frequently over the loss of him. She explained how he brought back the joy of dancing, how attractive she thought he was and how much energy he had. He made her feel young and desired, until he had rejected her. She loved Bill's daring ways and his in your face attitude. She told Sarah that she felt she could never love like that again. Sarah told Lillie that she had to do what she thought best, that only she could decide whether there was enough love for Devin that would make it ok to marry him. Sarah had Lillie list off the true reasons for getting into a relationship with Devin that were marriage worthy. She asked Lillie why she even went out with Devin in the first place. Sarah wanted Lillie to make her choice to marry or not based on simple love and respect and to not deny a good loving relationship due to lack of lust. The two of them made a list of pros and cons that made them both laugh, then they threw it into the ocean. They relished the comfort that their sisterhood brought them. Lillie decided that she probably should marry Devin. He was good to her family, would support her well and had always been kind to her. She could give him love and partnership. She had been living on her own for a few years now and had learned to enjoy it and was concerned about giving up her new found freedom. Sarah told Lillie to be honest with Devin about needing this freedom to make her own choices and to have alone time. She told her sister to watch how he responded to those requests before she accepted his proposal. And deep in her heart, Lillie absolutely knew she should not marry Devin Norman Blaine, but that she would do so any way. Lillie, and those who loved her, would stay in denial about her materialism for a long time. Lillie saw it as "bettering" herself and her children's opportunities. All knew how absolutely sweet, caring, loving and self- sacrificing she was. No one would ever see her as a "gold digger" because in truth, she unquestionably was not. Yet she was directed, motivated and moved by money and things in a powerful way that she did not fully understand. She was filling her insecurities about having enough and being safe with material things.

At the start of this relationship and then marriage, all went well. Lillie continued her nursing. She now was a nurse for a large company that grew mushrooms. Her job required her to provide first aid for injuries, counsel employees to determine if referrals to drug programs or counselors were needed, train staff on safety procedures and OSHA regulations and fill out paperwork for all of the above. Lillie loved this new position and enjoyed the variety it brought to her life. Devin owned several businesses nearby and sometimes popped in to see her, bring her flowers or lunch, and visit. Life was pleasant. Then there were the times that Lillie would overhear Devin on the phone with his employees and hear his terrible treatment of them, it made her sick. She put this out of her mind and lived in her denial world as much as she could. She could now see through his nice manners and caring attitude. To those he felt were subordinate to him, manners and care were not required. If you were deemed beneath Devin's opinion of success, he did not see you as a person of any value. He knew how to fake it and most people fell for it, seeing him as charming and kind. They did not hear how he spoke so poorly of them once he was home. They did not see his sneers behind their backs, but Lillie did. This side of Devin was thinly veiled once one got to know the true man. Lillie attempted to soften Devin and tried to encourage him to see the other's situation. She told him to be nicer and to be kinder. Flashbacks to similar patterns in her other lovers made Lillie fear that she had chosen the same type of man all over again. If she had only realized that she now had the epitome of the same man; personality, ego, wealth, stubbornness and mental illness were all the same only much larger in the form of Devin Blaine, she would have considered leaving, she might have run, but most likely she would have stayed anyway. Lillie's pattern of living had not changed.

Devin was good to Lillie's children and grandchildren so that made her happy. That brought her respect and gratitude for Devin. He appeared to enjoy visiting them and having them to the house. Devin often threw large parties and was sure to include all of Lillie's family. Thelma was still alive, but now lived in an assisted living environment spending more and more time in a wheelchair. Due to her lack of mobility, Devin had had a wheelchair ramp built leading to his deck and house. She was always concerned that Lillie was not being nice enough to Devin. Thelma had worried greatly that Lillie would not marry the wealthy business man and now continued her worry that Lillie would lose the guy. She even asked Kim if she thought Lillie was being good enough to him. "I fear that your mother will ruin this relationship, Kimmy. She's lived on her own for too long and wants things her way now," Thelma whined in her adenoidal voice of anxiety. Kim assured her grandmother that all was well and that Devin was lucky to have someone like Lillie. Lillie was the nicest and most beautiful woman that he had ever had. This gave Thelma a bit of relief.

Devin took Lillie on fabulous trips around the planet. For all of Devin's inflated ego, he was in awe that he had been able to get such a beautiful woman. Lillie was so sweet and fun to be with. He could not believe his luck at how adventurous she was and at how very little she asked from him. He knew she was the catch of a life time and he was driven to please her. They went first class, saw and did things Lillie never dreamed of. She loved the hot air balloon safari over the African plain. This was followed by a five star dining experience under some trees and shrubs in the middle of the African expedition. They were surrounded by silks, linen, crystal, china and guns. Animals prowled and growled nearby. Lillie loved the adventure of it all. Her heart broke and her mind was forever changed by the children of the villages. They lived in poverty and few of them had shoes. Their guide explained that the children had no idea that life could be different and this is why they were so happy in what we considered poverty. She could see the children were filled with joy and had an innocence that most children in the U.S.A. lacked.

They flew to China, bought leather coats in Italy and toured Vietnam. They always brought home something exotic and expensive. China shocked Lillie with the outdoor porta potties on random corners. Even in large cities, public restrooms were mostly unheard of. Usually the toilet was simply a hole in the sidewalk that one could squat over and relieve themselves, with simple walls around the hole. They had been warned to carry their own tissue as the porta potty would not supply toilet paper, soap or water. Hand sanitizer was in every American tourist's pocket or purse. Lillie relished these first hand learning experiences.

Every six months brought a new adventure for the couple. Devin was enchanted by Lillie, her physical magnificence, adventurous spirit and youthful approach to life was so refreshing to him. She was more than he ever dreamed he could have and he could not stop himself from trying to please her. Only one thing soured his relationship with this bewitching woman and that was the fact that he knew she loved her family more than she loved him. He felt that was a small price to pay and he thought he could handle it.

Devin responded to Lillie's love for her family, at first, by trying to please her with his support of them. A very noble gesture that pleased the entire Walloon family. He often invited the family over, both hers and his, and found he truly enjoyed it. It did please him to see Lillie's joy over her grandchildren's happiness and successes. Devin learned that Nick and Kim were taking little Amanda to see Beauty and the Beast in Chicago and stepped up to take Lillie and them to show them the town. They ate out and saw shows. They saw the sights and stayed in a hotel that he knew they could have never afforded. When the family would enter or leave the hotel, the bell hops would say, "Good morning Blaine family" or "Welcome back Blaine family". Nick and Kim were grateful, happy and had a wonderful time. They experienced life at the upper echelon and were shocked at all of the extra services and free stuff they got when being a part of that life with Devin. It was surprising how many people wanted to help out the wealthy and give the wealthy free things. Nick did insist on paying for their own tickets and meals. It was obvious to Devin that they were not ever going to "freeload" off of him and he admired that. Devin decided to continue to pursue Lillie's ultimate love by sending Matthew's struggling children to a private school for a few years that ended up being only one year as the children missed their home too much. He pulled them aside and gave advice and scoldings as he felt they required. He assisted with medical needs for the kids. When this pleased Lillie, but did not increase her love for him over the love for her children, his desire to please turned to rage.

Devin had had these problems with other wives and soon began to put his prior emotional sorrows in with his bundle of issues against Lillie and Matthew. He began to assume that everyone was after his money, as had happened to him frequently before. He found Lillie's concerns for her grandchildren annoying and as a call for more of his money even though he had stopped spending a dime on Matthew's kids. He soon began to see her money spent as his money spent. While Devin felt he could do however he pleased with his money without Lillie's council; she, however, could not spend a dime of her own money without his scrutiny. It bothered him that her money was in a separate account and that he could not control her spending on grandkids. He knew Matthew was not wealthy and began to feel that Lillie was sending him money as well, even though this was not true. As he became paranoid and obsessed with this little bit of money, it began to feed on itself and grow. It was a vicious circle that created arguments and pain between the couple. Soon, Lillie gave in and had her money put into Devin's account. She now had to ask him for her own damn money. She now had to answer for every check written. This was a flashback to her prior marriages and brought her the additional package of that pain to this relationship. Now Lillie's resentment grew. It would continue to grow and spread throughout the relationships she had with Devin and most of his family. Lillie knew that several of Devin's family members were fabulous people that she completely trusted, but they were few in number.

Devin respected Nick and Kim for being college educated. He struggled to tolerate Matthew simply because he had only a high school education and his children were not doing well in school. Matthew was quite intelligent and had chosen not to go to college, this was something that Devin could not understand or admire. Devin could see how much Lillie loved and catered to Matthew. This continued to eat away at him and he brought it to Kim's attention assuming she would be angry at her mother for spending more money on Matthew than she did on Kim. It unnerved Devin to find that Kimberly was not upset and fully realized any help her mother had given. Matthew was in more need at this time than Kim was. She did not resent any assistance her mother gave Matthew or his children. She and Matthew both were concerned over

Lillie buying his children cars and providing everything for them that he could not. Matthew had asked her not to do so much. He was worried that his children were picking up bad values and wrong expectations. He was correct in this. They had too much handed to them by their Grandma Lillie and they did not have to work for or earn anything at all. Lillie knew this in her head as well, but could not stop her heart. Devin became more agitated by this and was not quiet about his disapproval.

Lillie's Illness

Lillie had been coughing a lot each morning for a year now. This had been treated as bronchitis, but the cough continued and got worse. Lillie now would cough randomly throughout the day. Devin's local doctors could find no answers, so they went to specialists in Ohio. It was after much testing and discussion that Lillie was found to have something extremely rare and incurable. Lillie had Micropolyspora faeni, also known as "Mushroom Worker's Lung". The coughing was the result of her lungs attempting to get more oxygen. She also had experienced shortness of breath and a lower energy level.

Soon several other office co-workers were diagnosed with this as well. The current plant/farm grew mushrooms, but there was no evidence that these were a cause. The plant had been equipped and redesigned to prevent this type of contamination. Research proved that the old farm had grown Shiitake mushrooms in the past. These Shiitake spores had gotten into the ventilation system of the plant and had grown. Mushroom spores then would come out into the office air whenever the heat or air conditioning ran. Once cleaned and removed, most workers slowly recovered. Lillie and two other workers had more severe reactions due to allergic reactions. For Lillie and one other worker this entire health problem was exacerbated by the fact that they were smokers. Their lungs became chronically affected and doctors could only treat the symptoms with medications used for asthma and other lung diseases. Much of the treatment was trial and error.

Lillie was told that she would not recover from this and would most likely die from it. Lillie was told about a possible lung transplant, but really she felt too healthy to want to think about that. She was able to enjoy her life, but just had to limit her physical exertions. Lillie faced this horrible fact with her usual way of handling bad facts, denial. She was able to live in denial, use an inhaler and continue on. That is exactly what she did the first two years. Devin was able to continue to enjoy his relationship with Lillie except for the fact that she was now spending even more money on her grandchildren from Matthew. She had also insisted on buying many things for Kimberly, but not nearly as much as she did for the grandkids that always had tugged on her heartstrings. Matthew's children had suffered so much in not having a real mother, then having a strict and unloving step-mother, that Lillie never felt she could make up for it. She was hell-bent on trying to though.

Now that she knew she was ill, and had to face the fact that she was terminal, Lillie dealt with it by making sure all of her money was used for her kids and grandchildren. This infuriated Devin. Devin usually saved his evil ways and feelings for those in the community that angered him or got in his way. Kimberly, Nick and Matthew had witnessed several times when he took a neighbor or business to court, just to make them squirm. He took people to court even when he knew he would lose, just to make them spend money on attorney fees and to make them worry. When he would speak of doing these things, he would glow with joy and excitement. It made him giddy to talk about how he controlled others and how few dared to cross him or disagree with him. This behavior made

Lillie's family sick and disgusted. Devin's family either agreed with his behavior or was used to it. Soon, Devin was talking to Kim, Nick and other family members about Matthew and his kids. He was diligently trying to turn them against each other. He did not understand how most families were, especially the Walloons. His anger toward Matthew for being loved by Lillie was growing out of control. This was typical of the men Lillie chose. Devin was so similar to her other men. Controlling, needing to be loved to the exclusion of her son, perverted, egocentric, and mentally unstable were the characteristics that all of her husbands and boyfriends had shared. The attraction of those qualities to Lillie were obvious to her family by now. They had been tricked initially by every one of these men and by the time they saw the true colors of the sickness, Lillie was completely tied up in the relationship. The one difference with Devin was that he had more money and power in his community. He was able to intimidate people with that power. Any community member that was not controlled by Devin made honest efforts to steer clear of him and his family members. Lillie hated the way people did what Devin wanted and gave in to him without argument, even though she was often just like those people herself. Nick and Kim were treated very well by Devin because they were in education as was his youngest daughter. This daughter was his obvious favorite. Devin had been married five times prior to his marriage to Lillie and had eleven children from these marriages. He was good to all of his children, but had three favorites from two of his marriages.

This favoritism among his own children disturbed Lillie from early on in the marriage. She could not imagine treating some of your children so much better than others. This went beyond just money. Lillie heard Devin and two of his daughters, one biological favorite daughter and one step-daughter that he favored over other daughters, talking very poorly about Devin's second youngest biological daughter. They were laughing at her in a very mean way, making fun of her fat legs and ankles. It was so extremely juvenile and unkind. These were well educated adults. They were also planning a way to celebrate and vacation without inviting this individual, which would also exclude her husband and four of Devin's biological grandchildren. It was obvious that they had done this type of thing before. Lillie was cold with rage. She felt hatred toward these individuals that were now part of her family. She calmed her exterior and asked, with a smile, why they would want to exclude Karen and her family. They laughed and mentioned Karen's obnoxious personality and excessive talking. They could not stand that she would not be able to afford certain restaurants and activities and would complain if they went to these unaffordable places without her and her brood. Karen would indicate that Devin, her wealthy father, should pay for her family and help out. Everyone knew better than to ask or insist that Devin pay for anything. While he had always been extremely generous to all of his children while they were young and through college, once they were out of college, they were on their own. Lillie found no fault with that, it was the meanness of their talk and her knowledge of all that Devin did financially to help these two daughters out. Help he had denied to four of his other children, 3 biological and one other step-child. His third favorite child was his only son, Brett Blaine. This was his second oldest child and he bent over backwards to please this only son. He would tolerate all types of verbal and financial abuse from Brett. Brett had hated Blaine and all of his wives and nannies growing up. He had left home during high school and lived with a local family. This family was of modest means and was a kind, Christian family. Therein lies Devin's suspicion and automatic hatred of "Christian" as he determined. Even though he considered himself a Christian, it was those "do-gooders", those "sanctimonious hypocrites" that he could not stomach. The difference between a bad Christian and a good Christian was totally made up as Devin saw fit. Truth be known, this family had saved Brett's life and Devin knew it and resented that they could do something for his son that he could not. Devin had been quite absent during his children's youth. He was busy making more money and he really did not have much time to divide among the children or a wife. He would take them on fabulous family trips. He bought each of them a horse and paid for lessons for anything they wanted, but this was not what satisfied Brett.

Brett felt abandoned by his mother and his father. His mother, Devin's second wife, had divorced Devin and left Brett and his sister with Devin. He had actually chosen to stay with his father, he did not want to leave his home and friends. Anger he had toward his mother spilled out on Devin and anyone that tried to get too close. Step-mothers never had a chance and most of them did not want to bother. Nannies were afraid of him as they were reprimanded by Devin if they attempted to discipline the boy. Nannies quickly learned of the three favorite and had to let them do as they pleased. Brett pulled mean pranks in school and became suicidal. He had had a step-mother commit suicide at the Blaine mansion and thought he might try that too. This step-mother had a history of depression and lost the battle with her mental illness. Brett was not mentally ill, rather he was angry and wanted to show just how awful he felt about his life. When his friend's family listened to him and took him in, Brett felt loved and relaxed for the first time in his memory. His staying with this family was necessary and Devin knew it. He was good to the family at first, but as time went on and Brett stayed and was happier there than at home, Devin grew resentful. Brett's leaving for college helped to sooth Devin's feelings of embarrassment in the community.

Brett thrived in college and began to accept Devin as a father again. Devin, for his part, had gone out of his way to please Brett. He would show up to all college functions regardless of meetings he had to miss or horrible weather, Devin would be there. He took Brett shopping for a new car and allowed him to buy anything he wanted. Brett felt the power shifting to him from his father and he loved and used that power over his father as well as his sisters whenever he felt the need. This power shift was permanent and Brett wielded it with the same force and determination his father had. Brett became a dominant force to be reckoned with in the community as a powerful land owner and developer. Soon, the Blaine family controlled the county when they wished or felt they needed to. There were two daughters that were local medical doctors, Brett as a leader in the business community, two that ran successful businesses of their own, a teacher, a local judge and Devin himself. Whether people of the community knew, liked or worked for the Blaines or not, did not matter, everyone knew to not cross or get involved with the Blaine family if it could be helped. They had power; attorneys, police and judges on their side. Even if one were to win against a Blaine, they would suffer in the long run. There was no real winning against a Blaine.

Helping All the Way to Bankruptcy

Lillie suffered greatly to see Devin's children and grandchildren having so much in the way of material things and taking great trips. Even Nick and Kim would not be able to provide in such a way. Then to top it off, Devin would be sure to help out greatly and buy extravagant gifts for some of his children and grandchildren, but not for all of them. Lillie would feel desperate to ease Matthew's financial burden, to see her grandchildren have such things and opportunities, and to have her family take wonderful trips. She then began to run up her credit cards feeling like it did not matter because she would most likely die before she had to pay them off. Even with all of her help, Kimberly and Matthew's children would never see even the tip of what the Blaine family had. Lillie was fairly comfortable with what Nick and Kim could provide for their children, it was always Matthew and his children that broke her heart. Kimberly and Lillie had always strived to protect and help Matthew since he was a toddler. Those behaviors were not about to change and were often damaging to Matthew's maturing and independence. Matthew would often attempt to get his mother to stop these behaviors, but she would not, could not.

Lillie had to leave her job as a nurse a little over a year into her illness. She was able to continue volunteer work on a daily basis and she loved it, but her income was now limited to a disability paycheck and a small settlement from the mushroom plant. She lived well and had more than she needed or wanted because of Devin, but her credit card bills took all the money she had coming in. Devin was not about to help her with those credit cards because of what they had purchased; things for Matthew's children. He made it very clear to Lillie that he would not help and did not like that all of her money was going to this debt. He then arranged for her to declare bankruptcy so that her money would not have to go to paying off her debt for "those kids". In addition, he arranged for her small social security checks to go into his accounts as well. He was determined to control what she did and how she spent money. Lillie was humiliated and asked Kim and Nick to help her, but there was nothing that could be done aside from her divorcing Devin. They spoke with Devin regarding her finances, but he held to the story that he was helping her and would not be swayed. He did, however, agree to give Lillie some cash allowance for spending money. Lillie thought about divorce often and Nick and Kim offered to have her move in with them due to her health making it impossible for her to be completely independent and safe.

Lillie did not want to burden her children with anything. She also did not want to give up the beautiful home that made it so easy to have her entire family over. Her grandchildren could swim in the pool or the lake. They could roam the woods in golf carts, four wheelers or on horses all owned by Devin. Her children and grandchildren called the estate "Camp Blaine" and she loved the experiences it gave them. Then there was the house, large enough for many to stay the night and have their own bed and bath. The kitchen was massive and there were two dining rooms. Yet the Walloons always managed to squeeze everyone together into one room so they were not separated or did not leave anyone out. Christmas season brought the family members from all sides together for a large party where everyone could fit into the Devin Blaine living room with the large fireplace and huge Christmas tree. These opportunities and experiences were valued greatly by Lillie, above her own daily emotional comfort. So again, she stayed with a husband for material reasons. Her admiration for Devin had long since waned and her love for him was very thin. Lillie's disgust, humiliation, annoyance and resentment were growing and Devin could feel it to some degree. This brought Devin to be annoyed with Lillie's son and his children even more. Devin had given Lillie's children and grandchildren gifts and help on his terms and that help had stopped as his anger toward Lillie's love for Matthew grew.

Premonitions

Thelma's identical twin, Velma, had been depressed the last few weeks. Velma's husband, Elmer, had died a few months earlier and she thought perhaps that was why. It would make sense, but it did not feel like the same type of sorrow. This depression was a sorrow so deep in her soul, in her very cells. Then as she was standing in her daughter in law's kitchen, she felt herself float to a funeral. As real as daylight she was at her sister's casket. Thelma was dead and Velma was at a loss as to how to move or exist without her twin. She could smell the sickening sweet flowers and felt the prickle of her lace collar and the twist of her panty hose. Then just as quickly, without a seam, she jolted back to the kitchen with the smell of pot roast and her daughter in law chattering on about something, completely unaware of Velma's absence. Velma wobbled and tottered slowly to the phone, lifted the receiver and dialed a number that her fingers knew without her brain. She heard her sister's voice and felt the whoosh of relief. Her sister was alive, weak and in nursing care, but alive. Velma said only, "I am so relieved" and Thelma instantly understood her sister's premonition. She had felt the chill of death at the same time Velma was having the premonition. Both twins had moments of "seeing the future" if you will. When they had been small children and unaware that this was not a typical thing to have happen to a person, they had shared their "awake dreams" with their mother. When their "dream" happened, their mother pulled them close and whispered fearfully, "Please, girls, you must never ever share these things with anyone other than each other"! She had taken each child in her arms and looked them in the eye and asked if they understood. They had and they were frightened by their mother's reaction. They knew she understood them and suspected that she had these "awake dreams" too. They followed her instructions and never ever spoke of these happenings to anyone.

With Velma's dream shared, Thelma now realized that she would be the first twin to die. They also knew it would be soon. Thelma made sure to say what she needed to say and have things ready. It was two weeks later that Thelma passed away. She had slipped into a semi-coma state from her diabetes and never completely gained consciousness. Velma felt her sister's passing. She felt weakened, a bit frightened along with the joy of knowing her dear sister was in Heaven waiting for her. Velma's and Thelma's children and spouses had long since realized a bit of intuition existed between the sisters, but they had no idea how deep it ran. The sisters never shared with anyone outside of the two of them. Thelma had let on to a little bit of "seeing beyond" toward the end of her life, but never went into detail about it all. Both sisters always remembered their mother's fear regarding this ability they had. Their mother had told them that people would think it was of the devil and it would be awful to deal with the public and church people. They never pursued it further with her and were devastated when their precious mother grew ill and passed away.

Thelma had felt the passing of her mother and Velma had "seen" her mother dying during one of her "dreams". Velma saw her mother's passing three days before it happened. She had been sitting in a chair and talking on the phone to Thelma. She suddenly saw her mother's home. Velma was walking up the steps to the porch of the white clapboard farm house. She looked down and saw her own brown shoes walking on the grey floor boards of the porch. She felt the cold sweat of dread running down her neck and back. Upon entering the house, she heard birds chirping and could smell a pot roast in the oven. She walked to her parent's bedroom where she saw her mother lying in bed, taking a little rest after starting supper. Her mother's breathing was labored and she knew she was passing. She had made sure to wear her best clothing and had just bathed and washed and styled her hair. Oh, but she did look pretty and the house was spotless. Velma saw her mother's last breath and then came to consciousness to the awareness that she was on the phone to Thelma. Thelma didn't miss a beat, they were well versed in these occurrences through-out their lives. Many friends and relatives knew that the twins took after their mama in having these types of distractions, they appeared to others as though the person were having a small absence seizure or daydreaming. They were short and the person was able to continue on seemingly unharmed. No close friend or family member questioned the behavior anymore. Velma or Thelma would just kind of stare briefly into space for less than 20 seconds and then be back to normal.

Velma and Thelma made sure to take their families to visit their dear mother the next day. They brought pie and cakes and had that knowing look pass from mother to daughters. Not a word was mentioned about what the twins had seen and felt, their mother knew, they could tell. Their mother was at peace about it and quite happy for this last earthly visit. Velma and Thelma made sure to be together at the time of their mother's passing. They knew she wanted it this way; that they would stay with their families and wait to be notified. Velma's and Thelma's families were always amazed at how prepared those women were when it came to deaths and tragedies. In this manner, they felt that the twins had some sort of extrasensory perception. So when Thelma passed, Velma knew with certainty that her twin was gone before the news ever reached her by mouth.

Devin Shows His Kind Side

With Thelma's passing, her family was coming in from many states. Devin spoke softer to Lillie and offered her family refuge in his home. Lillie was grateful for this opportunity to have her family all together and Devin's home was a beautiful spot for all to come together to share and heal. Lillie's family thought that this was the true Devin and only her children realized the price she paid for living with him and accepting his help. Actually, her children only knew the surface; if they had known how lonely and sad she was most of the time, they would have snatched her right out from that house.

Devin had food catered in and most of his children and their families stopped by to pay their respects. Thelma would have been pleased with the family all being together, crying, laughing, and eating. Devin offered for all to stay the night and many did stay. Some went on back to their homes in nearby towns and a few relatives stayed in a nearby hotel with all planning on coming together the next day to eat and say goodbye. It was a lovely, bittersweet time. When everyone left, Devin spoke approvingly about Lillie's family. He had come to know them well over the years and did treat them graciously. Then he had to ruin it by twisting the knife about how Matthew had dressed and asking if the grandkids had asked her for money. She knew that he knew she had given both of Matthew's children gas money to make it to the funeral and visitation. He began one of his long lectures about how hard he worked for what he had and how many master and doctorate degrees he had. Lillie knew that Devin worked hard, but she also knew about his many shady transactions that brought him wealth on the backs of the poor. She also had seen those same people he had cheated having to stay quiet or get out of the county. Devin had some of the police and most of the attorneys in town beholding to him or just plain scared. Once one saw the devastation Devin could cause in a life, you learned to shut up and steer clear.

Kim and Nick knew of several instances of Devin's conniving and examples of the power and control he desired and had. Devin had shared stories of his power with them himself, thinking it made him look good and showed off his supremacy. The most alarming part of Devin sharing his tormenting of others was the absolute glee and delight it brought him. He would often share the stories repeatedly or repeat certain parts that gave him the most pleasure.

One story involved him selling some of the properties he owned. Devin owned a lot of property in northern and mid-Ohio as well as property in Michigan and Indiana. This particular parcel of land was huge and ran along some very popular industrial areas. A business had approached him to buy this property. What Devin hid, with help from his attorney and a neighboring business that was in on the deal with him, was that this piece of land was landlocked. When the buyers were given a tour of the land, they saw the wide frontage along the road and a wide path leading to the land. They were purposely led to believe that land was part of the deal. This "misunderstanding" was all intentional. The buyers were given verbal assurances by Devin and his attorney. There was no way for the business to legally access their land without buying further land from the other business owner or from Devin. Once the deal for the land was made and the company tried to access the land, they were stopped and told that they could not cross the land they had thought was the drive to the property. That was owned by the other business owner. Adjacent forested land that they thought they owned, was still owned by Devin. They all went to court and to make a long sad story short, the business ended up paying twice what the land was worth to the other business owner. Now, Devin may have lost some money on this deal, but he took delight in the misery this caused and he secured the other business man to owe him for future support. He was absolutely exhilarated each time he told this story. Kimberly and Nick did not know how to react. They had never met someone that was so bold about such meanness. Well, Lillie had topped herself with this choice of a man. Most likely mentally ill or deranged and a master at manipulating people and his local city and county. Like her other men, he had few, if any, values or morals.

Devin had once had someone taken to jail for screaming at him. That individual had made the mistakes of being poor and not knowing Devin's influence. When the police officer arrived, this individual explained their frustration with a business trick that Devin had pulled on them. They were shocked when the officer began to handcuff them. They yelled at the officer that this was a mistake. Charges were brought by the local prosecutor and no one would ever believe it, but this person spent 36 days in jail. Bond had been set high at Devin's request and the charge was disturbing the peace and resisting arrest. People were shocked and thought that this person must have done something really wrong to get this sentence. His crime was not realizing the crooked system that would support Devin due to past obligations to the man or fear of him. This man did not have money to pay bail or to get his own attorney. He was represented by a court appointed attorney that owed Devin a favor. When the judge finally saw the charges and questioned the prosecutor on why such a long sentence, and wondered what other charges there were, he was shocked that this was all there was. The judge asked the man if he knew Devin Blaine. The man had thought Devin was a friend and said he was shocked when he was tricked by Devin and then when he yelled at Devin, he was arrested. The judge told the man he was free to go. The judge was smart enough to not make a deal out of this, he could not afford to live in this area and have Devin or his family upset with him. Devin loved this story.

Nick and Kim knew that Devin was a larger than life version of all of the men that Lillie had ever dated or married. They knew that he would not be enjoyable to deal with as Lillie grew weaker from her illness. They did everything in their power to make her days the best they could. Until she grew too weak, they would take her on outings and small trips. They would remind her of her family and of how very much she was loved. They would often offer to have her come live with them, but she always said she absolutely would not do that. She would share a little of how unhappy she was and at one point asked them to help her find an apartment so she could move out. She was much too ill to be on her own at that point, but they checked into it and into having nursing support. She then changed her mind when she saw the apartment, she did not want to leave the beautiful home although it had never felt like her home. She was the proverbial caged bird. She was beautiful and afraid to leave her wonderful cage. Lillie's needs, fears, and insecurities kept her a prisoner in many ways. She had been so set on living differently and better that she had lost herself. Matthew had seen her pattern and had been able to recognize his mother in himself. He broke the pattern the only way he knew how, to commit to never marrying again. He was busy with family, work, hobbies and the occasional girlfriend that he would not let take over his life. He drew the line at living together or marrying and just moved on when the woman became too committed. He was honest with everyone he dated, they just rarely believed him. He found much joy in running his own life and doing things his way. In having his children and eventual grandchildren to himself without being told what to do was such peace and pleasure, he was not about to give that up.

The fact that Matthew, Nick, Kim and families attended church also seemed to irritate Devin. It was not at all like they talked about it or preached at anyone and Devin himself attended a church sporadically! It was Devin that would ask Nick to say a prayer before each large family meal. Devin took them to his church, but he had a difficult time accepting religion from others. It was as though Devin did church, religion and God right and others were just fanatics if they went to church more often than he. So when Lillie grew weaker and wanted to begin counseling with a pastor, Devin had just the guy. When Lillie felt uncomfortable with the recommended pastor and asked for someone else, Devin was very upset and rolled his hands in the air with his head and arms held high, he spoke arrogantly, "Oh, so he is not good enough for you. Who do you want? The Pope"? Holding his arms in the air and rolling both hands around was Devin's way of making fun of arrogance while being very arrogant himself. It was extremely irritating for everyone around him, except perhaps his three favorite adult children, and he did it often. A small child might even be mocked in this manner for not wanting the type of ice cream that Devin had in the house. "Oh, so this is not good enough for you? What, pray tell, do you want?" he might quip. Devin always needed to be the best and to be right. He was just smart enough to disguise it for a while. He would often follow a slight to someone with a smile and a laugh, as if to say how silly you must be to get offended by my word play.

Lillie was at a point where she needed much more medical attention and personal care than she was receiving. Kimberly feared that it may be time for her to go to a nursing care situation. She had come to stay with her mother many week-ends and often for weeks at a time during the summer, when Devin would take vacations that Lillie was not well enough to go on. No one faulted his need to get away. It is draining to have to care for a loved one that is critically and chronically ill. Matthew would take his turn caring for her and Lillie's sister would travel from South Carolina to visit and stay as much as she could. Lillie had even gone to South Carolina to stay with Sarah occasionally when Devin had business trips or vacations. Devin surprised them by arranging for help to come during the day, every day. This was due in part to the fact that Devin did love Lillie, in his own sick way. Just as her other husbands had loved her in their own warped ways. Devin also did not like the fact that other people were finding out that he was not answering Lillie's phone calls. As manipulating as he was, he still held on to a belief that others saw him as very noble. Lillie had been so desperate for help with her breathing, that when he had not answered all morning, she had been forced to call friends and his family to get help. Even one of his favorite daughters had confronted Devin on this, telling him to get some help for Lillie or to answer his phone when she called. He had stopped answering Lillie's calls because it was such a bother to have to listen to her needs and wants. Devin did provide top of the line care and doctors as he did hope to ease her suffering and would have liked her to be strong again. It all irritated him immeasurably. Lillie was growing older looking and frail. The illness was vicious and Devin wanted his wife the way she was before this all happened. He knew it was not to be and thus he began an affair with Lillie's health aide.

Brenda

This woman had always fantasized about the Blaine clan and at the wonder of their life style. Brenda came into the home and fell in love with the darling Lillie. She could see the sparkle of Lillie's faded beauty and enjoyed the charm and hospitality. She could see how frail Lillie was and enjoyed being able to ease her distress. Brenda enjoyed Lillie's families' visits. Everyone was compassionate and appreciative of all Brenda did. The family made sure to take over to lighten Brenda's load as well. Kimberly would assist Brenda in taking Lillie on short outings. These were usually just to a nearby store to shop or to a doctor's appointment. Lillie could no longer go without her oxygen at all and was on a large amount of steroids and frequent breathing treatments just to be able to get a shallow breath. Her doctors had advised that her lung capacity was reduced to less than 16% of normal. Lillie was no longer able to get around even in her wheel chair. She could barely stand to transfer from her wheel chair to another chair or bed.

For two years, Lillie pushed passed what might kill most. She was determined and set goals for herself to live to. She would say that she had to live to see this grandchild graduate or that grandchild get married and so on. Brenda entered Lillie's life during this second year of further incapacitation. Lack of oxygen took its toll on her body and her mind. She became forgetful and had difficulty saying things with her normal tact. Incredibly, several of Devin's children became angry with her for this. Devin himself became angry about this as well. Seemingly intelligent adults reacted with anger toward Lillie when she praised a granddaughter for losing weight. She told this teenager how nicely she was growing up and that she looked beautiful. Lillie had forgotten that she had been told not to mention this weight loss in front of the other grandsons as they had taunted this girl about being fat. Instead of being angry at the boys for laughing about "Grandma's compliment", Devin and the girl's mother became enraged and yelled at Lillie when the boys left to ride horses. These obviously irrational adults then walked together out to the garage where they continued their angry conversation about how cruel Lillie was. Their behavior resembled 7th grade mean girls and not the supposed successful adult, college educated humans.

This was the beginning of a family get together and Nick and Kim arrived with their children as this heated conversation was taking place in the attached five car garage. Not knowing what had taken place, Nick and Kim greeted the Blaine family members warmly. There were the usual hellos, distant hugs and quick conversations to catch up when suddenly, with all smiles, Devin exclaimed that Lillie was angry with him as he rolled his hand in the air. They knew Devin well enough to know that something had occurred that was inappropriate for Devin to be grinning about. That stupid big grin, like a small boy getting away with something. Kim could not get into the house fast enough to check on her mother. It nauseated her that Devin could be so evil and assume that all would support any behavior from him. She wanted her mother to agree to leave him and to come live with her. She decided to begin to work with her mother on leaving this insane man's house and coming to live with Nick and her.

Once inside, Kim found her mother sitting in the large sunroom in her lift chair. Lillie looked so sweet and frail stuck in that huge chair with her afghans and quilts cushioning and warming her. As she drew closer, Kim could see the tension in her mother's forced smile. Lillie then asked her daughter what Devin and the others were talking about out in that garage. She proceeded to explain to Kimberly the "goof" she made in her compliment to the granddaughter. Lillie was frustrated as she felt both guilty and ridiculed at the same time. She had realized quite some time ago that Devin's love and adoration of her was fading with her looks. She felt deceived by him; she often withstood hours of his ranting and yelling at her for infractions only he understood. Lillie would never divulge the mental and emotional abuse she suffered from Devin. She would certainly not want her children to feel bad about her situation. She did not want to live with her children as desperately as she did not want to leave this beautiful home. She had vowed to herself to never be an encumbrance to her family. And as sure as sunshine, Kimberly again offered to set up a room for Lillie at her home. She greatly wanted her mother's last days to be peaceful and happy, void of the fear and stress that she could sense went deeper than her mother would ever let on. She had seen this side of Lillie many times before, but how does one force a parent to do anything when you have played the obedient daughter for so long. She was afraid that insisting on moving Lillie to Michigan with her would solve one problem but create another. Lillie would no longer be able to see her beloved great-grandchildren as often. These darling little ones brought her hours of joy and wonderful memories. They were vital to her very existence in many ways, Kimberly could never deprive her mother of this essential joy. The alternative was to leave her in the care of Devin. Devin, who used to be so very loving and sweet and was now in the garage with his daughter complaining about and laughing at her precious mother. A woman that had embraced his children and family giving her love and joy to Devin's many grandchildren until this evil disease had robbed her of her filter and ability to reason. Any reasonably intelligent adult would see these changes and understand the correlation to the disease, but Devin and his family saw the changes and believed that Lillie was turning on them. Devin's own mental disorder and age had brought a paranoia. Lillie's behavior now made him even more so. He began to suspect that her entire family was only nice to him for his money, money that they all never dreamed of getting at or inheriting. Money that they did not even want from him. They treasured his ability to care for Lillie, love her and provide what she wanted and needed. They treasured the happy family times Devin provided at his house, not his money. This lack of desiring or scheming to get money was something that Devin could not understand and actually could not respect as Devin, himself, was always scheming and chasing after the "almighty dollar".

With the relationship of Brenda, Devin began to see new possibilities for a happier and easier life. He became more disenchanted with Lillie and her illness, it was no longer making him feel loving and noble to care for her and was now bringing him great frustration. Although Brenda was far from being as beautiful as Lillie and was not considered pretty by cultural standards, she was much younger, sixteen years younger than Lillie, making her twenty one years younger than Devin. This younger woman made Devin feel robust and desirable and he could barely stand having Lillie around. The house was huge and they could easily get away from Lillie's presence, until she would call for assistance. Something had to be done to get rid of her.

The Devil in Him

Devin began to increase the amount of morphine he gave to Lillie in one dose. He hoped it would cause her to be hospitalized or to quietly slip her into death. The morphine was provided by hospice as Lillie had gotten to that point five months ago. No amount of other medicine or oxygen could help her overcome the shutting down of her lungs and organs. Now it was time for comfort. Lillie knew this and fought hard against accepting the morphine. This resistance on her part gave Devin the ability to hoard up the morphine and then give it to Lillie all at once, in one huge dose, without being detected by the hospice nurse. It was going well for him, but Lillie had survived several of his attempts at a sufficient overdose. He was getting away with it until Kimberly came down earlier than expected. She had taken the day off of work to celebrate her mother's birthday and had done so for the last four years fearing that each birthday might be the last.

As Kimberly pulled into the long driveway, she noticed that Devin was driving out to the horse barn in his "gator". They waved to each other and went their way. Kimberly parked and went into the house entering through the sunroom where her mother now was confined day and night. Lillie had been unable to climb the seven stairs to the master bedroom for seven months now and thus slept in her lift chair in the sun room. The chair also had made it easier for Lillie to breathe at night as she could be propped up a bit and not have to lay flat. It was 8:30 a.m. and she intended to allow her mother to sleep until she awoke on her own. She grabbed some coffee from the kitchen and walked back toward the sunroom when she heard a strange noise coming from her mother, a strange sigh and wheeze sound. Rushing in, she saw Lillie struggling to sit up and kind of gurgling. Her heart screamed that this may be the end for her mother, was she truly going to watch her mother suffer, struggle and die? As Kim held her precious mother's head and small shoulders, she saw Lillie's eyes flutter. Lillie shook her head and spoke a mumbled sentence with only the word "wrong" understandable. Lillie's eyes would open for a few seconds then close, her body had strange twitches in it. Again, Lillie spoke with a slow, thick tongued, slurred speech, "What is wrong with me? Why can't I wake up"? Kimberly was reassured with the small improvement in her mother's speech, but she knew immediately what was wrong. She gave her mother a sip of coffee, got a cool cloth for her head and then raced to the large utility room where the emergency morphine was kept and recorded. The box of morphine was filled with empty vials that had not yet been documented as to time given. She knew then and there that Devin was overdosing her mother. Before she could think straight, she called the hospice nurse and voiced her fear and knowledge. The nurse shared her concern for Devin's ability to handle this time of sorrow, she knew better than to agree with Kim on any wrong doing on Devin's part. Anyone, could hear the concern and slight horror in the nurse's voice as the two of them concurred that Brenda and other part time help should be brought in to assist 24/7 at this point. The nurse said that it was too much for Devin to be able to handle during this time of such distress for him. Kim's stomach turned at the continued protection of this man that could be monstrous. She understood the fear of the people of the entire county. Devin could take your life and ruin you, even if it cost him a great deal of money, because winning, saving his sham of a reputation and getting his way was even more valuable to him than his precious cash.

Then in walked Devin. Kim turned and confronted him. She wanted to scream at him and punch him in the face and felt that she probably could get away with it. Devin had accorded her some respect and still wanted her to believe he was a good guy. She pulled herself together and let him know that her mother had been overdosed with morphine. She told him the symptoms she had witnessed and explained the large amount of empty vials she had found. She demanded that her mother be given around the clock care by some form of nursing staff or nursing aides. If she could have seen inside Devin's mind and heart, she might have not been so cavalier or careless about her own safety. He would have liked to have murdered them both and been done with all of this pressure and inconvenience. Fortunately, he was an intelligent man and was able to muster self- control to follow through on a plan, if not for that, both Kim and her mother would be dead and buried in a field somewhere. Devin Norman Blaine did not get what he wanted by being rash and impulsive. He put on a look of horror and mock disbelief. "Why, she must have gotten into that morphine during the night and overdosed herself by mistake!" They both stood there staring at each other realizing that the other knew Lillie could not walk to the restroom alone, let alone manage walking to the utility room to overdose herself. They stared at the lie as it hung there. Devin assured Kim that he would get more help to watch over Lillie as she sat there still twitching from his overdosing of her. Kim knew better and she would not leave until arrangements were made for 24/7 care of her mother. She knew then that Devin could not overdose her mother again as the medication would be very closely monitored. Devin made the arrangements and ordered food to be delivered for the three of them to celebrate Lillie's birthday. Family dropped in and out, cake was eaten and presents opened. Lillie laughed and had a wonderful time with her family and those darling little great-grand kids. Many found it odd that only two of Devin's children sent birthday wishes and one of Devin's grandchildren came over. The family discussed Lillie's care and Kim said she would wait until Brenda got there before she left. Kimberly was clueless about Brenda and Devin's affair. She could not even fathom such a thing and thus left her mother in the clutches of the devil and his mistress.

She would never make a scene about it, but Lillie was scared. She was frightened of this hideous disease and of her horrible husband. She refused to let on in front of her family on such a lovely day, but when they all began leaving she worried at what would happen to her. She knew Devin had given her too much morphine and she highly suspected Brenda of sleeping with that dirty old man. It was with this thought that her anger took over her fear and her common sense. She confronted Devin about the morphine and then when Brenda left to get a clean night gown for Lillie, she confronted him about the affair she suspected. It tore her up and fueled her anger when he just laughed at her and told her she was crazy. Devin then turned and walked out, going to the den in the basement where he knew she could not reach him. In five weeks, her life would change in a most devastating way; she could not imagine that it could get worse, but it would.

Dreams

Lillie was dancing in a glorious light. Her legs were not tired and her breath came and went freely and deeply. She was amazed at her new energy and felt surrounded by loving approval. She felt, more than saw, her entire family around her. It was better than Christmas get-togethers. She was wearing her ballet outfit from Swan Lake and the skirt floated and swirled as she spun and moved. Lillie looked up to see her dancing partner and was not surprised it was the one man she had always loved. She was pleased that he could dance this ballet with her and it did not strike her as odd. William had never danced this way before. He was more of a social dancer, but now he was lifting her and turning. She laughed and felt the lightness of her body and soul. Then came the crashing heaviness, the familiar tightness in her chest and she awoke to the sunroom that she had designed; never realizing that she was designing her own bird cage. Gradually, she came to her reality. Her sorrow was tempered by the beautiful memory of her fantastic dream and she decided to try to sleep more to escape and perhaps to recapture that feeling.

The Call/The Warning

Kimberly was in a meeting with several teachers when her cell phone rang. She excused herself and went into a nearby room to take the call. All of her friends and teaching buddies knew that her mother was very ill. On the other end of the line was her mother's voice and she was angry and crying. Devin was having Brenda take her to a nursing home and she was not prepared to go. Lillie was in shock and knew this event was a combination of her failing health and her confronting Devin about his affair with Brenda. None of Lillie's family knew of the supposed affair.

Knowing how poorly Devin was handling her mother's illness and fearing that he was trying to hurry Lillie's death, Kimberly was more than relieved to have her mother away from Devin and under supervising eyes. However, the terror in her mother's voice broke her heart. She spoke with her mother and told her that she would be down to check things out and that she was leaving now. Kimberly walked back to her small group staff meeting and told them through her tears that she had to leave. They all understood her heart ache.

She drove to Ohio alone and as fast as possible. She spoke with Devin as she drove and was relieved that he sounded calm and heart broken. He explained that this was just a respite for 5 days and that Lillie would return home after that. He was intending on using respite occasionally for a much needed break. Which would have made sense if he had been caring for Lillie, but Brenda and others had been doing all of her physical care. Devin had sat with his parents and a grandparent as they died and proclaimed himself an expert in the death process. He had frequently expressed his desire to be with Lillie upon her death and to hold her hand as she died so sending her away did not add up. Lillie had spoken with her sister Sarah and she had felt the same way Kim had. She and Kim both had reassured Lillie that the break would be a good idea. Kim had told her mother that she would come right down to stay with her for as many days as she could and that Lillie would be back home as soon as possible. Lillie had no choice but to go. Devin had Brenda pack up her needed clothing and toiletries and drive Lillie to the nursing home. He would not go with them and he strode out to the barn. It was the same nursing home in which Lillie's mother had passed away. Lillie cried and shivered all the way to her supposed respite care. In her heart she feared that she would never see her home again.

Kim arrived after her mother had been all unloaded and moved in to a rather nice room. They clung to each other and cried, gasping big gulps of air, but Kim pleaded with her mother to not be so devastated over this 5 day respite. She was going to stay with Lillie in the room with her for three days. Then, two days later, Lillie would be back home. It was then that Lillie told Kim about Devin's behavior upon her departure. He had told her that he could not handle having her at his house any longer and that he was not sure he could bring her back home. When she was sitting alone in the sunroom, she had overheard Devin speak with Brenda and heard him say, "Good riddance to all of this stuff…" It felt very final to her. Kim was saddened, but not surprised at Devin's callousness and feared that this was most likely true. Kim had been shocked to see her mother's expensive and heavy leather lift chair had been delivered along with much of her lotions, perfumes, personal pillows and quilts. It seemed like a lot to move for 5 days of respite care. The room had a wonderful and soft lazy boy type of chair already and Lillie could no longer utilize the lift chair as she could not stand on her own any more. Kim spent the next three days and two nights in the nursing home with her mother, leaving only to pick up some food and things her mother needed or wanted. The nursing home staff was kind to Kim and her mother, but they did confirm that this was not a respite situation. Matthew stopped in every day to visit as well. It was very difficult for Kim to have to leave, but she needed to get back to teaching and ready her students and room for Christmas break. Lillie was so comforted that Kim would have a break and could come back soon, she was supposed to be back at home and done with respite care in two more days anyway. As Kim drove away from the nursing home that evening, her freedom from the place felt strange after so many days spent there. She looked at the nursing home from the road and saw a large star, actually Venus, low and bright above the home's roof. It took her breath away and she had to stop the car on the side of the rode to stare at it. She was impressed with peace and knowledge that her mother was not going to live much longer. She wondered if her mother's soul was flying free right now and she cried and waited for her phone call from a nurse. The call did not come and she decided to continue her drive home, praying for her mother's peace, comfort and soul all the way.

Of course, the five days of respite care passed and Lillie was not taken home. Kim took yet another day from work that Wednesday to drive down and figure out what was happening for sure. It had been three days since she had seen her mother although they had been able to communicate by phone. Upon her arrival, she heard a nurses' aide speaking roughly and arrogantly to her mother about her mother's oxygen flow. Lillie was pale and clammy. She was being scolded, by this stupid aide, that her oxygen was just fine and had been all day. The uneducated, uncaring woman then turned to Kim and said, "She has been complaining about her oxygen all day and it is just fine! I have been in and out of here all day because of this." Kim was shocked at the attitude. She informed the woman that Lillie did not LOOK fine and asked if a nurse had been contacted to check her out. This insensible woman then went on about how that was not necessary as she knew what she was doing. Kim asked her to leave, but the fool continued on and on about the situation. She was then informed by Kimberly to leave immediately. She continued to explain to Kim that it was not the panic attack that Kim claimed it to be and that her medicines were not due for two more hours. At which point Kim put up her teacher hand, used her teacher voice and look to tell the woman, "YOU need to LEAVE NOW, you're blocking the doorway and I need out" repeatedly until the aide gave up and left. Kim ran to find a nurse and explained the situation. It took another 20 minutes before the nurse showed up with the anti-anxiety medicine. Lillie then relaxed and breathed more normally within 15 minutes. Kim filed an official report for what it was worth. When other family members arrived to visit over the next couple of days, they also were concerned about leaving Lillie there with that type of mentality lurking around. The aide was reassigned; the others appeared more competent, to a point.

Later that evening, Matthew and Kimberly were alone with Lillie when she began to struggle with her breathing again. Turning up the oxygen was not a good idea as too much oxygen being pushed in would result in a person getting something like the bends diver's get when they surface too quickly, knowing this, Kimberly pretended to turn up the oxygen. This sometimes worked to calm her mother, but did not work this time. She went to get a nurse. The nurse informed her that she needed to contact a doctor before she could give her any more medication and to try to distract Lillie. The nurse did check on her and agreed that something needed to be done. Matthew showed Lillie old photos and the three of them reminisced while Kimberly put a cold cloth to Lillie's head and neck. It seemed like forever and both were afraid that they were going to watch their mother struggle unto her very death. The nurse eventually brought the relief of morphine and Lillie relaxed and could breathe again. The nurse informed them that she had received permission to give the morphine as needed. This was a relief at the same time it signaled the end of their mother's life. The excess morphine caused Lillie's feet to point down into a position that looked very much as though she were about to get up and pirouette on pointe. This "mushroom lung" (any type of lung shut down) was cruel and such torment. They decided to ready her for bed. As Kim turned to put away the soap and washcloths, she saw her brother lift her mother gently from the wheelchair and hold her in his arms like one would hold a small child. It took her breath away and she knew she was witnessing pure God love;

soul touching soul, mother and son. She stood back silently, with tears streaming down and watched her brother place Lillie into bed and cover her up. Lillie whispered something and smiled. Matthew said, "...a story book rabbit" and smiled back. At this point, Kimberly sobbed and gasped. Her mother was playing out a moment from Matthew's childhood where he would ask his mother, every night, if he should be a real rabbit or a storybook rabbit. She had now asked her son which she should be. Lillie then went to sleep pretending to be a storybook rabbit. If life were fair, Lillie then should have passed away peacefully with her children standing near, waiting for her to go to sleep. That is not how it happened.

Enter Devil, Stage Right

Kimberly had to return to her classroom for two more days and then her break would begin. She was worried about her mother being left without a trusted loved one near. She had been in her classroom for only two periods when she received a call on her cell from a nurse. She informed Kimberly that her mother was very close to death and was requiring a lot of morphine. She advised Kim and family to get there tonight or tomorrow morning if possible. Within twenty minutes that nurse called back and said, "Just to let you know, if she were my family member, I would get here as soon as possible". Kim arranged to be able to leave early, called her family to meet her at the house to leave for Ohio to see grandma. She let them know that grandma was passing away. She and Nick wondered at the second call from that nurse. It was as though she were sending a warning and they wondered if Devin was up to no good.

Nick, Kim and their now young adult children, drove to the nursing home in Ohio. They told stories about their times with grandma and Kim tried to prepare them that dying could be difficult and that they could leave and go to the waiting room whenever they needed. None of them could ever be prepared for what awaited them. As they entered Lillie's room, she was in her comfy lift chair curled into a fetal position and barely breathing. It was granddaughter Amanda that first noticed the missing oxygen tubes and all could hear the silence of no oxygen compressor running. Lillie had been on oxygen for over seven years, so this was unusual. Kim found the oxygen tube and put the cannula into Lillie's nose as Amanda ran to turn on the compressor. They knew she was dying, but not like this. This is not what she would ever want. Nurses came in and began to attend to her and Kimberly noticed an odd sense of relief among them. After about an hour, Devin came in and shrieked, "What are they doing?" and he threw his coat against the wall! This was a man who had been a grandpa to Nick and Kim's three children and now they watched as their grandpa screamed and ranted about the oxygen being put back on. He had given the order to remove it and he was her husband, he had rights and they didn't. The grandchildren were in shock at this behavior. For all of his evil, this was the worst they had seen. He had been good to the kids for the most part.

The hospice workers took them all aside and spoke at length about why Devin was right to remove Lillie's oxygen. That this was for the best and she would suffer less. That did not make sense as the amount of morphine she was on would bring her comfort and stop the suffering. They would continue to push and argue for Devin's choice until Kim brought up the living will that Lillie had signed stating that she wanted everything done except intubation. She wanted her oxygen to the very end. Did they not understand the law? Devin and Kim had been their together when she made that living will. Hospice people then went into recovery mode and spoke with Devin privately. These hospice workers were not like any the family had seen before and it dawned on them that Devin's power had these people on his side for money or out of fear, or both. The oxygen was left on and people straightened up and left them alone. Lillie began to revive and gain some awareness. Sarah called and said her plane had landed and that she and Renee were on their way.

When she asked about Lillie, she was shocked to hear what Devin had done. Only hours before she got on that plane, she had asked him to do everything he could to keep her sister alive. He had to have gone right over to the nursing home and removed the oxygen, almost insuring that Lillie would not survive to see her sister! Sarah was livid. She wondered how anyone could be so cruel and conniving and why Devin would want to be that hurtful.

The next shocker came when Lillie's sister, Sarah, arrived with her daughter and Kim's close cousin, Renee. Devin spoke to them at length about how he owned Matthew's house. This had been a problem in the recent past as no one was sure how he had obtained ownership of the small home and several acres. Matthew had gone to his mother for help years ago when he was going through the divorce and somehow Devin had gotten involved and illegally obtained ownership of Matthew's home. Matthew had since been buying it back from Devin and only owed $30,200 to buy his house back, he had already paid over $65,000. With Lillie out of the picture, Devin informed everyone that Matthew had only been paying rent and that it did not go toward paying off the house. Renee offered to pay off Matthew's remaining debt so as not to have to deal with this horrible man any longer. Devin knew that Renee and her husband were wealthy and demanded $140,000 more for the house. So as their mother and Devin's wife lay dying, Devin was positioning himself to get the best financial deal he could and he wanted to make Matthew suffer due to Lillie's love of this son of hers. Devin confided to Sarah and Renee that he planned to evict Matthew as soon as he could and put the property up for auction. He actually chuckled with the thought of it. Right in front of Lillie's family that dearly loved Matthew, he chuckled and grinned about causing Lillie's son misery. Devin continues to twist the family around for the next two days as Lillie dies.

As they sat to discuss funeral arrangements, Devin announced that it was all taken care of and decided. He was going to have Lillie cremated knowing full well this went completely against her last wishes. She absolutely had an opinion and last wish and Devin was pushing against anything she wanted. He also informed the family that her ashes would be buried in a cemetery in another town right next to his other dead wife, the one that had committed suicide. Lillie had been promised by him to be buried in another cemetery plot. This decision of his would anger her and he seemed to get a jolly over having power over the most helpless of all, a dying and incapacitated woman. Sarah was sick and devastated and spoke to Devin about being an honorable man and being the hero. He agreed with her, but will do things his way because it is what he needed to help him grieve. Now he had the hospice staff wrapped around his finger as he howled and "cried" a tearless sob in the hall. Interestingly, the nursing staff turned a blind eye to Devin. They seemed to know more than they could ever be allowed to say. They made eye contact with Kim and the family and showed their appreciation to them in many ways. It was then that Kim understood that second call. These nurses knew the power of Devin and they were against his action of pulling Lillie's oxygen, but they were powerless against him. With the strength of Kim's family not being afraid of Devin and pulling out the living will, the nurses took solace in someone standing up to the great and powerful evil that is Devin Norman Blaine.

Lillie

The family is sitting around Lillie, as she is now awake and "chasing chickens" from the room, laughing and at peace within her morphine haze. Matthew and Aunt Sarah are discussing how Lillie sure knew how to pick the craziest of men. This family is close and loving; all who enter the room feel the love and harmony. Stories abound and then Lillie, who only ever and rarely drank wine or champagne, shouted out, "Does anyone know where I can get a beer around here. The floozies get in the way." She then turns to her beautiful and very well dressed niece and says, "Are you a floozy? You look like a floozy"! The entire room breaks into a much needed laugh and then cries. Lillie is at peace and she knows each person by name, so even though she is out of it, she is not gone. She kept telling Kim to bring in more trays of food for this party. Lillie began to speak of Jesus more and more. She inquired of others to see if they knew Jesus. Lillie smiled and said she wanted to see Him, her brothers and parents that have gone home to see God. She felt the love and companionship of her family around her and believed it was a family party. Her family sighed with relief to see that Lillie was ready to move on at last. Such bittersweet tears are shed and much hugging and love was shared all around.

Lillie crashed that evening and took a turn for the worse. Nick and Kim had run out to do some errands and grab food when they got the call that Lillie had passed away. It was devastating at the same time it was a beautiful thing to imagine Lillie in the presence of the Lord and God she loves. She was free and dancing with loved ones that have passed on before her. Lillie could breathe. Kimberly comes across a photograph of Lillie dancing at a party with her little brother, Babe. Boyd Jr., aka Babe, had passed away two years before his big sister. In the picture they are young adults, smiling and Lillie's dress is swirling around her. That is the image of their reunion in heaven. They are young, happy, at peace and Lillie's dress is swirling around her.

And dance

Lift high your
head, heart and pride

Pull from your core;
your being

Extend your limbs and soul;
fragile self and soul

en pointe
pirouette
glissade

And dance

P. K. Hubbard